UNDERGROUND
TEXAS

An Anthology by Members of
THE FINAL TWIST

L & L Dreamspell
London, Texas

Cover and Interior Design by L & L Dreamspell

This is a work of fiction, and is produced from the authors' imaginations. People, places and things mentioned in this anthology are used in a fictional manner.

ISBN: 978-1-60318-411-3

Visit us on the web at www.lldreamspell.com

Published by L & L Dreamspell
Printed in the United States of America

CONTENTS

Fifth!

This is the fifth annual anthology from Houston's The Final Twist writing group.

Previous volumes include:
2007—Dead and Breakfast
2008—A Death in Texas
2009—A Box of Texas Chocolates
2010—Twisted Tales of Texas Landmarks

The Final Twist started as the dream of one person who wanted an affordable Houston-area writing support group whose focus was helping writers succeed. Only a handful of potential members showed up at that first meeting, but she soldiered on. The dream has been picked up by others who have grown The Final Twist into a strong multi-location group of authors, aspiring writers, librarians, reviewers, publicists, editors, radio show hosts, and publishers whose purpose is to promote reading, support authors, and mentor aspiring writers.

The annual anthology and all the activities surrounding each year's call for submissions, writing workshops, story editing, and book promotion activities certainly goes a long way toward helping the group fulfill its purpose.

In three of the first four anthologies, new writers were introduced. It is our pleasure to announce that this fifth edition carries on the tradition. We're proud to introduce three talented newcomers to the world of published fiction: Natasha Storfer, Becky Hogeland, and James R. Davis.

We also have ONE writer with the distinction of having a story selected for each of the five volumes: Cash Anthony.

Congratulations to one and all!

FREEDOM TRAIN
BY CHARLOTTE PHILLIPS

Yesterday I bought a slave. I still feel dirty. Even knowing why I bought her, I feel dirty. I wish I could tell her that everything will be all right, that her life is about to get better. But I can't. I told so many lies yesterday; I can't bear the thought of telling one more. First I told Papa I needed a note for the bank because our money jar was low. Then I told Mama I needed the pony cart because Papa asked me to run an errand. At the bank, I tried to hold my tongue, but once I started telling tall tales, I just couldn't stop. Banker Morgan didn't even question me about the withdrawal, but I went ahead and made up a story about Papa, my birthday, and my unusually large withdrawal of two hundred dollars. At seventeen, I'm plenty old enough to know better than to build a foundation with lies. And Papa has told me, at least a hundred times, the end does not justify the means. But I didn't see that I had any choice.

Now I want to tell my slave that everything will be all right, she's on her way to a better life. But I don't know if that's true. We face a treacherous journey. So, I stay silent.

Yesterday, with my purse full of the family's hard-earned money and my stomach full of butterflies, I headed out of town toward the Double-Bar Ranch. Before I could scare myself out of my crazy scheme, I found myself standing on the sagging, wooden porch of the old ranch house.

Yesterday. Was it really just yesterday? The rancher didn't want to sell to me; didn't even want to speak to me. He didn't believe a family of suspected abolitionists would have any good reason for buying a slave. Besides, he said, he needed all hands to tend to his cotton and cattle.

I was persistent in my story—that with Papa ill and Mama running the store, we needed help. He finally relented but offered up only one option. We waited in uncomfortable silence for the overseer to fetch her. I was jumping out of my skin and wanted to move around a bit, but I made myself keep still.

The overseer hauled her to the porch by her hair. He held his arm straight down to keep the woman bent over, with her face toward the ground. He walked so fast she could barely keep up. When he got close, he gave her a shove so she tripped over the top step and landed on her hands and knees. When she didn't immediately rise, he kicked her and yelled that she should stand and face her master. She struggled to gain her feet. Her weak legs shook with the effort. I ached to reach out to her, but I feared doing anything that might give the rancher reason to change his mind. I stood still and focused on thoughts from the Good Book. I prayed for the strength to get through the day.

I took a good look at the woman's face and felt sure God had smiled on me. I was certain this was the right woman. This was Honey's mama. The woman I'd come to think of as Honey*Mutter*.

"What we have here is a fine ol' cow. She produces strong bulls and mighty pretty cows. She's a strong'un, too."

The rancher's words pulled me from my thoughts. When he grabbed her by the nose and chin so he could pull open her mouth and show me her teeth, I maintained my silence, but when he yanked up her dress so he could show off her 'fine, strong legs.' I protested, "Mister, please. Where's your decency!"

But my protest fell on deaf ears.

"When you're buyin' a cow, little Miss, you need to check it out. Your Papa should'a taught you that before he sent his little girl out to do a man's job. This here's a fine specimen. Worth at least three hundred, but I'll sell it to you for two-fifty." He hiked her dress up a bit higher and slapped her naked hind quarters.

That set my blood to boiling. Before I could stop myself, I stepped forward, yanked that dress out of the rancher's hands and thrust it back down to cover Honey*Mutter.* "You've made a mistake, Mister." My voice sounded a bit high and squeaky, so I swallowed before continuing. "I'm not as green as you seem to think. This woman barely has the strength to stand. She looks like you've been starving her. You won't get two-fifty for her, from me or anyone else. I'm offering fifty." I nodded my head for emphasis while I prayed that I hadn't just condemned Honey*Mutter.*

"She's much stronger than she looks just now, Miss. She's been in bed with a bit o' the sniffles for the past week or so." He hung his thumbs through the waistband of his filthy trousers. "We don't starve our property around here. I takes good care of my investments. 'Specially one that's birthed me nine strong calves. Eight o' them dogies and their daddy brought me a fine price a few months back."

Those words nearly toppled Honey*Mutter,* but the rancher didn't notice her knees buckle, the way I reached out to steady her, or my reaction when a simple touch told me she was burning with fever.

He was staring off at the far field and barked orders at the overseer to get out there and take care of something that didn't suit him. He returned to our conversation without bothering to pull his attention from the field. "This one will bring a fine price, too. Soon as she gits off her duff and back to work, she'll be on full rations again. I won't take less 'n two hundred."

"So, you have been starving her, and now you expect me to pay full price for damaged goods. My offer is seventy-five." I remembered Papa using that line when bargaining for our buggy pony. I silently apologized to Honey*Mutter.*

"Now little Miss, you don't understand how this works. I came down fifty, you should come up fifty. See?"

"That's a good system when both parties start out reasonable. But you didn't. If I follow your instructions, we'll end up at one hundred fifty. That leaves me over-paying, assuming I had that much to offer, which I don't. My offer is seventy-five. That's a fair price."

"That might be true, depends on how many uses you're willing to entertain. She can take care o' that house for you, sure. She'd make money for you if you rented her out nights. Might even produce a calf or two for you. One hundred's my final offer. I'll not take a penny less."

"Sold." I said.

He grinned at me, obviously pleased with the fine deal he'd made. She was so weak, I'm sure he believed he sold me a dying woman.

It didn't matter to me. I was certain I'd found Honey's mama. I wasn't expecting someone so small and sickly, though. Honey had described her mama as the family's strength. Still, I could see Honey in the woman's face, in the way she held her head, in the way she moved her hands. Honey is the escaped slave who kept my Papa alive through the force of her will. I intend to do the same for Honey's mama. But I still feel dirty.

I had to complete my business with the rancher and get away from that place. "I'll need proper paperwork before I pay."

That got his attention. He stared at me for a good, long minute before heading inside for the document. I used the time to remove one hundred dollars from my purse without giving him the chance to see I had more.

When he returned, we exchanged money for paperwork. I quickly read the document he handed me to make sure all was in order. I read the last line twice—missing big toe on left foot. I glanced down at Honey*Mutter*'s feet and saw, for the first time, the ugly wound where a toe should have been.

The rancher saw my reaction and said, "That's how ya keep 'em from runnin' when them damn Mex'can layabouts come round talkin' trash in their ears." He stopped to scratch his ample stomach and glare at me. "They sweet-talked her pretty lil' gal outta here just when I had some fine bids from some Louisiana businessmen. When I find that cow, I'll make her wish she'd never been born." He marched back inside, slamming the door behind him. It was done.

I'd started the day as the dedicated daughter of God-fearing parents—good, decent people. I'd ended the day as a liar, thief, and slave owner—owner of a disfigured slave. I knew I could make Papa understand and gain his forgiveness. I wasn't so sure about Mama. She was still recovering from the last time angry slavers visited our home in the middle of the night.

Before leaving, I asked Honey*Mutter* if she wanted time to say any good-bye's or gather any belongings. She responded with a barely visible shake of her head. With my procrastination options gone, I turned the pony cart around and headed home to face Mama. I owned a slave. Heidi Sturge owned a slave whose big toe had been cut off and the wound left to fester. I felt dirty.

I thought Honey*Mutter* might be as frightened as I was. In an effort to calm her, and myself, I used the ride home to tell her the story of how I came to meet Honey. The story started with a confession.

Eight months earlier I'd begged my papa to stop helping runaways. The conversation began at the dinner table. Mama asked Papa if he'd read the paper, said there was a new law. When they slid into rapid-fire German, I knew something bad had happened. I waited until they were too engrossed in their conversation to notice my absence before slipping away to find the paper.

It didn't take me long to locate the source of Mama's angst. Two stories ran side by side on the front page. The Republic of Texas had a new law. "Every person who shall steal or entice away any slave, out of or from the possession of the owner or owners of such slave, shall be deemed guilty of felony, and on conviction thereof, shall suffer death." Providing food and shelter to runaways was considered enticement. The other story concerned a suspected abolitionist in San Jacinto. A mob hanged him. The stakes had been raised. Papa was in danger.

He was a stubborn man, my papa—set in his ways and the

way of the church. He'd be hard to sway, but I had to try. Mama's rising voice told me Papa would soon be going for a walk; he always went for a walk when Mama's voice worked its way up to the high notes during their discussions.

Our homestead was a bit odd. Mama and Papa are farmers at heart. When we arrived in Texas, Papa bought a little bit of land just outside of town. It was too small to be a real farm, but big enough to keep us fed and sheltered. Since then, the town has grown around us, and Papa's turned the downstairs part of the house into a general store. We still have our little bit of land, where Mama keeps a vegetable garden, and Papa keeps two milk cows and horses in the barn, which doubles as storage for the store's dry goods.

I slipped out to the back porch to wait for him, paper in hand. I didn't have long to wait. That wasn't a good sign. It meant Papa thought there was little to discuss.

He stepped out and stopped to light his pipe. That's when I moved in front of him, waving the paper. "Please, Papa. Stop and think about what you're doing."

"I've thought about it. We'll continue to do what's right."

"But Papa, they may kill you. What would we do without you?"

"Selfish thoughts are beneath you, Heidi. We do what's right when it's easy *and* when it's hard. It's our way." Papa stepped around me and headed for our little barn.

I ran after him and said, "Papa, they hung this man because they *suspected* him. They didn't even have proof. He lived alone, but you don't. If they found one of the 'packages' here, they might hang us all. I'm scared, Papa. Mama's scared."

"It's okay to be scared, Heidi. I'm scared, too. But that's no excuse to not help God's children. He asks so little of us and offers much in return. He loves us all the same. God doesn't have favorites."

"But Papa, I'm not asking God to favor us. I'm asking you to love me more than you love strangers. I feel sorry for them, really I do. But surely God has a reason for giving them such a heavy burden."

Papa took his time in answering me. "Dear child, surely you know I love you and your mama more than life itself. It's that love that gives me the strength I need to do these things. Our time here on this Earth is short. But if we live right, God promises us all eternity in His house. I need to believe I've done everything within my power to earn the right for us to spend all eternity together. Promise me you'll think on that tonight."

What could I say to that? I said the words Papa wanted to hear, "I promise, Papa."

"One day you'll understand. Go back inside and help your mama." I was halfway to the house when I heard him call me from the barn. I ran back, hoping he'd changed his mind, but I was in for one of Papa's Life Lessons.

"Yes, Papa?"

"I've decided to leave the next package in your hands. I believe if you step into the empty stall, you'll find we have a special delivery. If you don't want to accept, just send him on his way."

I can't describe how happy I was in that moment. Papa had heard my pain and responded kindly, or so I thought. I gave him a big hug, then inched my way to where I could peer into the stall. I'd never seen one of Papa's packages before, but I'd read the descriptions of runaway slaves printed in the paper. I expected to find the usual adult field hand or a group of strong young boys. It would be easy, I thought, to tell them where they could find some food and ask them to leave. Instead, I found a little slip of a girl who stared at me with large eyes and trembled. She reminded me of the frightened kitten I'd found a few years earlier. My heart sank. Papa had tricked me.

I wiggled my fingers between the slats and ventured a greeting. "Hello."

No answer.

"Can you hear me?"

She nodded.

"What's your name?"

I had to strain my ears to hear her whispered reply. "Mama calls me Honey."

"Are you hungry, Honey? Would you like to come inside and have something to eat?"

"You gonna whip me?"

"No."

"You gonna send me back?"

"No." I walked to the front of the stall and held out my hand. "Come inside, Honey, and meet Mama."

When Honey stood up, I could see she was my height, and probably close to my age, too—sixteen or seventeen. She took my hand and let me lead her to the house, but she continued to shake something terrible. As we walked past Papa, I could see he was grinning. Mama wouldn't respond quite the same way.

Mama was still cleaning up supper when Honey and I slipped into the kitchen. I introduced them before sitting Honey in the chair closest to the stove, preparing a plate of sausages and sauerkraut, and placing it in front of her. Mama watched silently.

I sat beside Honey and spoke with a quiet voice until she trusted me enough to eat. She ate timidly at first, but was soon shoveling food with vigor. I left her to her supper and went to give Mama a hug. "I'm sorry, Mama. I couldn't send her away."

"You did right." That's all Mama said before returning to her chores.

Papa chose that moment to come back inside. Mama greeted him in German, but I don't know what she said. She used the voice she reserved for accusations and some words I'd not heard before. I got the feeling she was blaming Papa for my behavior.

Papa didn't respond. He was busy studying our guest. "What's her name?"

"This is Honey, Papa. Honey, this is Papa."

Honey looked up from her food and began shaking again.

"You're safe here, child." Papa's soothing voice had a calming effect. "Honey is a fine German name."

"Papa?"

"Honey Sturge is your cousin, come to visit all the way from New Orleans. Yes. That will work. After supper, you help her clean up and give her one of your old dresses—the one from *Tante* Gerta with that prairie bonnet. We'll need to burn the rags she's wearing."

I took another look at Honey. She was fair of skin, and her hair looked more like mine than hair I'd seen in drawings of slaves. Perhaps Papa was right. In different clothes, she'd look like one of us.

Papa's reason for such a bizarre plan was simple. We couldn't keep Honey hidden in the barn indefinitely, and we didn't know when it would be safe to travel.

Honey's stay stretched from days to weeks to months, and we grew close. I taught her to speak English with a German accent. Mama taught both of us some German phrases. Honey taught us some new recipes, which were delicious, and told us stories about her family. Our only real challenge was Sundays. There was no excuse, of course, for missing Sunday services. Mama came up with the solution. We simply told everyone that Honey was painfully shy and awkward. She wouldn't speak to strangers.

Somewhere along the way, I forgot the truth. I grew to think of Honey as my sister and made the mistake of feeling safe. That changed the day a young slave boy slipped into the store to warn Papa. A mob was planning a visit to our home; they thought we were hiding a runaway slave called Sarah2. The boy carried a wanted poster containing a crude drawing of our Honey. Honey explained that her family named her Honey, but the rancher who owned her family called her Sarah2.

Papa hadn't forgotten our predicament. He was ready with a plan. Amongst many tears and hugs, we packed Papa and Honey into our smaller wagon and sent them on their way. Mama and

I were to mind the store and tell anyone who would listen that we'd received word Honey's mother had taken ill and was asking for her daughter. Papa was escorting her as far as Houston. Papa didn't tell us where they were really going, but he did say he expected to return in a month. Papa felt certain this information would divert the mob from searching our home to patrolling the roads to Houston.

I took a break from my story telling then. I didn't want to tell Honey*Mutter* about the mob's midnight visit to our home or about my nightmares, but I'll tell you.

The men didn't come that first day after Papa and Honey went away, nor the second. When they came on the third night, they selected an indecent hour and made enough racket to wake the dead. The nightmare returns nearly every time I close my eyes.

I wake to sounds of whistles, shouts, and gunshots. I rise quickly and run to Mama's room. "Mama. Mama, wake up. They're here." When I touch her arm, I realize she is awake—and trembling. "Come, Mama. We have to get out. They may set fire to the house."

I dress quickly and then help her. Arm in arm, we make our way down the stairs. The front porch is in flames, so we run out the back door. Our barn is also on fire and we can hear the terrified animals inside. The bastards had not freed them before torching the building. Mama screams and falls to her knees.

Her scream alerts the men to our presence. One of them runs at us, waving a burning torch. "Get back inside." He jabs the flames at our faces, but I can't move, can't even yell for help. I'm frozen.

I wake up—heart pounding, dripping in sweat, gasping for air.

I wish I could say I was stronger in real life than in that dream, but I wasn't. We survived because the townspeople saw the flames and rushed to help. The cowardly mob ran and our friends saved us, most of our animals, and part of the house and store.

It took nearly two months, but with the help of the Miller

boys and the church elders, the store, the barn, and our home were restored to a workable state. I had to sleep with Mama because my bed was lost to the flames. Mama and I did our best to pretend all was well. We told each other every day that Papa would be home soon.

After I'd gathered my thoughts a bit, I continued my story to Honey*Mutter*. I wanted to give her hope, but she had to understand some of the risks. I skipped to the part where Papa didn't return when he said.

By the time one month stretched into three, Mama was beside herself with exhaustion and worry. I hired one of the Miller boys to do Papa's morning and evening chores so Mama could get some much-needed rest, but I can't say that it helped. Between her own thoughts and my nightmares, she didn't sleep more than a few hours each night.

In the middle of month four, I found a stranger in the barn, a new package. He raised both hands, as if to surrender and said, "Don't be scar't, Miss. I's jus' lookin' for my girl. You see a girl 'bout this high?" He held one hand out at about Honey's height and held up one of those runaway reward flyers—the one with a drawing of Honey. "Please, Miss. I jus' need to know she safe."

My heart told me this was Honey's papa, but my head said to take caution. He could be a spy for the slavers. "Why?" It wasn't much of a question, but it was all I could form into words.

"She my baby, Miss."

The flyer used the slaver's name for the girl. Only her family called her Honey. I asked, "What's her name?"

"She be my Honey."

The words were said with such love, I knew they were true. It broke my heart and tears threatened. I explained what happened and that I didn't know where Papa and Honey were headed, only that Papa had not yet returned—and he was more than three months late.

He rubbed his chin while he took in the news, then took

a look around the barn. "Beggin' your pardon, Miss," he said, "but I might know where they's headed. With your hep, Miss, we could look for 'em."

I listened to his plan as best I could, which wasn't easy with two thoughts running round and round in my head— "Mama will never agree to let me run off with a stranger," and "I have to go—Papa might need me."

If Mama hadn't been so exhausted, she would have stopped me. But she was worn out to distraction. I told her there was a man outside who could help me find Papa—and we could take some of the melon crop with us to sell along the way. I didn't mention that the man was not from our church, that we didn't know his family, that he was probably a runaway slave. Mama, in her distressed state, forgot to ask. "*Ja, ja,*" Mama said. "You find Papa."

A smarter person than me would have stopped to ask a few questions. What kind of a man would suggest an unchaperoned journey with a sixteen-year-old girl? Was he really Honey's papa? How did he know to come to our barn looking for Honey? I didn't give myself time to think about these things. I wanted to find Papa. The man said he could help. I needed to believe him.

I did make time to look after Mama. Mrs. Miller from across the way promised to check on her daily until my return and to arrange for another of her many nephews to come help with chores. I knew if I worried too much about Mama I would lose my nerve, so I worked hard to think only of finding Papa—and Honey. I knew the only cure for Mama was Papa's return. I had to find him.

Back in the barn, my new guide had the horses hitched and our bigger wagon packed in the most peculiar way—with great spaces between melons and blankets between the layers. He had broken into several crates of merchandise and was digging through the contents.

"What are you doing?"

"Pardon me, Miss." He stood and surveyed the barn. "It be a long way. I's jus' thinkin' what we need."

I hadn't given much thought to that. We had a wagon full of food. What else might we need? I looked around and spotted Papa's old hat. I suggested he wear it. Please don't think I was being kind. I thought the sight of Papa's hat would give me comfort and strength.

I still felt a need to hurry. I jumped in the wagon and placed my bag in the center of the bench. He took the hint, grabbed Papa's hat off the hook, and hopped in on the other side of the bag. He handed me the reins. I was just pulling out of the barn when Mama rushed out the back door of the house. I was tempted to pretend I didn't see her and hurry the horses along, lest she try to stop me. But I didn't. I pulled the team to a halt.

Mama rushed to my side and reached a hand up. "*Sichere Spielräume, Tochter. Gott sei mit euch.*" Safe travels, daughter. God go with you. The same send-off she'd given Honey.

I reached for her hand and gave it a squeeze. "Thank you, Mama." I felt her pull my hand. That's when I figured out she was trying to give me something. I tied off the reins, jumped down, and gave Mama a quick hug. She shoved her gift into my pocket and ran back to the house. I'm pretty sure she was crying. I peeked into my pocket and found a small gun and some money. It looked like she'd emptied the cash register and the cookie jar. I climbed back into the wagon and headed out of town.

For the first few hours, my guide and I had much to discuss. I learned his name was Sam. He told me the story of how Honey's family had lived most of their lives at the Double-Bar Ranch. He said it was a hard life, but they knew it could be much worse. The rancher was free with his use of the whip and used the married women for his own pleasure, but he also kept the slaves fed, sheltered, and clothed—and he kept his hands off the young girls.

Sam said the family often made up stories about what it would be like to be free, but they never seriously considered running away. There were too many of them to travel together, and his wife refused to discuss any plan that split up her family. That all changed when the gentlemen from Louisiana showed up. They were shopping for new girls for their houses—the kind of house where men rented women for a night. Both men took a shine to Honey, and a bidding war was underway. When word reached Honey's mama, her swift decision-making made heads spin. Sam would take Honey to a safe house that night. Sam and the boys would follow as soon as they could. They'd find freedom and a way to buy Honey's mama.

That was the night Sam had brought Honey to our barn and instructed her to hide and wait. But we found her. And the rancher did not take kindly to Honey's absence and the financial loss it represented. He had Sam's whole family whipped in an effort to get them to talk. When that didn't work, he split them up, selling the oldest son to one neighbor, Sam and the younger boys to another, leaving Honey*Mutter* alone. He continued to punish Honey*Mutter* viciously, to make an example of her to others who might be thinking about running.

The more Sam talked, the angrier he got, and so I changed the subject. I tried to get him to tell me about our destination, but he only shared bits and pieces. He showed me a map that I was to say came from Papa. We'd travel only during the day, stopping at night to rest the horses and to avoid the night patrols.

For the first week or so, Sam was able to guide us to ranches where we were welcomed, and I was given a place to sleep indoors. Sam always stayed close to the wagon. I tried to tell him to relax, none of our hosts was likely to steal anything, but he ignored me and kept to his ways.

At our last safe house, I had a nightmare. This time, I didn't wake up, but screamed out loud and my screams woke my hosts. Mrs. Schneider shook me awake. I was more than a little embarrassed. She kindly suggested that it was close enough to morning for the two of us to begin our day. I dressed and packed quickly, then headed for the kitchen. Mrs. Schneider was at the table, shucking corn. Pearl, her ebony-skinned maid, was hauling a large pot of water from sink to fire. I moved to help with the heavy load, but Mrs. Schneider called me to the table to work with the corn.

"Your dream is about the journey ahead?"

I nodded. I didn't feel I could trust anyone with the truth.

"You're smart to be scared. Indian country is no place for a young girl. You should send your man on ahead. You can wait here with us."

"Indian country?"

"Yes. That's what's between here and the next town—five days journey through hot, dry scrub. Indian land. The trip isn't a pleasant one. Pearl can tell you. She's been to Eagle Pass many times." I glanced at Pearl and wondered if we were now speaking in code. I was not familiar with Papa's abolitionist work. He'd kept Mama and me protected from that, until Honey appeared in our barn.

"I must go. I must find Papa."

"I'm sure your papa would wish you to remain here and send Sam alone."

That was true enough. But, she didn't know that Sam and Papa had never met; that I'd only met Sam on the day I'd left home. Our story had been that Papa owned Sam from before I was born. I hadn't considered the possibility of Indians. But I couldn't come this far and stop. I just couldn't.

"That's more than kind, ma'am, but this is something I must do. I hope you understand."

"I do, child, but I will continue to try to talk you out of it. Pearl, come tell Miss Heidi about your last trip to The Pass."

"Please, no." I pleaded. "I have enough nightmares, and it won't change my mind."

"Well, if I can't keep you here, I beg you to take Pearl with you."

I'd been staring at the table, refusing to meet her gaze, but when I felt Mrs. Schneider's rough hand on my chin, I turned to face her. She chose her words carefully. "Pearl is a good guide. She wants to go. Please take her."

I looked to Pearl for confirmation. "Please, Miss," was all she said. I nodded my head and wondered once again if we'd been speaking in the secret language used to move packages to freedom.

"*Danke*, Miss Heidi. You will not regret this." Mrs. Schneider gave my hand a quick squeeze. "If you two can finish making breakfast, I'll go talk to Mr. Schneider."

"Yes'm." Pearl spoke for us, and Mrs. Schneider hurried from the kitchen. "I best be tellin' Sam," Pearl said to me, then left me alone to prepare the morning meal and think too much about Indians.

I'd like to tell you I was brave and strong. The truth is, I shook with fear and nearly scared myself into waiting at the Schneider ranch. In the end, prayers and thoughts of finding Papa gave me the strength I needed.

After the morning meal, I offered to help clean up, but Mr. Schneider said we'd best be going. Mrs. Schneider and I walked to the barn arm in arm. She asked me again to stay. I didn't trust my voice, so I simply shook my head.

Sam had the horses hitched, and Pearl packed into the very back of the wagon. He was ready to go, but Mr. Schneider insisted we trade out Papa's team for fresh horses. He said we could trade back on our return trip. While the men changed out the horses, Mrs. Schneider and I moved Pearl to the center of the driver's bench.

"Sam won't like this." Pearl whispered. "He say I talk too much."

I laughed and carried my bag to the back of the wagon. Sam noticed and fairly ran to my side. "I pack the wagon, Miss," he said, and relieved me of my load. I shrugged, gave Mrs. Schneider another hug, and took my seat.

Sam and Mr. Schneider made some final adjustments to the team, and we headed out.

I won't bore you with details of the first four days, except to say they were long, hot, and mostly uneventful. The monotony was periodically interrupted by arguments between Pearl and Sam. They didn't agree on when to travel—during the day or at night, when to rest the horses and for how long, how hard to push the team, where to set up camp for the night, whether or not to light a fire. If there were two answers to any question, I could count on Pearl swearing by one and Sam the other. I began to wonder if facing Indians would be easier.

On the fifth day, with Eagle Pass nearly in sight, we were challenged by a band of slave traders. They lined up across the road, blocking our way. Sam pulled the team to a halt, and I greeted the men.

They ignored me and spoke to Sam. "Boy, you look like a runaway. Git on over here so's we can get a good look at you."

Sam took his time in answering, making a point of scratching his nose and pulling Papa's hat down to his eyebrows. "I's takes my orders from Miz Heidi."

"You get outta that wagon, boy. Ah'm gonna teach you how to speak to your betters."

I watched in disbelief as the man unfurled his whip and cracked it in the air. Luckily, Sam had a firm grip on the reins, for the noise scared the team. At the sound of more whips cracking, I looked around. Our wagon was surrounded by men itching for the feel of their whips against Sam's skin. The horses bucked something fierce. I was able to grab onto the back of the bench, but poor Pearl was thrown to the buckboard. I grabbed a handful of her dress in time to keep her from tumbling between the horses. Sam got the team calmed down, and Pearl crawled back to her seat. Sam moved to jump from the wagon, but I pulled him back and stood to face the horde. I shouted, "How dare you threaten to damage my property!"

My words were met by another crack of the whip, and the horses shied. It took a moment for me to realize I'd been struck. My hand was bleeding. Before I could react, Sam was pulled from the bench and surrounded. I hollered, "No! No, no, no!" They ignored me and cracked their whips in the air. With all that noise, the team bolted. Pearl grabbed for the reins and managed to bring us to a stop fairly quickly, but we had traveled a good twenty-five yards.

She clucked at the horses and drove the team in a wide circle that brought us closer to Sam. By then, most of the slavers had jumped from their horses and surrounded their prey. Sam had been struck several times, once in the face, but he remained standing.

I remembered Mama's gift and pulled the gun from my pocket with shaking hands. I fumbled with it and dropped it. Pearl grabbed the gun from where it landed between her feet and fired into the air. That stilled the men long enough for Pearl's voice to be heard. "Aaron Travis Smith, the Gov'nor won't take too kindly to you interfering in his business."

"Well, lookie here." Mr. Smith coaxed his horse toward the wagon. "If it ain't the Gov's favorite whore."

Pearl dropped Mama's little gun, reached into the wagon, and pulled out a rifle that I didn't know we had. She stood and aimed at Mr. Smith. "That's close enough."

Mr. Smith stopped, and Pearl ignored him. "Sam, get back up here." Sam ran for the wagon. Pearl continued, "Miz Heidi, we best get a move on. The Gov ain't known for his patience."

As soon as Sam leapt in beside Pearl, I grabbed the reins and started the team—a bit too fast. Pearl lost her balance and would have toppled into the wagon bed, had Sam not caught her. The rifle went off in the process and scared the horses again. As I fought to keep them under control, I heard the slavers laughing. I couldn't look back. I was focused on escape. Luckily, they didn't chase us, as I don't think we could have out-run them. Sam let me run the team hard for about five minutes before reminding me I could kill the horses pushing them so hard in the desert heat. I was shaking something fierce by then and passed the reins to Pearl, who seemed to know where we were headed.

I stopped my story there and glanced at Honey*Mutter*. She sat with hands folded tightly and her head bowed as if deep in prayer. I didn't know if I should continue my tale, but it didn't matter. That's as much as I was able to explain before pulling the pony cart into our back yard. Mama was on the porch. She took one look at us and said, "*Tochter*, what have you done?"

"This is Honey's mama. She's sick."

That was all Mama had to hear. She took charge, directing me to take Honey*Mutter* inside, sending one of the Miller boys for Doctor Kopf and another to tend to our horse and pony cart. Before Mama joined me in the kitchen, she banned Papa from the living quarters until the doctor could confirm I hadn't brought The Fever into the house. Papa had not yet fully recovered from his ordeal in Mexico. Mama didn't want him exposed to illness.

By the time Dr. Kopf arrived, Mama had placed a cold compress on Honey*Mutter*'s forehead, cleaned the wound on her foot, and was pumping her full of Mama's special tea-for-the-sick. Like many in our community, the doctor had developed a healthy fear of being charged with aiding escaped slaves. He asked for proof that Honey*Mutter* was not one of the increasing numbers of runaways. That's when Mama learned I'd bought a slave.

Mama's gasp made it clear to Dr. Kopf my news was a surprise. I blushed at the certainty that my family would be the subject of much gossip over the next few weeks, and it was all my doing.

Mama recovered, and the doctor got to work. The two of them conversed in rapid German that I was not able to follow. In the end, they dressed the wound, and Mama sent me to help Papa close the store and tell him he was permitted to come home, my only clue that Honey*Mutter*'s fever was not the dreaded yellow kind.

We sat to supper. Papa said grace, but before I could pick up a fork, he placed the bill of sale for Honey*Mutter* on the table, and said, "Explain."

"It's a long story, Papa."

"We have time, *Tochter*."

While Mama encouraged Honey*Mutter* to drink more tea and try some soup, I worked to gather my thoughts, but they were too jumbled to unravel. In the end, I just blurted out the story I'd been keeping from them—the last part of my journey to Mexico.

"You already know most of the story about my trip with Sam.

But I've been skipping over one part. I didn't want to frighten you." I looked at Papa, and he nodded for me to continue, so I told them, finally, about what happened between our first encounter with the slavers and my reunion with Papa.

"We could hear the river long before we could see it. The louder the river got, the more jittery Sam became. I thought he was just anxious to learn Honey's fate, but it turned out he was worried about the river crossing—and for good reason.

"Pearl pulled us off the trail and stopped. She explained we were approaching the safest place to cross the river because there was help nearby on the other side, and there were ferries we could use to pull ourselves across. She said the water was often shallow enough for the horses, but we'd do best to leave the wagon. Sam, of course, argued. He said we had to cross whole.

"Then Pearl explained this was also the most dangerous place to cross, because it was a known smugglers' route and a suspected runaway slave crossing. Slavers and bounty hunters on the prowl often lie in wait, she explained. She suggested that we either send one of us ahead as a scout, or wait until dark. Sam became more agitated with every word, until he grabbed the reins and ran us full steam ahead.

"As we approached the river, Pearl and I could clearly see the band of slavers that had challenged us earlier in the day. We tried to get Sam to turn around, but he just drove the horses harder—right into the river. The water was too deep and too fast where we went in.

"So many things happened as soon as we hit the water, it was hard to take it all in. The slavers shot at us, and they shouted for us to turn about. The wagon heeled over on its side and tossed us out. I managed to hang on, and that's what saved me.

"I pulled myself up so my head was above water. That's when I got my biggest surprise—Sam had been hiding his boys in that wagon. One by one, the boys popped up all around me, and the river carried them away. Sam and Pearl swam after them. I came to my senses just in time to catch the last one who was tangled in a blanket. I pulled him close and got him untangled.

"He did the bravest thing, then. With the slavers still shooting and riding toward us, he climbed on top of the wagon and made his way forward to the horses. Just as he managed to get them moving toward Mexico, gun shots rang out from that side of the river. At first I thought they were warning us off, but they weren't. The Mexican army was shooting at the slavers, and some of the Mexicans ran into the river to help us.

"I paid so much attention to the shooting, shouting, neighing, and rush of the river, that I didn't notice I'd lost my grip on the wagon until I went under. I kicked my feet and waved my hands as fast as I could, and I managed to get my head above water long enough to scream. That was the wrong thing to do, because when I went back under, I had no air left and blacked out. I woke up on the shore. Pearl told me it was Sam who left the safety of Mexico to rescue me.

"Pearl spoke enough Spanish to tell the soldiers we'd come looking for Honey and Papa. One of them knew where Honey was and offered to take us to her. Nobody mentioned Papa.

"The soldiers prepared our horses and wagon, then escorted us to town. I can't tell you much about the trip because my eyes brimmed with tears, and my heart ached knowing I'd have to tell Mama that I failed to find you, Papa."

I took a breath then and reached for Papa's hand. I often felt a need to touch him, to assure myself he was really home. He understood and gave my hand a quick squeeze before indicating I should continue.

I wasn't sure how much more to say about finding him. Papa and I had not told Mama much about Papa's injuries. I'd heard the story from Honey, so I knew they'd gotten to the river before a band of robbers pulled them from the cart, shot him in the leg, beat him, left him for dead, and stole the horses. I knew how Honey had dragged him onto the hand ferry, pulled herself and Papa across the river, and used Papa's sock money to hire help on the other side. I decided that Papa's tale was his to tell.

I picked up mine where I'd left off.

"Sam spotted Honey as soon as we reached town. She was standing in front of a store and waving to a woman across the street. Sam called out to her in a voice so loud, I believe the whole town heard. He jumped from the wagon and they raced toward each other, shouting and crying up a storm. The street filled with people who laughed and cheered their happy reunion.

"It took some time for Honey to notice Pearl and me in the crowd. As soon as she saw me, she pulled herself from Sam and rushed to tell me Papa was resting and would soon be well enough to travel."

I finally stopped my rush of words and found the courage to look at the people around me. Mama and Papa stared with their mouths hanging open. Honey*Mutter*'s eyes bored into my own, and she shook something awful. I placed my hand on hers. "Ma'am? Are you okay?"

"Her boys, Heidi," Mama said.

How could I be so stupid? "Yes!" I blurted. "All of them, and Sam, and Honey. All safe in Mexico. And Honey has her own store and cafe. They are well and waiting for you."

Honey*Mutter* slipped from her chair in a dead faint. I caught her just before she hit the floor, with only enough time to soften the impact. Mama's smelling salts brought her around. Papa carried her off to bed with Mama following on his heels issuing too many instructions.

With my story finally told, I found I had a hearty appetite and attacked my dinner like a ranch hand while waiting for Mama and Papa to return. I had emptied my plate and was sopping up the last of the gravy when I felt Papa's hands on my shoulders and his lips on my head.

"*Tochter*, I know you mean well." He gave my shoulders a final squeeze before reclaiming his chair. "You know the journey to Mexico. It's too dangerous."

"Yes, Papa. But we do what's right when it's easy *and* when it's hard. It's our way."

Papa sighed. "I have taught you too well, I think."

"You have taught me much, Papa. I will wait until she is strong enough for the journey."

"We will wait." Papa smiled at me.

"*Ja.*" Mama added. "We are family. We go together."

About Freedom Train

I was eight years old the first time I read a story about the Underground Railroad in a biography of Harriet Tubman. It started my fascination with the people who put themselves at risk to aid strangers.

I wondered if I would risk my comfortable life, and that of my family, to help someone else escape. I thought so, but I wasn't sure. I struggled with this. I read more about Harriet Tubman, who first took herself to freedom, then returned, many times, to guide hundreds of others to safety and freedom.

A few years later, I read the diary of Anne Frank and learned there were monsters and victims in my century—and people who would risk all to rescue those victims. I understood something more troubling; those who did nothing, those who cooperated, were obeying the law of the land. That little tidbit raised many more questions.

When The Final Twist called for Texas-based stories with an underground theme, the Underground Railroad leapt to my mind. In Texas, that railroad was called the Freedom Train. During research, Heidi emerged. She gripped my brain and would not let go until her story was told.

ALL THAT GLITTERS
BY SALLY LOVE

Sheriff Townes stepped out of his white Crown Vic cruiser, its light bar blinking, ticket book in hand. He pushed his Stetson up a notch as he ambled over to the aging Dodge pickup. "Evenin', Mose."

Moses Wiebe stared straight ahead, jaw tight. Silent.

Townes tapped gently on the closed window. "Fifty in a forty, Mose."

Townes hoped the county-born resident of nearly eighty years would be reasonable this time. "You were on the town council when we voted in the 40-mph speed limit."

Wiebe didn't even twitch.

"It was the school bus accident that decided it. Remember?" Townes figured he was wasting his breath—again. He pulled a ballpoint from his shirt pocket, poised it over the first square and wrote, "W-I-E-B-E, M-O-S-E-S." Townes entered the license plate number by memory. He tore off the ticket and slipped it under the windshield wiper.

Wiebe had long since refused to roll down his window.

The stubborn old geezer jutted out his jaw, gunned the motor and peeled out, leaving a layer of rubber on the asphalt.

"Ornery old coot," Townes mumbled as he eased the cruiser onto the highway. At least Wiebe could afford the accumulating fines. Rumor had it that old Mose still hoarded a fortune from the extinct Heath gold mine. Couldn't prove it by his rundown house or rickety pickup. The old-timers' gossip maintained that the Wiebes who came before Mose valued nothing showy but collected multi-millions from a lucrative partnership in the Heath Mine during the early 1900s.

Townes steered northeast, keeping a vigilant eye out for heavy-footed drivers, trash dumped along the highway, stranded vehicles and illegal hunting. The Sheriff's Department was charged with enforcing state laws as well as the county's. Since Llano County advertised itself as the Deer Capital of Texas, Townes also considered himself an unofficial, full-time game warden.

He slowed as he came closer to the construction area near the old Heath mine and flinched as he heard the blast and felt the rumble of an explosion. The Highway Department, now known by its highfalutin' new moniker, TxDOT, had let a contract for a new spur. A squad of blasters had cordoned off a wide swath of real estate to dynamite in order to remove rock for the roadbed. The new road would connect SH-71 south of town in a wide arc to SH-16 north of Llano. He doubted the state's wisdom, dropping millions on their little city. The existing roads worked just fine, but he welcomed the jobs. More work meant fewer burglaries and less general mischief in his county.

He continued on his rounds a quarter-mile past the construction. Townes stopped at the entrance to the old gold mine, closed since it quit producing in 1942. Four years before its closure, Townes' great-uncle Bauman and three other partners had given up on the petering-out Texas mine and headed for California where, talk was, lots of gold miners were fed up with scratching a living from small claims. California claims were plentiful...and for sale. Families of the four partners never heard from them again. Townes had grown up with the passed-down stories, enhanced with rumors, fortified with details of the families' search for the four men.

Three of the men had been married. One wife paced her porch for years waiting for word to join her husband until one dawn she jumped from the attic window. One partner left a freshly impregnated teenager who later delivered a child. They both died within a week. A year or so later, word came from El Paso that two men were found a hundred yards from the highway, throats cut. But no positive identification was ever made. If Townes had to put his finger on why he'd gone into sheriffing, it would be to find out what happened to Uncle Bauman.

Nowadays the mine was just a mysterious place for kids to double-dog-dare each other to break in and explore.

Townes drove past the locked gate at the turnoff road, braked, then pushed the gearshift into park. He stepped from the vehicle, stretched his long legs and stared toward the mine. He felt another shudder as the road crews dislodged more earth. The sheriff rattled the gate and tested the lock. It fell off in his hand. A quick inspection revealed sheared metal. Bolt cutters. Occasionally kids might squeeze through the gate. Only adults needed cutters.

He radioed his location to base, swung the gate open and drove the hundred or so yards to the mine entrance. Townes got out and walked off a wide circle, inspecting every inch of the packed dirt and weeds for footprints, listening for any sound. Nothing. He made his way inside the shaft and flipped on his flashlight, lighting up rock walls that hadn't seen a human being for decades. Or had they?

Another explosion rumbled from the highway construction a quarter-mile away. Townes ran the few steps back to the entrance as rock particles and dust rained from the ceiling. When the dust settled, he retraced his steps into the mine tunnel, careful to step over the ore tram tracks, choosing the first bend to the right. In an alcove, he spotted a fissure opened by the force of the blasting. He peered inside, then crabbed his way into the fresh opening. Two mining helmets drew his attention. Townes toed one of the helmets out of his way and continued. Ten feet farther, more rock dust pelted him. He laid his hand on the wall to steady his footing around a rusted pick and stepped into an area that must have held supplies at one time. Now it contained only remnants of wooden boxes.

Townes picked his way across the room, shined the light

around then turned to leave. He spotted something red and reversed. The sheriff fingered a piece of cloth caught beneath a crate, gently pulling it along the rock floor to free it without ripping. Along with the red cloth, he dragged a scattering of bones that at first glance appeared human. Townes knelt to get a closer look. If these were human, where was the skull?

After snapping a quick photo, he folded the fabric around the pile of bones and noticed something tied in a corner of the cloth. Townes slid his fingers inside the knot and pulled out a rock. Even without putting it under the light, he knew he'd found a gold nugget. He gathered up the bones and the nugget into the cloth and retreated.

Outside, he popped the trunk and pushed a hand into a latex glove. He spread the red cloth on the hood of his car, verifying that the assumptions he had made inside the dark mine were correct. After a closer look, he used his ballpoint pen to separate each bone from the group. Townes pushed the plastic tip at what he recognized as a shattered rib and separated a piece of lead that could only have come from a handgun. He then carefully folded the cloth around the find, slipped it into an evidence bag and stowed it in the trunk. He returned through the recently opened fissure into the bone room for another look with a more powerful Ray-O-Vac. He searched the grit and rock fragments that had fallen to the ground from the force of the blast. The sheriff spotted something resembling a smooth, limestone pebble no bigger than the end of his little finger wedged in a crevice. He pried it loose with the pen and dropped it in a second bag. Before he squeezed through to the mine exit, Townes shined the light around the open space again. There was no other exit from the small space, no signs of varmint activity. And there were no skulls.

Townes drove the long way back toward the Sheriff's Office and stopped at the cemetery. His mother's family was all in the ground. They'd all died not knowing what happened to their brother and son, Bauman. Townes knelt at the empty space saved for his uncle, next to his mother's marker. "I think I found him,

Mama," he said aloud. Townes removed his hat. "Looks like he never made it out of the mine. We'll know in a while." He stood, gave the headstone a loving pat and looked back at the graves. "I'll get the sonofabitch." He dipped his hat. "Pardon my language, Mama."

At the office, a deputy readied the bones, cloth, nugget and the chalky rock for the trip to the Department of Public Safety crime lab in Austin. Townes insisted on following procedure but figured he could save weeks and hundreds of county dollars. He had never seen Uncle Bauman without that oversized red square of a handkerchief. Summer or winter, he'd stop at the porch where Townes sat waiting, pull the cotton cloth from his back pocket, wipe his face and neck, then carefully refold it and return it to the pocket. Uncle Bauman would occasionally bring a stick of peppermint candy with a warning. "Don't tell yer Mama on me," he'd say with a wink. Townes had hid the candy from his sisters and eaten it in secret when everyone else had gone to bed.

Ten-to-one Uncle Bauman had been killed before he and the other three set a single foot toward California.

Once word of the find sped through the town, heated discussions would pop up throughout Llano over cups of strong coffee and stronger whiskey. Speculation about the gold mine bones would immediately surge to the first place gossip topic. The find would even top the upcoming start of deer season.

If the mine had only been broken into again, Townes could notify Wiebe by telephone. But finding the bones called for a personal visit.

Mug in hand, his chief deputy, Lyle Nesbitt, headed for the coffee pot. "How's Wiebe taking the news?"

"I'm about to find out." Townes slipped his hat off the rack and ambled out the door. Usually Wiebe could be found dishing out grandiose opinions to the captive customers in Elnora's Café and Ammo. Not today.

Townes circled the city, letting the cool air of late October remind him of the upcoming deer season. He'd spent the past few off-days sprucing up his deer blind and cleaning his rifle. He rested his arm on the open window as he drove past Carolfaye's Gift Emporium and Art Studio. After a quick radio check with headquarters and the five deputies, he left the city limits. The sheriff turned off the pavement onto Goldmine Road for another pass by the mine. Still no sign of Wiebe.

He made the turn toward Wiebe's place, driving along the winding asphalt, slowed by the surface aggregate made crumbly by years of travel. His vehicle rumbled onto sun-baked mud that formed misshapen bricks. Stretches had been rutted from the weight of loaded pickups. High spots between the ruts had eroded and sprouted Johnson grass, plus a few purple wildflowers.

A few miles later, Townes spotted Wiebe standing in his pickup bed by the side of the road. The old coot rested his elbows atop the cab, focusing binoculars across the hillside.

Townes kicked rocks and stomped shrubs as he made a path toward Wiebe. The man usually kept a rifle close by. Townes didn't see it in the truck's gun rack.

Sure 'nuff, when Townes came within twenty feet of the truck, Wiebe laid down the binocs and swung the rifle around. As Townes came closer, Wiebe inched the barrel up, targeting the sheriff's mid-section.

Townes stopped, then gazed around in a three-sixty turn. "Mighty beautiful county, Mose."

The old man hawked up a throatful of phlegm and spat it in Townes' direction.

The way the town gossip told it, when the Wiebes took over management as the last remaining mine partner, they ran Llano as a company settlement, squeezing more hours out of the hardscrabble workers and cheating them out of most of their dollar-a-day-and-found. Townes figured Moses Wiebe was just as mulish and conniving as his relatives.

"I checked the mine gate on my rounds. Came here to tell you the lock was cut off. The blasting for the spur opened a new break in the wall some twenty feet to the right. Opened a big break."

The sheriff paused, then lifted a boot to the running board. "Also found a pile of bones. We need to talk about those bones, Mose."

"Nuthin' to say," Wiebe grumped, shifting his rifle to his left hand.

Townes let his gun hand relax a bit. "We can do it right here, friendly, watching the sun dip or we can do it official."

"Bauman Leveritt was a shiftless, money-grubbin' leech," Wiebe growled.

"Really." Townes shifted his gaze from the rifle to Wiebe's face. "I mention bones in the mine, and you go straight to my Uncle Bauman."

"Evertime ya git near, it's about that mine. About them no-good quitters that lit out for Californey." He spat again at the hard ground. "Barely knew 'em."

The sheriff eyed the distant hills. "Bauman was on the job some nine, ten years before he and the others disappeared. And you barely knew him? You barely knew four of the men who invested and worked the mine? Who helped tote gold ore—"

"Did something stupid—hopped a freight, bar fight, jealous husband." Wiebe gripped the rifle tighter. "Them bones is prob'ly hobos—nothin' to do with them greedy traitors." He shifted the rifle. "If ya ask me, wuz hobos, knocked senseless, trapped by a blast early on."

Townes reached into his back pocket and pulled out a paper. He took a long step toward Wiebe, pushed the rifle barrel aside with an index finger. The sheriff held out the document.

Wiebe ignored the paper, never making eye contact.

The sheriff folded the document and slapped it into Wiebe's open shirt. "That's a search warrant, signed by Judge Carver. 'Scuse me a second, Mose. My deputies are waitin' for this call." He activated his radio. "Okay boys, come on up. He's been served. Is the other group standing by? Uh-huh. Nesbitt and I are taking the mine."

A sheriff's department cruiser sped into view, then turned down the road to Wiebe's house. Townes turned his back on Wiebe and waited until he saw in the distance his two deputies emerge from the vehicle. The men strode up to the porch.

Townes thumbed the mike. "Go ahead inside. Get pictures first. And take it easy with the breakables."

Wiebe recoiled, glaring, eyes rheumy and wild. He snatched the search warrant and crumpled it in his rough mitt, then threw it in the rocks behind. "You'll regret this. I'll see to it."

Townes pivoted, hands clenched. He heard the bolt action of Wiebe's rifle as he retraced his steps to the cruiser. At least his deputies would be close by, if Wiebe pulled the trigger. The sheriff straightened his spine and lifted his chin, letting his arms swing freely. He heard Wiebe start the old pickup and, out of the corner of an eye, Townes saw the old man rumble down the hill toward his house.

Townes stepped into the mine entrance, now lit up like a midnight madness sale at Walmart. Three of the deputies and the Llano County Medical Examiner stood in the main shaft, waiting for the photographer to complete his work. The sheriff moved forward, then led the way through the fissure he'd discovered the previous day. He posted a deputy outside in case Wiebe decided to show his face, but based on past experience, the man was not likely to approach head-on. Wiebe's usual M.O. had been to sneak around in the shadows, wheel and deal out of sight, come at a target sideways.

After more than four hours, Townes and his deputies had bagged and tagged three additional clumps of bones, plus remnants of the wooden boxes and mining tools—picks, shovels, detonator caps—plus tattered clothing and miners' helmets fitted with sodium lamps. The hidden room had protected the bones from predators who had found access to the main shafts. He signed the paperwork to transfer the evidence to the ME.

Townes headed back to Wiebe's house. Nesbitt had stationed the greenest deputy on the shabby porch, two feet from where the old man now sat, leaning against a weather-worn, paint-peeling, sagging post, rifle resting across both thighs.

Townes held out his hand, concentrating on the rifle.

Wiebe stayed motionless, staring toward the rugged landscape.

The sheriff bent, grasped the stock and pulled the rifle out of Wiebe's hands.

"Go to hell." Wiebe didn't resist.

Townes exhaled as he ejected the rounds, letting them scatter on the dirt below the porch steps. "You can pick this up at headquarters whenever it's convenient." He handed off the rifle to the rookie and went inside with Nesbitt.

When they finished the search and had loaded weapons and a scattering of documents relating to the mine, Townes and Nesbitt continued to inspect every room of the house, including the attic and crawlspace beneath the floor. Townes referred to the photographs taken before the search and recorded observations in his notebook. The deputies had carefully replaced clothing in drawers, re-hung pictures, stacked thawing deer meat in the outbuilding deep freeze and repositioned tools on pegboard. No way he'd give Wiebe ammunition to lodge another complaint against his department.

Wiebe was gone when they came out of the house.

Townes sent a questioning look to the rookie.

"Took off that-a-way when I was…you know." The red-faced rookie pointed toward the overgrown side yard past the two department vehicles where scrub cedar, oaks and weeds had taken over.

Townes tossed Nesbitt a key. "Hold on to that for me."

Three of the deputies unloaded ATV's from the trailer. Townes directed the four-wheeler past his cruiser and stopped, staring at the left rear tire, flat as a road-kill armadillo. He eased off the vehicle and examined the tire. He looked back at Nesbitt.

"I've got it, Sheriff." Nesbitt snapped a quick photo, then waved his rookie colleague over. "Get some official close-ups of this."

"Yessir," The rookie said. "Then change the tire and load this one in the trunk with the other evidence?"

Townes almost smiled at the young recruit. "Exactly." The sheriff led the way into the underbrush on his four-wheeler. Wiebe had inherited thousands of acres around Llano and had bought even more with Heath mine money.

The sheriff went to the public records office that afternoon. With the help of the clerk, he pulled every document on the mine. "Mostly I've found really old documents," the clerk said, "from the late 1800s. One or two from the beginning of the twentieth century."

Rather than get bogged down in legalese, Townes walked over to the District Attorney's office. Ira Bozarth had prosecuted every important crime in the county, from meth labs to drunk driving to the revival preacher whose converts burglarized stores during his sermon.

"In those days, the way partnership papers were drawn up was what you'd term 'loose,'" Bozarth translated, as he hobbled across the spacious office to his desk. He heaved his extra pounds into the padded leather high-backed chair, rocking back and forth as his toes left the floor, touched the floor, left the floor. "The thing was structured so that the major players received quarterly distributions based on when they became a partner. The early birds, including Wiebe, got the higher distributions. Cash call percentages were higher for newer partners, distributions lower. This one had a clause that awarded a deceased partner's share to the remaining partners, not to their heirs." Bozarth removed his glasses, rubbed a hand over his bald pate, replaced the spectacles, then picked up the magnifying glass.

"Still putting off the cataract surgery?"

Bozarth grimaced. "Can't get over the idea of a scalpel or some laser cuttin' into my eyeball." He shivered. "I'll keep what God gave me."

Seemed the mine had always been the source of curiosity and gossip. When Texas was still frontier, people settled in Llano because it was the end of the stage line—nowhere else to go. Some were lured by exaggerated claims of lost mines and hidden treasures of gold and silver buried by Spanish explorers in past centuries.

Townes prodded Bozarth for more background. "I remember when the four partners were declared dead."

"When Moses inherited the final piece of the mine, I looked into it," Bozarth said. "There were rumors of a suspicious death of another partner some ten years earlier. The man's body was found in an alley behind a beer joint. But he was well-known as a teetotaler." Bozarth rubbed his chin. "One of your predecessors dogged the trail, but he never could build a case against Wiebe."

The next morning, astride the ATVs, Townes and Nesbitt dodged low-hanging cedar branches and bounced over boulders for half an hour. Townes stopped and unfolded a fragile survey map. Nesbitt rolled up alongside.

Townes untied the shovel and stepped off twenty-three paces. "My best recollection is that it should be right about here." He scraped his boot sideways along a barely visible line in the dirt. The sheriff tossed aside a layer of brush, exposing a padlock. He reached a hand out to Nesbitt. "That key I gave you yesterday should come in handy right about now."

After unlocking and removing the padlock, Townes used a crowbar to jimmy up a corner of the double-steel door. He and his buddies had spent summers roaming the countryside, especially on the land they were told was off limits—the Wiebes' property.

Nesbitt grabbed hold of one handle, Townes the other. The two raised a door to a 1950s underground bomb shelter. Moses Wiebe had made sure in case a Russian nuke zeroed in on Llano County, the townfolk knew that no other surname would be welcome inside.

Townes descended halfway down the steps with a flashlight.

"Radio our GPS. Stay put and keep a sharp lookout."

Nesbitt's eyes grew large. "You don't think—"

"Makin' sure," Townes said. "Just makin' sure."

Townes flipped on the flashlight. He shined the light down and around, checking each concrete step before he put a foot down.

Nesbitt crouched on the top step, adding a second light. "I've got the bags ready. Holler if you need one." He turned his gaze to the far hills.

Townes nodded, his attention focused on the dark depths below. "You keep your eyes peeled for Wiebe."

"Yessir," Nesbitt said. "Whatever's down there must've been there a long time, right?"

"Maybe. Maybe not." Townes lit his way down the remaining steps. "So far, there's only rough shelves filled with canned goods—beets, hominy, chili." He made a quarter turn. "A row of gallon jugs filled with water. Another wall has cubbyholes filled with old newspapers, hunting magazines…and a Bible."

"That old outlaw owns a Bible?"

Townes reached the bottom of the shelter and picked up a corner of the book. Moldy, cracked leather stayed in his fingers as loose pages slid free. "Looks like it hasn't been read in decades."

"That I'd expect. What else?"

Townes walked a grid, stopping every few steps to focus the light. His foot hit something hard. He lowered the lantern on a pair of burlap bags tied with hemp. The sheriff shined the beam around. Everything was covered with a thick layer of dust. Everything except the burlap bags.

The sheriff crouched down, one knee on the concrete floor. He untied a bag and pulled out a fist-sized chunk of rock. Townes held it in the light as he turned it slowly in his hand. Just what I thought. "Toss down an evidence bag, Nesbitt. Any sign of Wiebe?"

"No, sir." Nesbitt tossed a bag at the light.

Townes dropped the rock piece in the bag, then climbed up the stairs and shut off the light. He scanned the nearby hills. The sun had dipped behind the tallest.

Townes and Nesbitt closed the heavy doors and replaced the camouflage shrubs.

"Throw a few shovelfuls of dirt over the top." Townes grabbed a small cedar cutting. He brushed their footprints out of the dirt. He took a step toward the ATVs and froze. "Nesbitt, pack up the shovel. We need to get out of here—now."

Nesbitt emptied the shovel, hurried to the ATV and tied down the tool. He started his ATV, then followed Townes' gaze and waited in silence.

The sheriff nodded across the field. "Second hill, right side, underneath the oaks." Townes paused, squinting to bring Wiebe's pickup into focus in front of the setting sun. "See it?"

"The dust trail?" Nesbitt steered a tight circle. "Is that Wiebe's truck?" "Yep." Townes started his four-wheeler and gunned the motor. "Good thing cross-country's always faster than the back roads." Nesbitt took only a few seconds to catch up.

Back in the office, Townes reread, then signed, the report that the printer had just spit out. The sheriff swiveled in his ancient wheeled chair, flipped open his notes and scrolled through his illegible shorthand. Something didn't sit right.

Moses Wiebe had always been contrary, but this felt different. The old man had forever been belligerent and hateful, but he hadn't discriminated. He'd treated every citizen of Llano County like scum.

Townes stuffed the notebook in his breast pocket and slid his keys off his desk. "I need some air."

Nesbitt put down his coffee mug and headed for the hat rack. "Not necessary, Lyle. I'll keep in touch."

"Yessir." Nesbitt frowned. "But what if Wiebe—"

"I'll be fine."

Nesbitt removed his hat from the deer antlers. "Time for rounds anyhow. You might keep your radio on."

Townes hid the beginning of a smile with a hand. "Good idea." Since he'd been elected sheriff, he'd worked hard at building a strong department. He insisted on knowing every detail of every investigation and adopted his own system of on-the-job training. He hired specialists—a card-carrying criminalist, a computer jock, a weapons expert, a Llano County good-ole-boy, and a college woman who could drag a confession out of a fence post. And he'd backed his deputies to the hilt. Wasn't a day he hadn't looked forward to coming to work, not a night he hadn't hit the sack exhausted.

This investigation had started with the new fissure exposing four skeletons in the mineshaft. Best thing to do was to retrace his steps and try to make sense of the old crime. Townes drove toward the mine, keeping an eye on his tail and listening with one ear to the radio chatter.

At the mine he transmitted his location, then took a walk around the entrance, just as he'd done days earlier, surveying the area, checking for any new signs of traffic. None. He retrieved the Ray-O-Vac, a small hammer and a chisel.

Townes ducked under the crime scene tape. He sucked in his stomach and exhaled to wedge his chest through the fissure. A quick pass of the light revealed what his gut had told him. He ran his fingers over the new chips in the old wall. He shined the light at his boots, over the small rocks that had fallen, along with larger flaked-off pieces. Hammer and chisel in hand, the sheriff broke off a slice, then slid it into an evidence bag with a palmful of fallen rock shavings.

As he eased through the fissure to the exit, Townes heard a rifle shot in the distance and the unmistakable sound of a bursting vehicle window.

Townes clicked his speaker on. He peered into the bright sunlight from the dark of the mineshaft entrance. "Townes here. What's Wiebe's location?"

"His pickup's still in front of Elnora's," the rookie said. "Nesbitt's on his way out the door to verify."

Townes remained inside the mine. Sticking his nose out in the sunshine wouldn't be smart. He spotted the glass shards around the Crown Vic. "Damn him." Those new cruisers cost the county twenty-one thousand, not counting the interceptor packages. The sheriff squatted down near the exit and scanned the territory between the mine and his vehicle. From the looks of the glass splinters, the shot had come from the nearby mountain cedars.

He stood and edged a few steps closer to the way out.

Nothing moved, not even the cedar branches.

"Sheriff," his radio crackled.

Townes pressed the mike. "Go ahead."

"Nesbitt here, Chief."

"Ten-four. Where's Wiebe?"

"M-I-A. We lost him."

"Round up the CSIs and head out here."

In department lingo, "The CSIs" meant all five deputies. Townes had standing county approval for crime scene training and took advantage of the updates offered.

"Bodies or clues?" Nesbitt asked.

"Clues. And have somebody order replacements for my driver and passenger side windows."

"Wiebe?"

"Most likely. Send a couple of cars to track him down and bring him in. Go easy."

Townes inched closer to the entrance, searching the distant landscape. There it is. Or were his eyes playing tricks on him? There. There it is again. A flicker. He stared at the spot. He'd swear he had spotted the reflection from a scope.

The sheriff gave his shattered windows another glance. A very accurate scope. He pressed his speaker again. "Cancel the last order. Don't come here. I'll meet you at headquarters." No way he'd provide extra targets for the guy behind a scope.

Townes stayed motionless another couple of minutes, hoping the reflection would appear again. No such luck. He bent low and ran to the cruiser, boots sending glass shards flying. Once inside, he ducked down, started the engine and hightailed it away from the mine.

When he passed the city limit sign, Townes activated his speaker. "Nesbitt, update me on Wiebe."

"Still looking, Chief," Nesbitt said. "He's not at his house. Or his usual hangouts. His truck is still at Elnora's. But Elnora said the truck was already parked there when she opened up this morning."

"Did anyone—" Townes slid his thumb off the mike button as he scanned the hillsides.

"Canvass the other stores? Yessir. Nobody's seen Wiebe today."

Townes pressed the accelerator down. Something weird was happening. Either Wiebe was gearing up for a major fight, or somebody had finally had enough of the old goat and—he wasn't ready to go there yet. "Any word on the analysis of the rocks?"

Nesbitt repeated the sheriff's question to the other deputies. "No, sir. Not yet. But you remember the little piece we thought might be chalk or limestone?"

"Right."

"Turns out it's a calcified molar—a tooth."

"Thanks." The sheriff digested the news and clicked off the speaker. "Where are you, Mose, you pigheaded old degenerate?" Townes let the autumn breeze from the blown-out windows focus his thinking. He drove to Elnora's.

Wiebe's pickup sat empty, nosed into the curb between Bozarth's new Caddie and Carolfaye's flamed-up, white PT Cruiser. Townes parked down the block, then strode inside the café. Elnora placed a Styrofoam cup of fresh brew on the counter in front of him. He asked the standard questions Nesbitt had asked hours earlier and received the same answers. The sheriff took a gulp of coffee, picked up his hat from the counter and walked out the door.

Townes circled Wiebe's truck, noting that the gunrack was still empty, surprised that the old sorehead hadn't stopped by for his cache of weapons.

The sheriff fetched a slim jim from the cruiser trunk and jimmied the locked pickup's driver-side door. He glanced at the floor behind the bench seat, finding only wrinkled, faded, ratty lengths of camouflage canvas—Wiebe's deer blind tarps.

Townes lifted a corner. There was Wiebe, stuffed into the space, a bullet hole in the head. Sticky blood had formed a thick trail down the side of the old man's grizzled mug.

After the coroner collected Wiebe, Townes searched the pickup. The glove box burst open, spewing every gasoline receipt the old hoodlum had ever possessed. The sheriff scooped the receipts into a brown evidence envelope. The cracked floor mats were practically glued to the metal chassis with barbecue sauce, beer spills, and cigarette butts from the overflowing ashtray.

He added the HandiMart receipts that Wiebe had clipped to the sun visor to the evidence envelope.

"Need some help, Chief?" Nesbitt asked, through the open vehicle door.

"Take this stuff over to the office and log it in."

"Yessir." Nesbitt took the envelopes.

Townes walked to the rear, let down the tailgate and jumped into the truck bed. He adjusted his latex gloves and unlocked the storage bins bolted inside the pickup sidewalls. He unloaded Wiebe's tools, one by one. Nothing.

The sheriff jumped to the asphalt, raised and secured the tailgate. He walked a three-sixty around the truck, inspecting every scrape and scratch. Townes stopped at the rear spare tire holder and stared under the pickup bed. He picked out the tire tool from the toolbox and knelt under the tailgate, fit the tire-tool on the nut and removed the tire. A plastic-wrapped package fell to the road. Townes picked it up. He peeled off the brittle plastic, then slipped out and unfolded the yellowed document inside.

He read each page.

Inside the courthouse, Townes stalked toward the DA's office. His Stetson shaded his eyes from the fluorescent lighting as he marched by the gatekeepers without a word.

The sheriff looked down a good three feet and read the

name-plate: Ira Bozarth, Llano County District Attorney.

Townes pushed his hat brim up, then reached into his pocket. He unfolded the document and tossed it, face up, onto Bozarth's desk.

"What's this?" the DA said.

"You know exactly what this is, Ira."

Bozarth slid his pudgy fingers toward the document.

Before he reached the edge of the paper, Townes slammed his fist in the middle of the document. "I said, Mister District Attorney, you know exactly what this is. Don't you?"

Bozarth gasped, wheeling his chair back until it hit the wall. "How dare you speak to me this way."

"I'm not even close to how I plan to speak to you." Townes pulled his handcuffs from his equipment belt and closed the space between them. "Ira Bozarth, you are under arrest for the deaths of—" He paused, turning the document to the next-to-last page. "For the death of Moses Wiebe, and by extension, William Fisher, J. George Walker, Granger Gordon and Bauman Leverett."

Bozarth jumped to his feet. "Wiebe killed them. He killed them all."

"Sit." Townes growled.

Bozarth froze.

"I said, sit."

The DA sat, hands trembling. "I never touched them."

"What happened, Bozarth, did Wiebe get tired of paying for your silence?"

Bozarth opened his mouth to speak.

"You drew up this agreement, 'Partnership Agreement, Heath Mine.' Your clerk witnessed the document." Townes pointed to his signature. The sheriff flipped to the final acknowledgment page. "Your secretary/notary acknowledged all the signatures."

Bozarth gulped but didn't try to speak this time.

"Thanks to your malpractice," Townes continued, "Wiebe confiscated every dollar the mine produced, instead of sharing with the families of the partners as this legal document clearly requires. And he paid you off to deprive the heirs of their rightful shares.

"After he killed the other partners, Wiebe told everyone in the county that the mine shares reverted to the remaining partner—himself. Everybody knew Wiebe's reputation for violence and nobody challenged him. Now, it falls on you." The sheriff pointed his finger in Bozarth's face. "You said nothing."

The DA shrank into the chair, chin quaking, eyes brimming.

"You miserable coward. You were the one who shot out my windows. I saw the scope reflection. Wiebe didn't need a scope. Get up, put your hands behind your back before I forget I'm the law around here." Townes marched Bozarth toward the door. "One more thing, Mister District Attorney. Wiebe kept every piece of paper he touched. Along with the agreement, there's a box of cancelled checks made out to you, including a big one the day after the four partners 'disappeared.'"

Nesbitt came into the office. "I'll take it from here, Chief."

Townes turned his back on Bozarth. "Get him out of my sight."

Two weeks later, the original copy of the assayer's report arrived at the sheriff's office. Townes opened the envelope and pulled out the report. The new fissure exposed in the mine had traces of gold, silver and copper. The vein found in the chiseled-off samples, identified as "hard rock titanium," would pump money into the heirs' bank accounts and into the county's coffers for decades.

Townes circled the mine in his cruiser. The experts had gathered for days, and were still testing, surveying and analyzing the titanium find. He rolled up the newly installed driver's side window and pointed the cruiser toward the city limits. He detoured to the cemetery. Hat in his hand, he walked gingerly between the graves of the Townes family plot. He paused at his parents' spaces: J. C. and Minnie Leverett Townes.

"Mama, we got 'em. Both of 'em. Finally." The sheriff swiveled toward the fresh dirt mound and wilted flowers covering the space next to his mother—Bauman Leverett's resting place.

Townes slid two peppermint sticks out of his pocket. He laid one on Uncle Bauman's headstone. "Don't tell Mama on me." He nodded respectfully to his uncle, patted his Mama's marker, and settled his Stetson on his head. Sheriff Townes opened the other peppermint stick, slid it in his mouth, and returned to the cruiser.

About All That Glitters

ALL THAT GLITTERS was an out-of-the-blue suggestion from husband Lou to write about a Texas gold mine, a small town sheriff, and a murder. A quick search through the state bible, The Handbook of Texas, revealed few places where even a speck of gold could be found, much less a working mine. Seems oil was called "Texas gold" for a reason. Llano, a small town in the Hill Country near my hometown of Austin, had a profitable gold mine until the mid-twentieth century.

Photos on the Llano County Sheriff's Department website were reminders of the no-nonsense, hard-working, honest people of my mother's family and of the Louisiana-born Loves. The years of visits to grandparents, cousins, and other kin provided a solid foundation for the sheriff who would never quit.

DIGGING FOR THE TRUTH
BY MARK H. PHILLIPS

By the time I got to the church, the paramedics had cut Pastor Holt down. As they wheeled him past, I could hear him mumbling, "Blasphemy. Horrible blasphemy." I looked at his wild, staring eyes and decided I would get nothing useful from him until later.

I stayed well back while the CSI people worked their magic. Sergeant Robert Colby found me and filled me in. "Janitor found him twenty minutes ago, Lieutenant, around two a.m." Colby handed me a photo of the pastor, crucified with duct tape to the life-size figure of Jesus on the cross high on the wall. His attackers had turned Jesus to the wall and bound the pastor with his front to the back of the statue, the pastor's pants hanging around his ankles.

"Make it clear to everyone that if this photo makes it to the papers, careers will end."

Colby shrugged and held up a sheet of paper. "It's too late. These are turning up in mailboxes all over the neighborhood. Around the same time the janitor found Holt, the community's private patrol car spotted a young white male distributing them. The culprit escaped. But for that lucky break, we wouldn't know about the flyers until tomorrow. Unfortunately, the whole neighborhood has been alerted, calling one another. There's no chance that we'll be able to contain this."

I put on latex gloves before taking the photocopied 8½ x 11 sheet from him. A color image of Holt on the cross occupied the top half of the document. Below that to the left was a cartoon image of a fat, bearded man in drag. A dialogue balloon contained the typed words, "Reveal Bobby's grave and confess, or there will be more of these." The cartoon figure pointed to the bottom right of the sheet, where there was a color photo of a grave, complete with wooden cross, inverted. I squinted to read the writing on the cross. "A tooth for a tooth." A bloody human tooth was glued to the paper as punctuation.

"Was Holt missing a tooth?"

"Nope. It belonged to someone else." Colby held up three more identical sheets, all with a tooth. "I'll bet there are thirty-two of these sheets out there, minus however many our mailman failed to deliver."

"Ouch."

A uniformed officer rushed in, nearly crashing into me. He pointed to the piece of paper in my hand. "We've found the grave, sir. It's in the backyard of a house on Forsythe, just three blocks over."

Outside the church we elbowed our way through a growing crowd. I ignored a hundred angry questions. Colby was already calling for more officers. I pointed out one hysterical man in pajamas who clutched in his fist another sheet with another tooth. Colby grabbed a uniformed officer just getting out of his patrol car and sent him to get the evidence and take a statement.

It took us far too long to travel just a few blocks. Residents were milling about in the streets, and our siren only attracted them to the patrol car. The young officer nearly ran some residents down. Angry fists pounded the car as we pushed through.

Colby was still on the phone demanding more officers when we made it to the backyard burial site. There weren't enough police to keep neighbors from rushing in, trampling the ground. Two residents with shovels maniacally dug at the grave.

"Are you people insane? This is a crime scene. Get back to your own homes." The crowd ignored me.

A burly, bald man in a bathrobe grabbed me by the arm, dragged me over to the grave, and pointed. By the light of several

Coleman lamps I could see a tube, a section of green garden hose, emerging from the ground. The two men dug around it while another held the hose gingerly erect.

The bald man shook my arm. "My son is missing, and someone is breathing through that tube."

When a phalanx of officers arrived to clear the yard, I let the father stay and the diggers continue. Within another five minutes, they had the boy out. Paramedics took over. The victim was wrapped like a mummy in duct tape, one end of the garden hose firmly secured in his mouth. They cut away just enough tape to reveal the teenager's face. When the tube came out, the boy screamed. I could see that all of his teeth were gone, his mouth a bloody, gaping pit. He was still screaming as they put him in the ambulance and roared away.

I sent Colby to the hospital to organize security and interrogations. He was in his element, turning chaos into order. I called the chief to get her up to speed. As expected, she red-balled the case and gave me the resources I would need: Ramirez and Falcone to canvass the neighborhood; Michaelson and Outlaw to start interviewing at the church. I took Mr. Gauge, the father of the buried boy.

He sat on the concrete in front of his garage, keys in hand, crying. A police car boxed him in, and he was unable to follow his son's ambulance to the hospital. When I helped him to his feet, he staggered and had to lean against the garage door to remain standing. I shined my flashlight in his eyes and watched the pupils. He was drugged. Now that the adrenaline was leaving his system, he was disoriented.

"Mr. Gauge, I'm Lieutenant Louis Farrell." He wiped at his eyes. I noted his wedding ring. I raised my voice. "Where's your wife?"

He looked at me. "Upstairs. I couldn't wake her up."

I hurried upstairs. It was a cool evening, and the air-conditioning was off. When I entered the bedroom, I could still smell the anesthetic gas. I made a mental note to have the crime scene people take air samples before it completely dissipated. I picked up the sleeping Mrs. Gauge easily—she couldn't have weighed more than a hundred pounds. Her dose-per-bodyweight had been significantly higher than for her heavyset husband. Outside, sitting beside him in the fresh air, she recovered quickly.

I sat down on the rough cement. "Mrs. Gauge, your son has been injured. Deliberately. Pastor Holt was also hurt. I'm going to get you and your husband to the hospital as soon as possible, but first I need you to answer a few questions. Whoever attacked your son and the pastor left us a note. It threatened more attacks unless someone reveals Bobby's grave and confesses. Do you know what that message means? Do you know who else is in danger?"

Mr. Gauge grabbed her arm, pulled her closer so he could whisper something in her ear. She listened until a scowl crossed her face, and she shook him off.

"Not when other boys might be in danger," she hissed. Mrs. Gauge turned to me. "Mark had four friends who may need protection. Theo Kendall, Jason Mitchell, Bryce Rasmussen, and Samuel Nolan." She continued talking to me, but kept her eyes on her husband's face. "That's all I'll say until I've seen my son. Just see to those boys."

I had a squad car take the Gauges to the hospital. Mrs. Gauge's info came too late. The units I sent out reported that all the boys were missing. All of their parents were recovering from anesthetic gas.

At Memorial Hermann Hospital, Colby and I exchanged information. Pastor Holt had given him the same list of boys needing protection but was otherwise uncooperative. Mark Gauge was still being treated. "The docs are testing for whatever the attackers used to knock the victims out. It looks like both a gas and an injection. The Gauge boy probably was out when his teeth were removed, thank goodness. Whoever did it used gauze and Superglue to stop the bleeding, or the kid might have drowned in his own blood. Holt was unconscious when kidnapped from the rectory and when they crucified him. They never saw their attackers."

"How many perps are we talking about?"

Colby shrugged. "Six separate kidnappings, performed simultaneously. I can't imagine fewer than three people involved in the crucifixion, and at least two for each of the boys. Ballpark, maybe thirteen?"

"Impossible to keep a conspiracy of that magnitude secret for long. What next?"

"Michaelson and Outlaw are getting nowhere at the church—I thought I'd pull them in to help interview the parents of the kidnapped boys. Sharon Holt, the pastor's wife, is in the waiting room. I think the pastor has told her to keep her mouth shut, but she's mad as hell and getting madder. I've been letting her ripen a bit. She may just be angry enough to tell us something useful."

I smiled. "Good. I'll take her."

Mrs. Holt was indeed red-faced, mumbling-out-loud mad when I got her alone in one of the doctor's offices. Her first words were, "It's those damned queers. Who else would commit such a blasphemy?"

"Why would the queers do that to your husband?"

Sharon Holt looked at me as if I was dim. "Donald has a national reputation among the spiritual for the zeal with which he denounces the sin of homosexuality, and for the effectiveness of his interventions to redeem the sinners. Our Redemption House removes the tainted appetites from sinners and returns them to the natural attractions sanctioned by God."

"You're sexual reprogrammers?"

Sharon's eyes gleamed with her fanaticism. "*De-programmers* is more accurate. Once you strip away the filthy propaganda that has corrupted our young people, God's innate programming remains strong and true. The homosexual conspiracy inundates teenagers with pro-queer material in movies, TV, music, and print media, until they begin to think of that abomination as 'natural.'

They openly advertise the 'joys' of degradation. Obviously, my husband's mission was so effective that the homosexual underground struck back."

"Why did this 'homosexual underground' attack Mark Gauge and kidnap the other boys?"

Sharon squirmed in her seat, not looking me in the eyes. I let the silence stretch; let her need to vent her anger and her husband's injunction to keep her mouth shut fight it out. I sensed that Sharon Holt was unused to keeping her mouth shut.

"Mark and his friends helped out at Redemption House. An important element of the therapy is to integrate the patient into a supportive Christian, heterosexual peer group. The boys help the patient by consistently modeling correct heterosexual behavior. Positive, supportive peer pressure is a wonderfully successful technique to prevent backsliding."

"I'll bet. So tell me what went wrong with Bobby."

"I'm sorry. Bobby?" Sharon's attempt at disingenuousness was laughable.

"Come on, Mrs. Holt. The flyers circulating among your parishioners talk about Bobby's grave. Did Mark and his friends go too far with their supportive peer pressure? When Bobby couldn't pretend to be cured convincingly enough, did they beat him to death and bury his body?"

Sharon Holt's eyes went round. Her surprise was genuine. She grew terribly pale. It was finally dawning on her why her husband had demanded silence. She grabbed for a nearby trash can just in time to catch the results of uncontrollable vomiting.

When her face finally came back up from between her knees, I caught and held her gaze with mine. "Give me Bobby's last name."

Sharon shook her head. She whimpered. "I have to talk to my lawyer."

She shrank back as I leapt out of my seat to tower over her. I kicked the trash basket over so her vomit spilled onto her shoes and spattered across her dress.

"Give me the fucking name," I roared.

"Hawkins. Bobby Hawkins," she shrieked.

A half hour later I was sitting in the living room of Connie and Edward Hawkins. I had woken them up. Connie was shaking with anxiety, while Edward hid his worry behind a stoic mask. We drank Connie's too-strong coffee. I asked them about Bobby and his time in Redemption House.

Connie said, "They did their best to cure Bobby, but he's been...that way from an early age. Pastor Holt explained to us how the homosexual underground deliberately targets children. Before Pastor Holt opened our eyes, I had no idea that one of the Teletubbies was gay, or that Sesame Street's Bert and Ernie were really a gay couple. Of course, Bobby watched all of that. I watched it with him and didn't suspect. It's insidious."

Edward took over. "Bobby was becoming militant. I blame his high school. Imagine allowing a club like the Gay/Straight Alliance. He sewed one of those damned triangle patches on an army surplus fatigue jacket, on the shoulder where the flag is supposed to be. I burned it, of course."

Connie laid her hand on her husband's arm. His face was red. He shrugged and sipped his coffee while she continued. "We committed Bobby to Redemption House for their six-week program. He was furious. Several of Bobby's so-called friends from school came to the house to try to tell us all kinds of made-up horror stories. Ed chased them away. After the initial program, there was follow-up outpatient therapy. Some of the boys from church mentored him."

Edward smiled. "It was great to see Bobby hanging out with good, clean-cut kids. They took him to football games, a sock hop where they encouraged Bobby to dance with the girls, needled him until he got a decent haircut, even took him hunting. I've been trying to get Bobby to go hunting with me for years."

Connie took Ed's hand in hers. She wiped away a tear as she continued. "Then Bobby ran away. Pastor Holt warned us that it was a risk; that a small percentage of graduates revert to their perverted lifestyle and run away from home rather than submit to further treatment. Bobby didn't even take any of his stuff. He left all his clothes behind, his stamp collection, his PC. He sent us a postcard from San Francisco a couple of weeks later saying he was with his own kind now and would never see or speak to us again. I worry that he's caught AIDS or is doing drugs. His handwriting was so shaky, I could barely read it." Ed held her close as she wept.

I set my coffee cup down carefully. "There exists the real possibility that Bobby never went to San Francisco." The Hawkinses looked at me, confused. "The postcard may have been a forgery. An assailant attacked both Pastor Holt and Mark Gauge and left a note implying that if no one revealed Bobby's grave and confessed to his death, there would be similar attacks."

Edward sat up straighter. "You think those boys murdered Bobby and then made it look like he ran away?"

"I have no hard evidence except for the attackers' accusation, but I'd be lying to you if I told you I thought Bobby was still alive."

"Oh, my God." Connie looked at her husband, then at me. "The pastor told me not to think of Bobby living on the streets in some far-off city, but instead to think of Bobby as having died of cancer. He said that I should get on with my life and that wherever Bobby was, it was in accordance with God's will. It seemed an unusually harsh thing for Pastor Holt to say to a mother, and he said it in such a strange way."

She thought a moment before turning back to her husband. "And remember how Gus Rasmussen behaved at the barbecue last week? He avoided us like we had the plague. You said you saw him later in his car in the church parking lot crying, and you were too embarrassed to go ask him what was wrong."

Edward exploded off the couch and threw his coffee cup against the wall. "Those bastards killed my boy?" He paced up and down behind the couch.

Much as I thought Edward had it right, I didn't want him going on a rampage. I already had enough militant vigilantes. "All we've got so far are allegations. It's my job to find out exactly what happened and who did what to whom." I assigned an officer to stay with the Hawkinses for a while just to be on the safe side.

Three hours later, the *Houston Chronicle* and the CBS and NBC affiliates called to report receipt of new communiqués. Thankfully, the pathologist had removed the eyeball from the one Colby showed me. The cartoon transvestite said, "An eye for an eye. When I said to reveal the location of Bobby's grave and confess, I meant within hours, not days." He pointed to three more fresh graves. I could see the jerry-rigged breathing tubes emerging from the dirt even in the grainy, photocopied images.

At the Rasmussen home I had a uniformed officer sit with Mrs. Rasmussen while Colby and I took Gus to the kitchen. I sat him at the kitchen table and put the communiqué before him. When Gus was crying and mewling, holding himself and rocking back and forth like an insane man, I gave him a form to sign waiving his Miranda rights and a legal pad and pen to write out his confession.

When I had Gus's confession, I tried the same tactic with all the other fathers. If a father refused to cooperate, I brought his wife in and showed her the communiqué and let them hash it out. Gauge and his wife lawyered-up—they knew where their son was. Mitchell and Nolan either had no knowledge of what their boys had done or were excellent actors. But after his wife raked his face with the fingernails of both hands, I got another confession from Kendall that agreed on all particulars, including the exact location of Bobby's grave.

Colby and I stood well back while the pathologist's team dug up Bobby Hawkins' grave site. The TV broadcast trucks all had their microwave towers extended into the late afternoon sky. I told them they would have their scoops for the five o'clock broadcasts, but all of them were interrupting programming with breaking news coverage. Coiffed reporters narrated our progress before the cameras.

Colby was watching the ABC crew. "So why didn't ABC get an eyeball note? We got three communiqués, all with an eyeball from a different kid. There are three graves shown. There should be four."

I shrugged. "Maybe they saved one back, just in case we found the graves before we got the confessions?"

"We've got Rasmussen, Kendall, Gauge, and Holt in custody as accomplices after the fact, withholding evidence of a crime, illegal burial, and whatever else the DA can think of. He'll charge the Gauge kid with second-degree murder and raise the ante with a hate crime upgrade when and if the kid is sane enough to hear the charges read. Same for any other boys we eventually dig up."

I sighed. "What gets me is how those fathers excused their kids. 'It was an accident,' my ass. Sure they were beating Bobby Hawkins with rubber hoses, but that was for his own good. Who knew he would fall and crack his head open on the pavement. Just an unfortunate act of God. Could happen to any decent group of kids beating a fag."

Colby nodded. "Pastor Holt didn't learn about it until after they buried Bobby. If he goes with a sanctity-of-the-confessional defense, we might not be able to convict him of anything. Possibly we can get him for inciting the hate crime in the first place?"

I shrugged. "They're pushing that up in Canada to reign in religious hate speech. There are First Amendment issues here. Do you want preachers to get government approval before they can deliver a sermon?"

"We've had that argument before. We'll agree to disagree."

Before the evening news at ten o'clock, anonymous tips led us to the graves of Theo Kendall, Bryce Rasmussen, and Samuel Nolan. All were alive, barely. Around two a.m. a patrol car picked up Jason Mitchell wandering down a country back road, disoriented but apparently intact. After the hospital had checked him over, I put Jason in an interview room at headquarters. I read him his rights, and we waited patiently until his father's lawyer showed up.

Jason sweated and fidgeted. I sat silently across the interrogation room table from him, tapping a pen monotonously and staring at him as if he were a bug I was preparing to dissect. Colby came in and showed me a printout of an e-mail. It read, "Jason Mitchell is the biggest fag of all. He and Bobby were doing the dirty from the start. I'll bet you anything that Mitchell is the ringleader of the local homosexual underground. I'll bet you he's responsible for these attacks on decent Christian folks."

Colby leaned over and wrote, "Credible?" on the sheet.

I took his pen and wrote, "Who knows. Get a warrant to search Mitchell's house. Use Judge Schumer—he owes me." I was thinking about an anomaly I had noted in the report from the hospital.

When Jason's lawyer finally showed up, I left for a while so they could converse in private. When the interrogation resumed, Jason was pale and shivering.

"Your lawyer has explained the various charges against you?" I waited for Jason to nod. "Good. Are you willing to give a statement?"

Jason's lawyer answered for him. "My client declines to give a statement concerning any aspect of the crimes alleged against him. He will, however, be happy to help in any way he can to assist in the capture and conviction of his kidnappers."

"Okay. What can you tell me about your kidnappers, Jason?"

"Nothing. I went to sleep night before last and woke up on the road where they found me. I don't remember anything in-between." Jason's voice was panic-fast and squeaky.

"Turn your hands palm up."

Jason obeyed my command before he thought to check with his lawyer. The hospital report had been correct. Jason looked blankly down at the blisters on his palms and fingers.

"Been digging recently?"

The lawyer sputtered and closed down the proceedings in a hurry.

When Colby and I appeared at the Mitchell residence and presented Jason's father with a search warrant, he was shaking with impotent fury. "This is outrageous. You've got my son in custody already for one set of crimes, and now you accuse him of faking his own kidnapping? It's insane."

My team searched Jason's room with little result. It was Colby, searching in the basement who found the locked door. It took Mr. Mitchell almost half an hour to find the key, muttering all the while about how it was just an old coal room locked up for decades.

Mr. Mitchell stood completely stunned when he opened the room to reveal what could only be described as a shrine to Bobby Hawkins. There were photos of Bobby on the wall clipped from various yearbooks and surrounded by typewritten love poems and erotic sonnets. On a little table there sat a manuscript printout of Jason's diary describing in intimate details his love affair with Bobby and how he had concealed the affair from his heterosexual enforcement squad friends. There were wild outpourings of grief over the beatings until Bobby's death precipitated a descent into madness. He outlined the entire revenge plot against his former friends, although specific names of the accomplices Jason had recruited from among his former victims were missing. We found the bloody instruments used to extract his victims' teeth and eyeballs, a shovel, cut lengths of garden hose, the roll of duct tape. Everything turned out to have his fingerprints all over them.

Weeks later I was with Colby when we read the news that Jason Mitchell had been arraigned for the kidnappings and mutilations of his former friends. Colby folded the paper and put it aside. His voice was carefully modulated. "So you're satisfied that we have the ringleader?"

I shrugged. "That's for a jury to decide. I suppose Jason's story could be true. According to him the kidnappers did have him unconscious all that time. They could have easily created the blisters on Jason's hands, put his prints all over the evidence, and set up that shrine in the basement. It all seems rather elaborate to me. I find Jason's alleged journal convincing enough."

Colby shook his head. "The journal is just a printout. We didn't find the computer that contains the original. The writing style is more advanced than that of Jason's school essays. What about the explicit testimony of Jason's several girlfriends? If he was gay, he certainly fooled them. Then there's the lie-detector test Jason passed."

"Lie-detector tests aren't admissible evidence. All the rest was brought out at the arraignment and will be brought out at the trial. Maybe a jury will acquit Jason. Even if he's acquitted, I suspect he'll live under a cloud of suspicion the rest of his life. And an acquittal on the kidnapping charge would increase his chances of being convicted for Bobby's death. Of course, if we track down any of the other kidnappers, they can confirm or deny Jason's involvement."

Colby's stare was intense. "You sound like you don't think we'll ever find the other kidnappers."

I returned his stare. "I'm extremely pessimistic. Is that going to be a problem between us?"

Colby looked at me for a long time. No matter what he decided, he would hereafter see me differently. He would see himself differently. He finally shrugged. "No, Louis. No problem at all."

After I turned out the light, we kissed, and I held his naked body tightly in my arms until the tension slowly drained from his body and he fell asleep. I lay awake for a while, thinking. Finally I drifted off and had the blessed sleep enjoyed by all cops with a clean conscience.

GOOD
BY CASH ANTHONY AND L. STEWART HEARL

The summer sun beat down on Houston, and I wanted to curse the light. That was illegal, though, so I kept my thoughts to myself.

Not yet seven on a Monday morning, and already the mercury had passed eighty-six degrees at the Big TravelPort, the Net announcer said. The A/C in our dwelling segment labored as it had all night, and sweat prickled the back of my neck. I mopped at it with my hand, angry. In the year 2145, someone should have been able to manage climate control better than this. At age 39, I shouldn't have to live in a dump like this, either.

"Why can't you get up for once and drop me off at work?"

The lumpy figure in the bed stirred. A plump brown hand emerged from the covers, waving me away. "Don't be late tonight. It's soufflé day."

"At least get up and enable the superlocks behind me. There's an alert for more alien contact today." For whatever that was worth.

This time I got no more than a shrug. Screw it, I thought—why should I care, if she didn't?

Still, her indifference made me mad. I dried my fingers on a bamboo fiber towel, then threw the soiled item into the laundry hamper for the house machine. I ran the lint-collector roller over my suit jacket, hoping to make it last a few more months. Folding the garment neatly over my arm, I carried it, a fresh shirt, and my antique Countess Mara tie—one of the few items left from my days of wealth and glory—downstairs.

I was late, but I detoured by the aquarium and sprinkled some food in the dish for Cindy's pet crab Mikey. I don't know why she bought him. She'd brought him into our relationship, but I never saw her express the slightest affection or concern for him. In my opinion, she only wanted a crab because it was fashionable among her crowd to keep rare wetlands creatures, and because she could use it as a food tester.

Mikey's presence made me question why she was interested in me, for that matter. Was it my position as supervisor of state field food inspectors? None of my previous girlfriends seemed impressed by my job. Maybe it was that steady paycheck; Fredericka had informed me she was too "sensitive" to work. Instead, she stayed home perfecting recipes when she had the energy to cook, and when I had the money to buy the esoteric grocery items she needed. Who eats rocky mountain oysters, anyway?

It was time to leave. My jacket, shirt and tie in their travel bag for later, I spoke the basic lock command to the house, and began to walk. Three steps and the heat plowed into my chest like a truck. I could only push back, drop my head, and keep going. At least my neighborhood had daylight, which beat the alternative, and these morning exposures keep the color on my face and torso even.

I turned the corner. Hugo Montoya, my neighbor, pushed his bicycle half a block ahead. I didn't hurry to catch up. We'd meet anyway at the bus stop, the Far Westside Lower Level station.

FWLL would remain my bus stop for only three more days, thank the gods. That was how long it was going to take to replace the clutch that Sleeping Brunhilda had burned out on our Volvo Air Rider. Three more days of primitive, surface-bound transportation. Crap.

Montoya saw me and waved as he waited in line to catch a level shooter to the FWLL platforms, where the underground Metro lanes from several routes converged. He motioned that I should jump the queue and catch up with him. Not on your life. Besides, while I waited, I turned 180 degrees so that the sun would hit my pecs and abs and the area under my chin.

I was keenly aware of the other commuters. This morning I was lucky: no Sub-People hanging around, begging and smelling like filth. The other commuters were all struggling Upper L's like me. We waited in silence to descend to platforms where a bus-shaped volume of air conditioning would eventually arrive. Everyone watched his Personal Media Link, catching up with Net news and the sports results from last night.

As a result of the burgeoning Houston population, the city had added a second level to its main streets starting in 2106 . At many points, the original paved lanes still ran like fortified tunnels thirty feet below the surface, in perennial dark.

"Hey, Boss." Hugo always called me Boss, probably because I was a few shades darker than him and he'd been raised to give respect. "You got any candy on you?" Every day he burned calories in the hundreds before noon, and he was always snacking.

"Not today, Hugo." I should get Fredericka to make something up for him.

He started to walk off, then stopped and came back to huddle with me, so that no one else could hear us talking. "Did you hear the aliens are back?" He made it sound spooky and mysterious.

I laughed. "Oh, is it the big invasion they keep talking about in Washington?"

"It's already started, they say." He looked worried.

"If it's so big, where are they? I think the feds are crying wolf. It's a social control mechanism."

"They say they're darker than us, covered with blue scales, and they don't even care." The farther the conversation went, the more paranoid Hugo looked. "They think indifference to color is the mark of a higher culture, a better character." By now, I could tell he was pulling my leg.

"Shows you how ignorant they are."

"You know what you'd be to them, Masterson? A primitive. A throw-back."

"And you're so well acquainted with alien history and customs, how?"

Montoya grinned and wiggled his eyebrows. He was a slippery

guy, moving between cliques and companies as unnoticed as a shadow, doing his courier thing. Whatever he'd heard, I saw these rumors merely as attempts to tempt the isolationists to come out of the closet and be re-socialized. And it was a highly unlikely scenario, anyway; we hadn't had any alien contact in three decades, and Hugo Montoya certainly couldn't know what they thought, even if they were back.

Hugo might rag on me about my sensitivity to skin color, but there was a reason the Sub-People were supposed to get a permit to stay in the light for more than a few minutes: genetic purity rested on identifying a mate within the range of your racial matches, on which so much of our civilization was based. No one wanted them to get dark—as if!—and pass amongst the rest of us. These days, if you're black, brown, or at least well-tanned, it shows you belong to the Upper L's. And all of us can spot a fake tan in two seconds flat.

Interbreeding is the only way the Sub-People can hope to subvert the system, but it's strictly forbidden; and besides, who would want to?

"How's your girlfriend…Freddie?" Montoya had a mind like a steel trap when it came to storing the trivia of others' lives. Official papers weren't all he carried around.

"Fredericka. She's so entrenched in my life, you couldn't get her out with a stick of dynamite," I said. "I guess she's all right."

Hugo commiserated. "Hard to move up in the world carrying somebody else's baggage." Once he got downtown, his whole day would be spent racing up and down from the tunnels and double-decker streets, all under his own steam, doing exactly that.

As soon as I followed Hugo out of the level shooter, I found myself mouth-breathing and disciplining myself not to gasp. The air was dense not only with heat but also with a terrible stench anywhere the Sub-People lingered. It was sweltering in the gloom.

Once he was on the platform, Montoya went off to find a snack for the ride in. I almost tripped over two rag-clothed figures passed out in a heap, but I finally found a place to stand in

sweaty isolation, holding my bag. I flicked off a drop of sweat
that had fallen onto the toe of my right shoe and tried to think of
icebergs floating clean, blue, and cold in Arctic waters. It didn't
work. It was just a daydream of an earlier time and place that
was no more.

Down here, in addition to heat exhaustion and foul smells, I
also had to beware the ear worm: the memory of a musical phrase
that eats your brain a cell at a time for hours, because you happened to overhear a song you don't quite know. If I knew the lyr-
ics and could sing the damned thing through once, it tended to
diminish its power over me; but if I only knew snatches of a pop
song that played relentlessly in my environment, I was subject to
its wormy authority, and control of my mind was gone.

It irritated me no end that the city piped instrumental music
into the LL stations. It was a mistake because, instead of soothing the savage beasts, it drew the Sub-People to them to party.
Summer nights, they liked to gather and dance there until they
fell into a stupor. They would sleep where they fell, or crawl into
the doorways of the few businesses that struggled to operate
down here. For that reason, except for an occasional emergency
purchase at the Circle K convenience store, I never gave any of
the LL places my custom.

Today the song was a real relic: "Down in the Boondocks,"
a fitting refrain for FWLL, I admit. "...Something, something,
but I don't fit her society..." Crap.

To distract myself, I let my attention drift to the stores that
lined this section of the Lower Level and formed a dilapidated
cluster of commerce. They ran about two blocks out on each side
of the station. Because it was Old Westheimer Road, the LL rents
way out here were too high for a lot of businesses, and many had
folded in the tough economic climate.

This week, the survivors included that die-hard Circle K with
its small, anachronistic parking lot; and next to it, a strip center
that contained a liquor store, a laundromat, and a 24-hour phar-
macy. The trade for all three was slow but steady during rush hour.

The last structure belonged to one of the economy's victims. A stand-alone storefront with a side window for drive-through service, it had been a donut shop for a hundred years, I'd heard. Despite what you'd expect was a captive market of walk-in commuters and a product that should have survived any recession, the donut shop had been closed as long as I'd lived out here. Not that I was any financial wizard, obviously, but I'd always thought it was odd.

Montoya sidled up to me with a paper sack of candy in his hand, humming along with the song coming through the transit station speakers. He offered me a piece, but, without even looking at the contents of the sack, I declined. Fredericka, my half-breed, Irish-Algerian girlfriend, was a former pastry chef. I'd thought that would be a plus when, on impulse, I'd made the mistake of asking her to move in six months ago after tasting her baklava. Now, after many servings of her pies, tarts, cakes, Napoleons, croissants, ravioli, chicken and dumplings…well, you get the idea. At work, I'd had to give up donuts. And bear claws, and crullers, and kolaches… The arriving Metro bus drew my mind back to reality.

Hugo and I climbed on the bus and waited for the driver to return from his break. He continued to hum that damn song and only stopped after a brown UPS Combo-truck pulled up and angled into the Circle K parking lot, honking the horn.

In a moment, two men in brown uniforms—shorts and tank tops, thank goodness—emerged and began unloading boxes. When they had a sizable stack piled up, they carried them across to the donut shop and through its front entrance.

"Hey, somebody's leased that shop. Gonna cost 'em plenty for supplies way out here."

"It's a good omen, but I hope it's not donuts again. I've got no will power against that."

"Is that what it is?" Montoya poked me in the belly, an unwanted touching I let pass. When I could eat in a kitchen that I knew absolutely was clean—like my own—I made it count. You wouldn't catch me playing Ipecac Roulette. Besides, Fredericka's experiments sometimes came out great.

The ride downtown was slowed by construction. Hugo dozed off, while I linked to today's editorial posts. One caught my eye, warning that the Sub-People still refused to cooperate with the Earth Agency for Alien Contact, a bureaucracy established to discourage immigration. The writer insisted that some of the Sub leaders hoped to establish a pact with the foreigners, sell them parcels of land on Earth, maybe even persuade them to supply arms for an uprising.

Well, so what? What could the Upper L's do about it, anyway? We all gave up our rights to private weapons after the Civilian War of 2068, so we had to depend on diplomacy. Good thing they didn't ask me to do that; I'm not exactly the most diplomatic person you'll ever meet.

The link indicated I might even end up with alien neighbors beneath my place.

I shuddered. If I thought I even had Sub-People within 30 feet of my dwelling segment, I'd have to move. The bright side of that scenario was maybe Fredericka would have put down roots in it by then. She'd have to assume my lease, and I'd be free again.

The bus reached my stop at the Milam LL station, and I found a place in line for the level shooters. Up in the daylight, every hover jitney I saw was full, so I trudged the five blocks to my office over on Caroline, ducking under the sombreros and parasols of other pedestrians for shade. The haze was gone, and sunshine poured down. I wanted to appreciate it, but it was going to be a scorcher.

I entered my building through the revolving doors and paused in the lobby. The cool air was heaven. I handed the attendant my travel bag and was routed through Security and the Biocell X-Ray Screener for a minute or so, then collected my bag and went into the Changing Room. A small coterie of management was engaged in buttoning shirts and tying ties, just as I did. One of them looked admiringly at my Countess Mara, and I gave him a nod of shared appreciation for his Calvin Klein.

I headed for the banks of interior level shooters. A chime announced the Bottom Basement at my floor. A faded sign on the wall said Earth Division-U.S. Food and Drug Administration. Beneath it was an arrow. I followed it, just as I did every day.

The air in the corridor smelled of pencil lead, hot electronics, and dust. This floor was deserted and would be until nine-thirty or so; but I was expected to set an example, a perk of my exalted supervisory position. I walked down the hall and pushed open the double glass doors that led to our part of the building. At Juanita's cubicle, I stopped to gaze at the picture of her daughter Carmen.

Ah, Carmen! I'd lusted and pined for her for almost a year.

We'd met but once, in the lobby; her mom had brought her in, but it wasn't to meet me. Juanita was grooming Carmen to mate with an Upper L trophy bachelor, and she wasn't about to bring her down to our level to look over the unwed staff. I trudged past the A/C maintenance room, the storage room, the back-up server room for document storage and overflow word crafting, and the toilets. All the way to the back, bottom corner of the building.

The tarnished brass plate on my door read "Walter Masterson, Field Food Inspection Supervisor." It was as high as I'd ever go.

I knew there were no openings in the bureaucracy above me to move me from the Field Food Inspection department to the Food Inspector Training department, or really onto any other upward career path. By now, it was clear that my job would never give me a reason to engage or change. I just tried to keep my output constant and my workplace neat.

The bus ride home was not pleasant. I spent it wedged into a seat between the window and the Fattest Man in the World. He scowled at me every time I took a breath. Each time the driver opened the door, the putrid LL air wafted in and discouraged breathing in any case. I didn't ask the fat man to autograph my ticket stub.

Past Gessner, the nose of the bus dipped as it rolled down onto Lower Level Old Westheimer for the seventeenth time. I realized we must be near my stop, and I was hugely—ha—relieved when it finally pulled up. I headed for the door, dreading what was to come. Sure enough, the driver flipped its gaskets open, and I stepped back into the blast furnace.

Mouth open again, I scurried across the platform to the level shooter. I turned the corner expecting to get into the closest car, as I did every night, only to find it barricaded with tape and a sign that read, "Out of order." Crap.

Across the westbound lane was the donut shop, still closed. However, the familiar "Donuts by Alice" sign was gone, replaced by a white sign with four large, dark letters that spelled one word: "GOOD."

An adjective? A proper name? Not even GOOD'S? No, just GOOD. It got my curiosity working. And I have to admit it, I was still holding out hope that a donut shop might open there again.

I took a look around but spotted no Sub-People nearby, upright or prone. I walked over and looked in the store window. A display rose from the red velvet that lined the bottom shelf. It was constructed of small gold foil boxes. Most were wrapped with a red velvet bow, but a few were open to show the contents. Each box contained a cluster of what looked like something no longer produced anywhere in the world: M&Ms! Only without the M's, and just a bit larger than the pictures I'd seen. Not a donut in sight.

On the top row of boxed candy, on a brass stand, was a sign. Red letters on a white background. It said, "GOOD." Beneath it was a smaller sign that read "USU-5 Each."

In my capacity as a Field Food Inspector, I had seen some pretty unusual displays in my day, but I'd never seen anything like this. Finally I decided to go in.

I palmed the door and waited. It didn't open. A sign on it read 7 AM—5 PM, MON—SAT. Closed Sunday. I checked my Personal Link. Five thirty-three, Earth Central Time. I looked in again. Five units each. Astronomical! How good could they be?

Then I remembered that Fredericka was waiting, and she'd warned me not to be late, as her soufflé would fall if she couldn't serve it as soon as it was done. I tore myself away from the window, joined the queue for the only working level shooter, and headed home.

Fredericka was in a surprisingly tolerable mood when I got home. She didn't gripe about my being late. She didn't even seem to care that I had forgotten to pick up a gallon of milk. I admit it, GOOD's intriguing display had distracted me. That I forgot something didn't surprise me, but that she forgot to berate me amazed me. Normally, she would have sent me right back down to the Circle K to get it, soufflé be damned, and then sulked because it fell.

The next surprise came when I went into the kitchen. I can't help being fastidious. An inspector, after all, inspects. Normally my nagging about spills and waste recycling fell on deaf ears when Fredericka went into a cooking frenzy. Today, the place was spotless and cool. Almost cold. Well, well.

"Kitchen looks good," I said.

"I got the A/C man out, too." She stood at the doorway, watching me survey the countertops and cabinet fronts. When I moved toward her, I caught the scent of bath soap and shampoo. Amazing! I felt a sudden rising optimism.

Before it could pass, I opened the freezer chute and programmed the code for two faux-vodka tonics. Thirty seconds later, they dropped into our delivery port. I cracked them open, handing one to milady. I told Fredericka about my day, a recap that took all of a minute, as usual. Then I remembered the new business at the donut shop. It was the only anomaly that might entertain her.

"Oh, I know all about that," she said as soon as I spoke the words 'donut shop'. "Mary Beth Wilson was at the Grand Opening today. The candy costs so much, she had to try it." Her tone implied that her friends weren't cheapskates, like me. "She gave me one."

"Oh? How was it?"

"I didn't eat the whole thing. I broke off a piece for Mikey." I glanced at the aquarium. If I hadn't been so tired that my perception was whacked, I would have sworn the crab waved a claw at me.

Two hours later, she said, when she was sure it wasn't contaminated, she ate the rest. "It tasted all right, but it left a slightly tart after-taste. It was good. Not worth five units, though."

"Even of someone else's money?"

She blinked in reaction. I'd reminded her how her appetites were satisfied. Instead of picking a fight, though, Fredericka laughed with sheepish recognition and blew me a kiss.

The night got better and better. Dinner tasted fine. We watched the projection wall for a while. After I ordered the superlocks on and the lights off, she surprised me with a request that kept me up for two more hours. I fantasized about Carmen and didn't regret missing the sleep.

Morning arrived. Fredericka said something like, "Nice day," before she dosed off again. I didn't bother to answer; I'd given up expecting a ride. I sprinkled fish food into the aquarium before I left. Mikey appeared to be doing calisthenics, so I guess he was fine. I did the basic lock-up and picked up my routine right where I'd left it.

Today the city piped a Bob Dylan song into the FWLL station. The chorus ended, "Everybody must get stoned." I laughed, knowing the words to this one. My father had sung it to me when I was only a babe in arms. Before the government took over distribution of all mood changers, American laws had punished people for satisfying their need to narcotize. Today's psychedelic drugs were tested by the FDA and sold in government stores. Only Upper L's could buy them, of course.

That evening, at ten minutes before five, I stood outside the GOOD shop once more. The window display was the same. I made up my mind. I put my palm on the entrance control. It whispered as the gasket opened for me, and I walked into an oasis of air conditioning unknown in the Lower Levels. It was even cooler than my place. When the chocolate molecules hit my nose, I realized the reason for that hugely expensive luxury. Of course. The candy perfuming the air would melt in the station's scorching temperatures.

Perhaps to enhance a sense of cool relief, the store's lighting threw a blue light over everything, turning the red velvet into a riot of deep purple.

As with the donut shop, only the storefront and its drive-through window, which snapped shut between deliveries, were open to the public. The production kitchen hid behind a parti-tion. Large hypothecary-style canisters lined with foil paper sat on shelves on the rear wall, preventing me from seeing their con-tents and further hiding how the product was made.

Soon a mulatto girl of about twenty came out. She leaned against the display case, her pink lab coat turning lilac under the lights, her hair bleached a defiant blue-blonde, her skin chalky. She looked bored.

I browsed, but there was really nothing to see. Every display case contained more of the same product, packaged the same way, differing only in amount. I was bored, too.

I was about to leave when I noticed that the girl in the pris-tine uniform wore scuffed-up, out-dated shoes that could fall apart at any time. She really needed to make a sale. I cleared my throat. "I'd like some, please."

She turned around to assist me. Her expression didn't change. "How many?" she asked.

"What kind do you have?"

"Just one kind. Five units each. How many?"

"That's a lot of money for candy, isn't it?"

"Satisfaction guaranteed. No samples. How many?"

The girl was making me feel the way Fredericka had when I first met her: intimidated. I stood up as tall as I could and said, "Half a dozen," instantly regretting the words as they left my mouth.

The girl put the candy in a small brown paper sack but kept it on her side of the counter. "That will be thirty-four units, with tax," she said. She watched me fumble for my wallet.

I handed her my units card to swipe, and she gave me the paper sack. The girl said, "Don't eat more than one a day. You'll just waste 'em."

I didn't open the sack until I found a seat on the bus. I sat down feeling stupid. Thirty units for six pieces of chocolate? Was I out of my mind?

And what was that "only one a day" thing about? I reached into my pants pocket for a clean handkerchief, and from my travel bag I pulled out my spare Nitrile gloves. I gloved up, opened the sack, and extracted one of the candies, placing it in the middle of the linen square.

With a forefinger, I turned the candy. It looked normal enough. I could have waited to clear it through our lab, but something told me not to be too quick to bring this to the attention of my agency. I bought it, I wanted to try it myself. So, instead, I placed it in my mouth. I didn't chew. I let it lay on my tongue. I left the candy in my mouth for almost two minutes. It didn't melt. I removed it and examined it. It looked the same, only wet. I placed it on my tongue again.

Finally, I bit into it. The initial flavor was a combination of chocolate center and crunchy candy shell. Those flavors passed, however, and as if urging me to swallow it, a distinctly tart taste replaced it. My mouth salivated, and almost unconsciously, I swallowed.

Nothing happened. The tartness remained. It wasn't unpleasant, but it was, as Fredericka had said, hardly worth five units. I tossed my gloves into the bus's clean machine, wondering if I should use that guarantee of satisfaction. Ten minutes later, I changed my mind.

I noticed that something was different, but I didn't know what. My environment looked and smelled exactly the same; but by the time I reached my basement corner office, the world didn't seem as oppressive as usual.

Two hours later, I was certain something was in the candy. It didn't take a genius to figure that out. I didn't feel stoned or even high. I wasn't speeding, nor was I tranquilized. I didn't feel drugged in any way. I just felt…good.

I took out the brown paper sack, opened the gold foil box, and poured the candies into my bare hand. The remaining five looked exactly like the one I'd eaten. I felt like I'd broken a law of consumption or at least an FDA regulation, but I couldn't decide which one.

By afternoon, I observed another anomaly. The tart taste had stayed with me all day, unlike any other candy—or for that matter, any other food substance—I'd ever consumed, even in a field test.

I should have dropped the candies off at the FDA lab, and I should have reported the store. But I didn't. I just did my regular job. My real focus was on the composition of GOOD. I had no idea my day's production had increased until I tallied the OUT box that evening.

When I got home, things were back to normal: dirty plates in the sink encrusted with food, crumbs on the floor, a hungry crab. I remained remarkably calm and communicative, even when Fredericka yelled at me for spending thirty units on GOOD. Arguing with her about how I spend my own money, even when I'm totally right, is a waste of breath, and tonight, I didn't want to, anyway.

When her temper cooled and the kitchen was sufficiently sterile, I offered her one of my five remaining candies. She made a sarcastic remark about my self-indulgence, but she ate it anyway.

Ten minutes later, the bomb was defused! It was amazing! We made love for the second night in a row. Once Fredericka had drifted off to sleep and was snoring with enthusiasm, I found myself wondering whether Carmen had a boyfriend, and whether she would go out with me, if I got up the nerve to ask her. I fell asleep and dreamed we were on a date. It was great.

The next morning Fredericka got up when I did. It was the first time in months. She even made breakfast, part of which was GOOD. I passed on it, leaving my piece for her.

I got to the FWLL station by seven twenty-five a.m., but there was already a line outside the GOOD candy store. The customers weren't Sub-People or even druggies, just Upper L folks from around my neighborhood. The line moved quickly, and people came out with enthusiasm showing on their sweaty faces. The store's instant success made me feel adequate, too. Perhaps even hopeful.

Hugo almost missed the bus, but when he sat down beside me, I saw that he a small paper sack of GOOD candy in his hand. "Tried it yet?" he asked. He offered me one, but I declined, knowing what that expense must mean to someone living on a courier's pay.

"It's all right." I shrugged it off, but I was curious. "Did you feel any kind of...reaction to it?"

"I don't know, man. I finished my day early yesterday, so maybe it's like an energy bar."

The GOOD shop made the local news the next day. A riot had broken out over the noon hour, forcing it to close for two hours. A lot of depressed people were desperate, I guess. By that evening, the store had hired a cop to monitor how many customers entered at one time; and it had expanded its operating hours.

"They ought to close that GOOD shop down," Fredericka said that night, placing a slice of Key lime pie with Oreo crumb crust and chocolate drizzle in front of me.

"Why? Success breeds success." I looked closely at the tines of my fork, then dipped them into the pale green filling.

"All that money coming in. Mary Beth says it's got to be illegal."

"And you go along with her?" The texture was perfect, though the tang of lime lingered just a bit too long to my taste. Overall, it was O.K., but it had a ways to go.

"Yeah. I didn't finish mine today."

"Are you crazy? Only an idiot would assume a successful venture has to be a scam," I said.

"It's essentially a drug delivery system, Walter. You know it's not just candy. You only wanted to be with me last night because of that stuff."

Maybe, but so what? "You don't have to eat it if you don't want to. But your attitude about it demonstrates why you aren't a successful chef somewhere. As far as the food *business* goes, you don't have a clue. So you might as well shut up about it."

Oh, it was stupid, I know. And I paid for it. She gave me the cold shoulder that night, and whatever had been good for a while was gone.

Another change was in the works. The next day, the Volvo dealer called to say our Air Rider needed repairs I couldn't afford. Instead of blowing up, I walked around the block. After work, I couldn't wait to see how the GOOD shop was doing. There was no sign of a slump in business there.

To Fredericka's disgust, on Friday I decided to sell the Air Rider and take the bus regularly. Heat or no heat, it made my day to see customers exiting the little store with smiles on their faces.

Waiting on the platform two weeks later, I noticed that the air quality had improved. Hugo showed up most days, still working his courier job, but he sometimes carried a travel bag for uptown clothes as well. I had the feeling he had a line on a new career, or maybe a new potential mate. He was rarely without a little bag of GOOD. I confess, now and then I bought some, too.

Some of the Sub-People who were FWLL regulars also showed signs of better grooming. A few had started sidewalk businesses in the station, including one older fellow named Jake, who sold ice chips. Jake rationed it out in cups and, to his fellow revelers, handed out free sterile water and soap, too. I had even seen Jake replace two burned-out light bulbs in the station, presumably with bulbs he'd paid for himself.

If this was a cumulative effect of GOOD, I wished I could get Fredericka back on it. But she'd turned against it and me, too. We shared a space, but we no longer spoke. Poor Mikey had become frenetic; I wondered what she was feeding him.

Six weeks after my first taste of GOOD, Francisco Salado, Vladimir's flunky, came by my office and told me N'tashia Ferguson wanted to see me. Foolishly, I took this to be a good thing.

Ferguson was my supervisor. I spoke to her maybe three times a year at office parties and during my annual performance review. I did my job. She did hers. There was little reason to talk. Aside from those meetings, we were strangers, and it had never occurred to me to change that, until today.

I took the level shooter to the eighty-seventh floor. I turned toward Ferguson's office, looking forward to the conversation. I didn't know what this all about, but I wasn't worried. I hadn't done anything I felt guilty about, or nothing she could discover, and civil servants like me were almost impossible to get rid of. In fact, this might be the perfect opportunity to ask about moving into that empty office one floor up.

Ferguson's door was open. She invited me in with a wave, but she didn't look happy at all. She opened a small bag and poured twelve pieces of GOOD onto her desk. "Ever see this stuff before?"

Deciding to play dumb, I said, "No. What is it?"

"The product name is GOOD. It's sold as candy."

"Is it?"

"Yes."

"No, I mean, is it candy?"

"Mostly. Seems to be chocolate wrapped around a center of mixed amino acids, with a hard sugar shell. Some fairly unusual amino acids, I might add."

"Anything illegal in it, ma'am?" I looked at Ferguson. She was paler than usual, a bad sign.

She shook her head. "Not that we can discover."

"So what *is* in it?"

She pushed back from her desk. "It acts as some kind of euphoric. Effect lasts for some ten to fourteen hours after eating one. The effect isn't cumulative. The lab boys are still working on it. Looks like some designer chemist's work."

"So what do you want me to do?"

"Walt, this is an election year. We can't have someone selling designer drugs at the transit stations, and mobs of people storming the Lower Levels to buy them. It doesn't look good. It upsets public policy."

"Against what? It's not really a drug, is it?"

"Of course it's a drug!" she shouted.

Someone must have been leaning on her pretty hard. I'd never seen her face quite that shade of purple before. Suddenly, I was reminded of the girl in the GOOD shop. I played my hunch. "Wait a minute. Are you telling me there's a truly foreign substance in this, something we can't identify?"

She clammed up at once. "We have the best lab on Earth, and it's given me no indication that there's anything strange in GOOD."

"You haven't tried one?" Actually, I knew the answer to that.

"No, and I don't intend to! It doesn't matter what the active ingredient is. GOOD's not properly labeled, and I want you to shut them down! Their store on FM 1960 has a line a block long in front of it, day and night, and I know this is just a start."

"Shut them down for what?"

"You're bright, Walt. Figure it out."

"What about Houston's finest? Isn't this more in their line of work?" Now that I was finding a little more self-worth, I realized I didn't want to get blown away in some undercover police operation.

"It's precisely our jurisdiction, so of course they want us to handle it. Look, if GOOD isn't illegal now, it will be by tomorrow. But changing the law will only drive the market underground and discourage the law-abiding citizens. I want you to come up with a plan to put an end to this stuff!"

I didn't care to be shouted at. I rose from my chair and looked down at the candies on the desk. I resisted tasting one, for I'd already had my ration that day, and she might have already tagged the samples with the radioactive tracer FDA used. I left her office not knowing quite what to do. Evidently the makers of GOOD had established a local chain, and my store at FWLL was only the first. I checked my pockets. The small bag in my pocket from my most recent purchase held three pieces. Only three? I might run out! It took a nanosecond to realize that, in less than two months, never getting stoned or high or truly euphoric, I'd still become addicted to GOOD.

I thought about what Ferguson had said: that GOOD wasn't illegal but it would be soon.

My Personal Media Link reminded me that I was supposed to meet Carmen for lunch. She'd accepted my calls and various propositions beginning a week before. It looked like I would have to tell Fredericka I was moving out soon, but first I wanted to seize the opportunity that had landed in my lap.

I left work early that day and stopped at the bank on my way home. By the time I got to my stop, the candy store at the FWLL station had a fair-sized line in front of it. I waited. After half an hour, the police officer waved me inside. The gaskets opened as I approached, and icy air enveloped me at the same instant the odor of chocolate tickled my nose.

The girl behind the counter today wasn't chalky. She looked deeply tanned, with an attractive burgundy undertone that I attributed to the shop's distinctive lights. Her skin didn't have that smell of tanning dye that we all recognize from our nannies; I guessed she'd been on an island vacation with some Upper L guy. Then I took a second look. Yes, this was the same clerk who had seemed so bored during my first visit to the GOOD shop. Now she looked alert, sweet, and engaging. I wondered how in the world she'd accomplished that so fast?

On the other hand, her conversational skills had not improved. I approached to offer a compliment on her tan, but she said, "How many?" and that short-circuited my impulse. She showed no surprise when I said a hundred. She swiped my card and handed me a large cardboard box.

GOOD made the Net again that night. Fredericka watched. "Do you think it's a plot?"

"What's a plot?"

"GOOD. Mary Ellen says that's how they'll take over our whole way of life, you know."

"Who?"

"That's just it. Nobody knows. I hear it makes you want to have sex with the wrong people."

"And yet you forget to arm the superlocks when I'm gone?"

"Well, you've locked them now. Want to go to bed?"

I wanted terribly to have sex, but only with Carmen. The idea of Carmen smelled sweeter than roses to me. I cleaned the oven and hung out in the kitchen until Fredericka was asleep.

The next morning's office memo copied me on a press release announcing an FDA investigation into GOOD. Over a hundred stores had opened across the country, and an estimated three hundred million "Goodies", as they were now known, had been sold. Well, I fairly beamed. That took me and my team off the hook. Being an interstate problem, the Washington office would deal with it now. We would "await instructions."

Carmen met me in the lobby after work. "Did you hear? They're pulling GOOD off the market. A lot of the stores will dump their supplies at a fraction of the original price, taking a chance they won't get caught. If we act fast, we'll be able to buy as much as we want!"

"How much do you want?" I got the answer I expected.

"Oh, just one a day, like always," she said.

Like always? She'd eaten her first GOOD piece, one I gave her, only a few days before. I was happy to oblige Carmen's appetites—all of them—but the reality was that even my hundred-piece stash wouldn't last forever; and when it was gone, Carmen might go, too, unless I had an impressive number of units to my name, so as to supply her with the next trendy thing.

The next morning, I borrowed against my retirement plan and bought five thousand pieces of GOOD. I was betting there were addicts out there who would drive the price of GOOD sky high once it became rare. I didn't have to make a killing to be satisfied.

By the time the Washington office shut down all the GOOD

stores across the U.S., I was one of maybe a dozen guys who had cornered the market.

For the first time in my life, I congratulated myself on my financial foresight. I kept the temperature icy at home and put a lock on the door to my private bathroom, where I had stockpiled all those gold foil boxes beneath the sink.

I had to hold my breath to do it, but a week later, when I knew any serious addict would be aching for a fix, I put on my Nitrile gloves and approached Jacob, who lay sleeping on the FWLL platform. "Hey," I whispered. "You want something GOOD?" I shook him fully awake and put a quarter of a piece of candy in his palm.

His face lit up with hope. He tried to pat my shoulder with his dirty, pale hand. I dodged it, but I told him, "Meet me here at five tomorrow morning, and I'll tell you how you're going to earn your cut."

It was genius. For almost a year, the GOOD store at FMLL—and eventually the whole chain—remained closed. I know, because every time I passed it, I would still see those four big red letters on a dangling, broken sign that no one cared enough to fix.

I didn't need a sign for my business, though. I had Jake. Each week, he met me near an Upper L hangout. We assessed a price to Subs of USU 12 per piece of GOOD, and I set up an underground network with other hoarders to assure I'd have a steady supply. We all dreaded the day that it would run out, but the feds were sniffing around anyway. Shutting down the operation before we got caught was the preferred way to fold. I was rolling in dough.

On the domestic front, I hired a housekeeper for Fredericka and to see that Mikey was fed, and instructed her to blend a piece of GOOD into Fredericka's slushy each day. My break-up fight with Freddie a month later was more like a talk; she took the news with equanimity, asking only to assume the lease and keep all the kitchen equipment I'd bought for us. I took these hints that she planned to work as a chef or caterer as mainly wishful thinking, but at any rate, I was off the hook.

Carmen and I moved to the Heights, an Upper L area with

real flowers and trees. We had a private car with a driver, a pool, and a patio, and we were both dark as fiends. Things were going good…until I looked at the headlines this morning. "Earth Division-Immigration Service says negotiation with aliens breaking down." If the damn bureaucracy didn't stop, they'd force the aliens—yes, authorities admitted there are *some*—to deal with the Sub-People instead of us! Who knew what would happen next?

Then my Personal Media Link buzzed. "Boss, you need to get over here," Jake said. "You got to see what's going on."

I summoned my driver and asked him to bring the Jet Rider around. At FWLL, I signaled him to descend and then pull in to the Circle K. I stepped out into the stifling heat. Jake appeared beside me. The music coming from the station speakers was "Sunshine Superman."

"What's going on?" I asked.

Jake pointed to the donut shop. The old sign had disappeared, and the door was open again. I walked over and looked in the window. The candy and the display seemed exactly the same as before. A pretty girl who resembled the clerk from the GOOD shop handed two gold foil boxes to a spiffy Hugo Montoya, dressed in a business suit and a Donald Trump tie that was worth a year's allotment of units. As he exited, he already had one piece in his mouth.

"Hey, Hugo. What's new?"

He stopped, swallowed carefully, then smiled and gave me a big thumb's up. "You're all right, Walt. Never thought you really meant all that racist crap you used to spout. I'm glad I was right."

As I looked around, Fredericka came out of the production side. She stopped short when she saw me. I almost didn't know her. Her dark blue hair was long, clean, and shiny; the body under her lab coat was sculpted like a black goddess's. Her face was stunningly beautiful, too, dark with an almost purple sheen under the weird blue lights.

"Hi, Fredericka," I said. I smiled. She didn't. I pretended to look around the shop, mentally singing, "Could have tripped out easy, but I, hum, hum, hum." I was uncomfortable at seeing her success, though I couldn't say why.

I wondered who had financed the deal for her. Before she could stop me, I slipped behind the counter where a series of framed photos hung, the kind that usually show Little League soccer teams or baseball teams with their sponsors' names on their equipment or awards.

A row of pictures showed the two of us in the production kitchen she'd created in our dwelling segment, just before I moved out, sheets of candy—I had ignored them—all around. *I was her patron?*

I turned back to ask her about it and noticed that she carried two signs in her scaly blue hands. She put them on the counter. The larger of the two signs said "BETTER." The smaller one said "USU—10 Each."

"How many?" she asked.

About GOOD

Over twenty-five years ago, L. Stewart Hearl joined a writers' group that I was starting, the Gulf Coast Writers Workshop. He wrote the original version of "GOOD" at that time.

Over the years, Stewart and I continued to read and critique each other's writing, until we both joined The Final Twist.

When the theme "Underground Texas" was announced for the 2012 anthology, I remembered it and asked him if it could be updated and expanded for this collection. He graciously allowed me to play with it, and we ended up collaborating on the new version. Since I'm not ordinarily a science fiction writer, creating an underground world for Houston in the distant future was huge fun. *Cash*

THE FRITZ RITZ
BY MARK H. PHILLIPS

I stared down at the body on the slab. How many bodies had I seen during this war, bodies torn and mutilated? I thought when I lost my eye and got shipped back to the States, I wouldn't have to see any more young men ground up by the war. Yet here I was in a stifling hot Texas POW camp standing over another casualty. Had he too thought his war was done when he was shipped here from the African desert? Had he thought he was safe at last?

"Sum it up for me, Doc."

The camp physician, Webber, was old and stooped. He affected old-fashioned pince-nez glasses and a little white goatee. "Here we have Sonderführer Bernard Holtz of the *Afrika Korp. Pionier,* what we would call a sapper or combat engineer. Model prisoner, designed and built the band shell you saw on the way in, improved the latrines, fixed our plumbing. Like a lot of prisoners, he was allowed out to work as a trustee. Worked on some nearby farms, helped lay sewer pipe in town. He participated in camp classes and learned English. He also learned to paint. He did a portrait of me and my wife for our anniversary."

Dr. Webber opened the autopsy file and pulled it close to his myopic eyes. "Last night he was attacked in his bunk. Blunt instruments, probably baseball bats, axe-handles. At least one weapon had four-inch nails sticking out of it. They didn't set out to just beat him and overdid it. They intended to kill him."

I rubbed at the scar above my eye patch, sensing another migraine starting. "This happened after lights out? What did the other thirteen men in the barracks do? Just lay there while their comrade was beaten to death?"

"That's exactly what the other prisoners did. Colonel Jenson likes the camp orderly. Letting the SS and Wehrmacht officers, mostly fanatical Nazis, handle internal discipline guarantees order. He doesn't care whether they occasionally beat to death one of their own. A prisoner criticizes the Führer or prefers listening to jazz instead of Wagner. The most fanatical officers—the men call them the Holy Ghosts—convict the dissident in their secret kangaroo court and send their thugs in the night, either to beat the tar out of him or to kill him as an object lesson. Most of the killings are made to look like suicides. We'll find the victim hung in the latrine with a note saying how distraught he was at no longer being able to serve the Fatherland in combat. The other prisoners know that we won't protect them, so they keep their mouths shut and just try to survive."

"It just isn't right. Murder is murder. I fight the Nazis to free Europe, and then come home to find them terrorizing and murdering right here on U.S. soil?"

Webber took off his glasses and gave me a sympathetic look. He shook his head. "I read your file. You were a district attorney before the war. I know it goes against your grain, but there are different rules in here. Colonel Jenson won't appreciate you stirring up trouble with an investigation, especially when you just arrived here. Even if you caught the murderers, the Army won't hang them. The brass are too scared the Germans will retaliate against our boys in prison camps over there."

Later that morning I started interviewing prisoners from Holtz's barracks. Word got around quickly. I could see the prisoners walking through a gauntlet of imposing bullies to get to my Quonset office. The implied threats worked. I got only stony silence. No one had heard or seen anything.

The last man I interviewed used the bunk below Holtz. Tears running down his face, he told me that he had slept through the whole incident. "I saw nothing. I do not know who would do such a thing."

"Come on, Ritter. I asked around. You were good friends with Holtz. You played chess with him every day. You gave him all your beer coupons, because you don't drink. Are you really going to sit there and deny your friend justice?"

Ritter shrugged his shoulders and wiped away his tears. "I am not a Nazi. I never joined the party. Bernard joined because he had to. He wanted promotions, wanted to make the military his career. But in his heart he was no Nazi. You let the real monsters continue to terrorize us. You cannot protect me. You will put me back in the same barracks, and the Holy Ghosts will kill me if I talk."

"I could say you talked anyway. I could give you special privileges, tell the guards right in front of your fellow prisoners to watch over you because you have been so helpful. Then it would be in your self-interest to betray the Ghosts before they got to you."

Ritter looked at me like a puppy that I had just kicked. "Now *you* talk like a Nazi. We've taught you Americans all too well. Will you also threaten to kill my family after the war?"

I felt myself flush with anger and shame.

Ritter smiled. "You can still blush. My masters do not blush. I doubt they ever could. Bernard is dead. It is horrible, but I can do nothing. I no longer care for justice. I only want to survive and someday, God willing, see my wife and child again."

After I dismissed Ritter, I went outside to smoke a Camel. I wanted to think of Ritter as a coward. How much of my own "heroism" was just no one at home to worry about? The migraine flared every time I caught a reflection of the brutal sun, and there were reflections everywhere. I felt sick, hot and cold at the same time. I pinched off the half-smoked cigarette and returned it to the pack.

A tall man with short-cropped black hair standing just inside the fence motioned to me. I had a guard get him and bring him to the hut. Maybe I would finally get someone to talk. I needn't have bothered. He introduced himself as *Sturmbahnführer* Albrecht, SS. We spoke in German. "I could have saved you the trouble of interrogating all those men, Major Price. But you are new to the camp and needed to see for yourself."

I forced myself to sit calmly behind my desk. A desk between him and me might just keep me from trying to strangle him. "Just tell me why Holtz had to die. What had he done that was so terrible?

"An army cannot tolerate traitors. They are like cancerous cells in the body—the only option is to ruthlessly cut them out. Of course I know little of these supposed 'Holy Ghosts.' Who knows what exact offense brought down their wrath. But I have utmost confidence that it was the sure, swift hand of military necessity."

"Before the war I was pretty good at hunting down gangsters and thugs. I watched them pee their pants and cry for their mommas when I had them electrocuted in the chair. During this war, so far, I've gotten real good at killing Nazis. It feels just the same to me. I dream of the day when I crush the last of the scum who prey on their fellow men."

Albrecht threw his head back and barked out a laugh. "You are naïve. You yourself are a predator, Major Price. You hunt your fellow man as ruthlessly as a Gestapo agent. You hope to sculpt a perfect world by erasing everything in it you hate. We are the same. We eliminate all that is weak, so that what remains will be strong, pure, and clean. I admire your drive and your hatred. Unfortunately you are a wolf in a country of sheep. Look at the way you treat us. You feed us better than you feed your own citizens."

"We follow the Geneva Conventions to the letter."

"Nonsense. You are simply afraid to treat us as you think we deserve. You are afraid that we will mistreat the American GI's who are *our* prisoners. I saw an American gangster picture once where the criminal boss lived like a king in prison, because the authorities feared he would use his influence to harm their loved ones."

"What happened to the gangster in the film?"

Albrecht grinned at me. "I believe fanatical policemen, those who refused to be intimidated, gunned him down like a dog."

Touché." The damn Nazi clicked his heels, saluted, and left, still smiling.

Within five minutes, Colonel Jenson stormed in. He had a decided limp from his artificial leg but refused to use a cane. He returned my salute with an angry gesture. "Who authorized you to investigate the Holtz death? Who authorized you to interrogate Albrecht?"

The migraine was still building, fraying my nerves. I held my temper by its last tattered shreds. "Sir, I was assigned to camp security. A prisoner murder is a security issue."

"No, Major Price, it is not. Your duties are to see that no prisoners get out and no contraband gets in. And all of your duties are subject to my authorization. The death of Holtz does nothing to undermine camp security. It's a German affair. You will shut down your investigation as of this moment. Understood?"

"Perfectly, sir."

"Look, Price. I understand this is new and different for you. I have three thousand German prisoners to guard. Most of my men are unsuitable for combat duties. I get too few, and the few I get are the bottom of the barrel. You're an exception, and I was happy to get a decorated combat officer. But you've got to understand that we cannot control or secure a camp of undisciplined, uncooperative Germans. I need the German officers to keep their own men in line. I let them keep their command structure for sound tactical reasons."

"I understand, sir."

"Good man."

"Oh, sir, one more thing. I understand the Holtz murder is a closed issue. But I've become interested in the fact that he was a sapper. Several of his engineering unit are here in camp. As you know, there hasn't been an escape attempt in weeks. I'm concerned there may be tunneling. I want to interview Holtz's sappers, backtrack their work schedules, see if any patterns emerge. Would you have any objections, sir?"

I could see that I had him. No way would he shut down that line of investigation and then have prisoners later escape through a tunnel. He gave me a withering look but finally just growled and left. I took that as overt approval.

After lunch I reviewed the work logs for Holtz and the other sapper prisoners. I found that *Feldwebel* Schroeder had worked with Holtz on several outside jobs: the city sewer dig, several plumbing jobs, digging a well on a farm, harvesting apples. Schroeder was currently working on a farm just the other side of Fredericksburg. Maybe if I could interview Schroeder off the base, he would be more open.

I requisitioned a Jeep and made it out to Mr. Samuelson's beet farm in less than twenty minutes. I found Schroeder in back of the large whitewashed farmhouse. He had stripped to the waist and was broiling under the vicious sun, chest deep in a large hole he was digging. Mr. Samuelson was right beside him in the hole. They could have been father and son, Schroeder blond and blue-eyed, tall and rangy, Samuelson an elder version, hair gone gray.

Samuelson clambered out of the hole and, after wiping the dirt off his hands with a red bandana, shook my hand. His voice was hoarse and deep. "Building a septic tank. I'm a goin' to have me indoor plumbing before I die."

I gestured to Schroeder, who had so far pointedly ignored me. "How is Sergeant Schroeder working out?"

Samuelson wiped muddy sweat from his brow. "Best damned worker I ever had. Worth ten niggers. Had to get used to the idea at first. A Nazi, no guard on him, and me having to pay him the goin' rate. But I'm getting way more'n my money's worth."

Mrs. Samuelson came out the back screen door holding a tray laden with a pitcher of lemonade and glasses. I declined, but Samuelson and Schroeder finished off the whole pitcher in a minute. As Schroeder handed back his glass, she asked, "Are you sure you don't want the radio again, Sergeant?"

Schroeder's face paled beneath his sunburn. He gave me a wild glance and shook his head vehemently.

Mrs. Samuelson turned to me. "Had to run an extension cord yesterday so's he could listen to that radio all day." She shrugged at the eccentricity and left.

I took Schroeder off to the shade of a huge live oak to ask him what he knew about Holtz's murder. We sat on a wooden bench built around the tree. He knew little English so I conducted the interview in German.

At first all I got back was a growled, "I will say nothing."

"Your officers don't know I'm here. They would have no way of knowing that you identified the murderers."

He looked at me and then down at the ground. "None of that matters. After the war, I will hunt them down, every one of them. You need not concern yourself. They are dead men already and do not know it."

"Fine. Just tell me why he was killed."

"I cannot. If I did, they would know who told. It is too late anyway." He hit his thigh with his fist, hard. "I tell myself it is already probably too late, but who can know for sure. But I cannot die like Bernard, not after everything I have suffered and survived. I've never even seen the daughter that waits for me in *München*. Not telling will haunt me the rest of my life. Bernard was a better man than I will ever be. He was a true Christian."

I drove for a while, not wanting to return to the camp. I parked in a residential part of town under a shade tree. The street was deserted. The bungalows around me were little one- and two-room shacks with loft bedrooms, weekend houses for the farmers who lived many miles from town, used only when they made the trip in to shop and go to church.

I laid my forehead against the steering wheel. If the migraine became worse, it would incapacitate me, possibly for days. I needed morphine and not only for the migraine. I had already gone through the entire prescription Doc Webber had given me. I knew he suspected. If I asked for more now, he would spot me as an addict.

I leaned back and closed my eye, watching infinitely complex geometric mosaics dance behind my eyelid. If I could only think straight. Why would the Holy Ghosts know that it was Schroeder who talked? Why did Schroeder think it might be too late? Too late for what? And what was that business with the radio?

I went back to the *Haupstrasse*. Why should an American town have a *Haupstrasse* instead of a Main street? Damn screwy, setting up a POW camp for Germans near a town filled with German immigrants. They called their oldest church the *Vereins-Kirche*. I had read in the little pamphlet the Army had given me that the church's bells had come all the way from Brenham in Germany. Half the town still spoke their own odd Texan-German dialect. Maybe I was in the midst of a morphine trance—maybe I was still in Germany, delirious on a hospital bunk, caught halfway between the dream of home and the nightmare of ravaged Europe.

I threw off the fantasy of delirium and forced myself back onto the case. I went into the post office to get directions. Soon I was headed towards the lone radio station in town, KNAF. The dusty, ramshackle building stood next to a towering steel antenna. The receptionist was gorgeous, and the small fan on her desk did little to keep her sweat-soaked blouse from sticking to her skin. She flicked back her Veronica Lake hair so she could assess me with both eyes. She smiled and batted long lashes. A beautiful girl flirting with me, and all I could think of was my throbbing head and the little damned pills I needed. Just to keep up appearances, I did take her up on her offer of a cold Coke from the icebox down the hall, and I got her name and number.

The station master/DJ found us before I would have had to refuse additional offers. He was a young man with long pomaded hair and an outlandish checked suit. He spoke with an odd slur. I looked at his eyes and saw the pupils contracted to near pinpricks. "What can I do to help the Army today?"

I made sure the receptionist was out of earshot. "I need two things. First, what you were broadcasting yesterday?"

The DJ looked at his wristwatch, held up a finger to indicate he needed a minute, and rushed back into the booth. I watched through soundproof glass as he went through his patter and changed records. When he returned he shrugged and said, "Usual stuff. Mostly music, polkas, crooners, some swing when they let me get away with it. We do the news every hour. Round lunchtime, we do the commodity prices and farm report. Oh, and yesterday I broke in from time to time with reports about the Johnson girl."

"Tell me about that. I missed the broadcast."

"You don't take the local paper up there at the base? This little Negro girl, maybe five or six years old, disappeared. Emilene Johnson. Everybody round here knows her father. He works lots of odd jobs 'cause it's nearly impossible to eke out enough to eat from that supposed farmland. Emilene's mother did a lot of dressmaking until she passed a couple of years ago. Anyway, the little girl disappears. Weren't no strangers come through town. None of the other kids seen her. We thought maybe we had a kid-down-a-well story for a while. It wasn't much of a well, just a dry hole. Her father found a torn piece of her dress stuck to a broken board near the well mouth. The sheriff and Johnson climbed a ladder down the well and found the girl's doll at the bottom, but no girl. We had reports all through the day yesterday, but we've tapered off today. Ain't nothin' new to report. Anyway, what was the second thing you needed?"

Back in the car I downed several of the pills I had bought. Outrageous price. In Europe I could get what I needed for next to nothing. I took just enough to keep the pain at bay. I needed to stay alert.

I thumbed through the work documents on Holtz. He had been on Johnson's farm recently working on that well, with Schroeder for a day, and then by himself for nearly a week. Following the directions in the file, I drove back towards the camp, turned off on a dirt side road, essentially circling the camp, continuing up a little rise and into some dry scrub woods. Johnson's tar-paper shack stood in a copse of desiccated oak trees. His fields of withered lima beans stretched a few acres behind the house. Dust was everywhere, coating everything. But I was excited. From his farmhouse, I could see directly into the camp.

Johnson came out of the shack. He was a large coal-black fellow in faded dungarees. He wore a big Mexican straw hat that had seen much better days. "Any news of Emilene?"

I could hear the desperation in his voice. It looked to me as if he hadn't slept for days.

"I'm sorry, Mr. Johnson. No news."

"I'm beside myself with worry. She's all I've got."

"I am sorry, Mr. Johnson. I'm here on a different matter. You had one of the German prisoners help you dig a well recently?"

Mr. Johnson, with some difficulty, pulled his thoughts from the abyss where they dwelt. He turned and walked me over to a wood platform with an open trapdoor in the middle. One of the boards at the edge of the trapdoor had broken. The top of a ladder just poked over the edge of the well.

"As you can see, the land round here is just too dry. But the trees got me thinking there must be water down there someplace. I had Old Tom come out with his dowsin' stick. He thought he got a faint reading right here, but I got to admit that he said it was at best a one-in-seven bet. The Kraut done a good job. The sides is all reinforced with strong timbers to keep it from collapsing. He went deeper than I ever would, but it turned out to be a dry hole. All that money I paid him, all for nothing. Then I really cursed my luck when I thought Emeline had fallen in. This one board was rotten and I found a scrap of her dress on the splintered end. The sheriff found Emeline's doll at the bottom, but no Emeline."

"Mind if I take a look?"

Johnson shrugged. He got me a lantern and lit it. I descended the rickety ladder. I fought off the dizziness and nausea from my migraine and somehow made it to the bottom. The floor was dirt, but the walls of the shaft were wood beams. There was barely room to turn around.

So what now? I had no idea what I was looking for. I knelt down and felt the dirt. I was no expert, but it felt wrong. It was churned up and then tamped down, as if Holtz had dug deeper and then filled it in. I started tapping at the walls. Nothing. They all seemed solid. But the wall nearest the camp leaked dust-dry dirt when I tapped it. I looked closely at the wall and gave it a good rap with my fist. Again, choking dust emerged outlining a barely visible seam that shouldn't have been there. I pushed at various places until I felt a slight give. About four feet of the wall at face level was a cleverly disguised panel on a central vertical pivot.

I pushed again and dirt streamed out both sides. Then the panel split with a sound like a gunshot. A torrent of dirt hit me in the face and chest and slammed me against the opposite wall. I tried to yell but dirt filled my mouth. Within a fraction of a second I was buried. I desperately fought off the panic-urge to breathe, which would only have sucked the dirt into my lungs.

The only part of my body I could move was my right hand, which was raised high above my head. It must have been sticking above the cave-in. But that was all I could move. The geometric patterns were turning to bright flashing stars as I began to suffocate. Then I felt a strong hand grasp my free hand. I willed myself up, straining every muscle to assist. The crushing soil moved, lurched, and then my head was free. I spit out clods of dirt and sucked in the dusty air. I choked and gagged, but the stars receded. More dirt poured in, but Johnson was dragging me up faster than the hole was filling. More beams cracked around us. We both clambered out of the hole just before the entire well collapsed in on itself.

Johnson brought me water from the rain barrel next to his house, and I washed the soil from my mouth. When I could breathe without coughing, I thanked him profusely and then roared off in the Jeep. I tore back to Samuelson's farm.

Both men were still hard at it. I apologized to Samuelson and took Schroeder back under the shade tree. He looked at the state of my uniform, my hair still white with dust. He held his face in his hands. He finally pulled his hands back across his hair and sat up straight. "You've been to the well."

"I found the secret entrance. Holtz worked it from Johnson's end while you and the others worked it from the camp end. There was a cave-in."

"Our officers wanted a mass escape. They said it was our duty to escape and cause chaos. The ground here is too dry, too sandy. We were short of suitable lumber. We took what lumber we could from the barracks to shore up the tunnel, but there were still cave–ins. The tunnel was nearly finished but too unstable. Then Bernard and I got the job with the *Schwartze* farmer. The site he had chosen for his well was fortuitously close to where we had left off digging the tunnel. We made him buy way too much lumber and then sawed the beams into thinner planks, which we then used to reinforce the tunnel. What you see lining the well are mere facades."

"I know. The damn thing collapsed in on me. The cave-in on the other side of the secret panel finally broke through when I shifted it just a little."

Schroeder looked at the ground. His voice grew sad. "Bernard heard the story about the little girl from some guards first and then on the radio. I listened here until I could no longer stand it. Bernard was convinced the little girl had fallen into the well and somehow found the panel. It should have been secured from the inside, but perhaps Bernard forgot to lock it. She tried to escape by going into the tunnel. Crawling around in there triggered a cave-in. We did not know there was a cave-in at the well end. There was a cave-in a mere thirty feet from the camp entrance. Perhaps the entire length caved in burying the little girl instantly."

I put my hand on his arm and made him look me in the eye. "But Holtz thought there was just the cave-in at the camp end. He thought the girl was trapped, probably injured somewhere in the tunnel between the cave-in at your end and the panel."

"He told our officers that the little girl's life was more important than our attempt at escape. You can imagine what they thought of that. Albrecht laughed at him as if he were telling a joke. Why should they ruin military plans for the insignificant life of an enemy child, a child of an inferior race, no less? Bernard tried to tell the guards, but the officers caught him. When he still would not obey, they killed him."

"Listen, Schroeder. What if Holtz was right? What if there were two separate cave-ins? The girl triggered one at the well end, which prevented her from returning to the well, but she wasn't buried and continued through the tunnel, causing another cave-in close to the camp. This time the cave-in forced her back, and now she's trapped between the two."

Schroeder looked away. He didn't want to think about the possibility. "It is unlikely. Even if it were so, her air would be exhausted long ago. She is dead. Buried or suffocated; what difference does it make now?"

"Suppose she was unconscious, breathing shallowly. She's a little girl—she wouldn't use as much air as a full-grown man. There could be hundreds of feet of tunnel between the two cave-ins. That could give her just enough air." I pulled his face roughly towards me, forced him to look me in the eyes. "Show me the tunnel entrance in the camp. Help me dig. Let's try to save her."

"I can't. I'm afraid."

"Be a man. Be a good Christian. Holtz knew right from wrong. You know right from wrong. Think of your own daughter. Think of what Johnson is going through right now. You would let his daughter die because you are scared of monsters like Albrecht?"

I didn't wait for a response. I dragged Schroeder towards the Jeep, stopping at the pit to grab a couple of shovels and a pickax. I yelled my apologies to Samuelson and roared off towards the camp. I skidded to a stop in a shower of gravel inches from the camp gate.

Sergeant Yates opened the gate. I pulled the Jeep inside, shoved the tools into Schroeder's arms, dragging him after me, and gave Yates his orders on the run. "I want ten men, armed with Thompsons and sidearms, and I want them now. We've got a tunnel."

By the time we got through the wire and into the barracks,

I had my escort. Yates handed me a web belt with .45 automatic and extra magazines. I strapped it on. POWs flooded out of the barracks, milling around us, but Yates and his men forced them back. The tower guards had their big machine guns pointed at the POWs, itching to give us covering fire.

"Where is it, Schroeder?" When he said nothing, I spun him towards me. "We're saving that girl. The girl, Schroeder. Help me save a little girl."

Someone in the crowd yelled at Schroeder to remain silent. I pulled the .45, released the safety and chambered a round. I aimed it towards the voice without taking my eyes off Schroeder. Out of the corner of my eye I saw Yates, on his own initiative, muscle his way into the crowd and pistol-whip the man who had yelled the threat to the ground. Yates managed to get back without anyone trying to take his weapons. Stupid move, but luckily effective. The crowd backed further away from us in deathly silence.

Schroeder stood tall. He looked at the faces of his fellow soldiers. Albrecht had forced his way to the front of the mob. He said nothing, but he and Schroeder locked eyes. And the threat was transmitted clearly. I saw Schroeder pale and shiver.

I had had enough. I marched over to Albrecht, put the pistol against his forehead, and blew his brains out. Fucking Nazi. I looked at the stunned POWs in front of me. Nobody moved. Nobody breathed. I very deliberately made the Sign of the Cross, but stopped before I reached the Holy Ghost and spit on the twitching corpse at my feet instead. Yates came up beside me, and I handed him the pistol.

Schroeder took me to Barrack 13 and showed me the concealed entrance to the tunnel cleverly hidden in the latrine. I had Yates and his men tear up the barracks for boards, go for saws to cut them to the right size, and gather as many flashlights as they could find. Schroeder organized his fellow sappers. Schroeder went in first, with me behind him. The tunnel was barely big enough to crawl through. Schroeder's men followed me in a long daisy chain, shuttling the boards down, shoring up the tunnel as we moved.

When we reached the cave-in, Schroeder dug like a madman. We feverishly scooped dirt back along the line and jammed boards against the walls and then wedged boards above that rested on the wall boards. The soft dirt flowed in through gaps, more like water than solid soil. Dust made us choke and gag, blinding us despite the flashlights. So many men using up all the oxygen in the confined space made those of us at the front gasp for air.

Then Schroeder yelled that he'd broken through. I wanted to follow him in, but he shoved me back with his feet. The stale air ahead made breathing almost impossible, but he managed to gasp out, "Let me. You'll bring the whole thing down if you follow."

I ordered everyone behind me out. I shined the flashlight ahead and watched Schroeder slither along. The inadequate boards around him creaked and bulged, dust and dirt raining down on him until all I could see was a cloud.

I waited. I listened for the sound of another cave-in ahead, intending to follow and maybe try to pull Schroeder out. Fresh air came through the shaft from behind me. I waited some more.

Finally I saw dust moving ahead, billowing back towards me. Then I saw Schroeder's boots. I crawled backwards out of the tunnel as Schroeder did likewise. Eventually I got to the bend to the surface, lying on my back and thrusting my legs up the hole, so men above could grab my ankles and lift me out. Then they dragged Schroeder up. He had a limp little body in his arms. I shoved men aside and knelt beside Emeline Johnson. Germans and Americans, all covered in dust, crowded around, watching as I felt for a pulse. They roared and cheered when I smiled.

They continued to cheer as we hit the yard. Col. Jenson had arrived with reinforcements. He had the POWs well back, but they could see Schroeder as he carried Emeline to the fence. The guards opened the gate and escorted him to the infirmary.

I blinked even in the dim setting sun. My migraine was back. Jenson had Yates and several of his men escort me to the brig, a little single cell at the back of my own Quonset office. I was allowed to wash up and change my uniform before they locked me in for the night. Later, Doc Webber brought me more pills, and I dreamed of bliss.

Emeline recovered completely, despite a broken leg. Jenson let me out long enough to see Schroeder carry her to the gate and hand her to her father. Jenson personally drove Johnson and Emeline back to their farm.

Yates told me there had been twenty "suicides" while I slept, groups of five men hanging side by side in the latrines of four separate barracks. All the "suicides" were hardened Nazi fanatics, officers and their enlisted thugs alike.

I was court-martialed, of course. My defense attorney played up my injury-induced migraines. He mentioned that I was up for the Medal of Honor for my heroics in Europe. The fact that I had rescued the Johnson girl and foiled a mass escape helped. It saved me from hanging. I was given a dishonorable discharge. I didn't fight it. It sounded more than fair.

As the years go by, I still wonder about the odd human practice of carving our visions of the future by slicing away the human flesh that disagrees with us. Is it the particular vision which justifies the carving in human flesh? Do we need to cut away the tainted to make way for the healthy? Most world leaders, then and now, think they are heaven-sent surgeons, and chop away with gusto. My own vision increasingly longs for a world without such butchers. How do you butcher butchers without becoming a butcher? I took Albrecht and his thugs out of that game at the same time I took myself out. At least I did that.

Many years later, I was bumming around Europe. I had moved on from morphine to heroin by then. Schroeder was both glad to see me and shocked at how far I had sunk. After the war he had returned to find his wife and child safe. Holtz's wife had been killed by Allied bombs. He had tracked down Holtz's orphaned daughter and adopted her. When Ilsa Holtz Schroeder Silverman had a daughter of her own, she named the child Emeline. Little Emeline hopes to be a surgeon some day—the real kind. I'm content.

MEETING MISS BETTIE
BY SHIRLEY WETZEL

I first met Miss Bettie Brown when I was six years old. Miss Bettie had been dead for forty-six years on that spring evening in 1964, but I didn't know it, and I didn't care. She was beautiful and exotic and as full of life as a dead woman could be. As time went by and I got to know her better, I decided I wanted to be just like her.

It all began when my parents took my older brother Sam and me to a grand ball at the El Mina Shrine Temple in 1964. I was awestruck by the gilt and glamour of the building. My mother, an expert on Galveston Island history, told me the temple had started its life in 1859 as the home of James Moreau Brown, a wealthy Galveston businessman, and his family. They named it Ashton Villa. Mother was BOI, part of the exclusive group who were Born on the Island, and what she didn't know about the unique and colorful history of the island wasn't worth knowing.

Sam and I were dressed in our Sunday best, a velvet suit for Sam, who hated dressing up, and a lacy organza dress with lots of crinolines and shiny Mary Janes for me. Mother, knowing Sam's penchant for getting into mischief and my inquisitive nature, told us both to look her in the eye. "Promise me you will NOT leave the ballroom for any reason. Miss Bettie might see you, and she does not care for strangers traipsing around her house."

"Who is Miss Bettie, Mommy? I thought you said the Shriners owned the house. Is she a Shriner?"

"Never you mind, Sarah Jane, just do what I say. You and

Sam go over there to the children's table and have some punch and cake while Daddy and I visit with our friends. And *don't* get punch on your clothes!"

She knew it was a lost cause, but she had to make the effort. Within ten minutes my pretty pink dress was splattered with red punch, and Sam's velvet suit was rumpled, the crisp white shirt untucked and his shiny shoes scuffed. Ten minutes after that, we were totally bored. Toni James, a snotty brat with a bad overbite, said "If you're so bored, why don't you sneak out of here and go see the rest of the house?"

Sam and I looked at each other. Then Sam said, "You know we're not allowed to leave the ballroom!"

Tommy Smithers joined in. "Are you scaredy cats? Are you afraid a ghost will get you?"

"There's no such thing as ghosts, you blockhead!" Sam was rational and scientifically inclined from birth. Even as a little boy, he knew there were no monsters under the bed or in his closet. I wasn't so sure about that, but I was, after all, only six.

"Are too! This place is haunted, my mama said so! If you're so sure, why don't you prove it? I dare you to just go through that door and to the foot of the stairs."

Sam's face was turning red. He was never one to back down from a challenge. "Okay, I'll do it. Just don't tell my parents, and watch Sarah Jane." He glanced around to be sure the coast was clear, and made his way around the edge of the dance floor to the massive doors leading into the main part of the house.

Even though I was only six, I didn't want to be left out. The older kids abandoned me as soon as Sam was out of sight, and I scampered across the middle of the floor, dodging the wide satin and chiffon skirts of the ladies and the tuxedo pants legs of the men, slipping through the heavy doors just as they were about to close. In the dim light of the entry hall, I saw Sam standing at the foot of the grand staircase, staring up at the landing in disbelief. Quietly, I crept up beside him. "What are you looking at, Sam?"

He jumped at least a foot, then glared down at me and said,

"I told you to stay put!" I heard a noise, faint, there and gone in an instant. We both turned our gaze to the second floor landing. A beautiful lady looked down on us, a finger to her lips, shushing us. Her blond hair was piled high atop her head, and she wore a turquoise dress, the prettiest dress I'd ever seen, long and flowing, lace and ruffles everywhere. She wore a heavy gold necklace and gold bracelets on both wrists. I thought she might be an angel.

Sam took off like the devil was after him, leaving me to my own devices. I stood there for several moments, feeling no fear, only wonder. "Are you Miss Bettie?"

She smiled and gently nodded her head. The lights flickered, and when I looked again she was gone. I made my way back to the ballroom. The doors burst open, and my parents were there. My dad, panic in his eyes, scooped me up in his arms. "Didn't your mother tell you not to leave the ballroom? You could have been hurt, or…or…" Sam stood behind them, a guilty look on his face. Mother didn't look panicked at all, just curious.

"Mama, I met Miss Bettie, and she didn't mind at all that I was there. She smiled at me."

Sam and Dad both spoke at once. "She didn't see anybody!" "There's no such thing as ghosts!"

Dad glared at Sam. "You're old enough to know better, son. We left you in charge of your little sister and look what happened! We're leaving right now, and I'll deal with you when we get home."

Looking over Dad's shoulder as he carried me out, I saw in my mother's face her conflict. She tried to scowl, but a smile crept across her face and she winked at me. I knew then that she'd met Miss Bettie, too. Rebecca Ashton Brown died in 1920, but James Brown's headstrong daughter didn't let a little thing like death keep her from letting the world know Ashton Villa was still *her* home.

My own home at the time was in Houston, fifty miles north of Galveston. I was asleep before we even got over the causeway, so the parental lecture promised to me and Sam was put off until the next day.

Sam, Mother and Dad, and I sat at the red linoleum and

chrome dinette table, and I started eating my oatmeal, served in my favorite Annie Oakley bowl. The December sun shone brightly through the bay window of the breakfast nook, and I was happy. Then Mother looked at Dad in what I called a Meaningful Way, and he cleared his throat and began to speak.

"About last night…"

I jumped right in. "Oh, it was the *best* night ever. I got to wear my favorite fancy dress, and I danced with you and I met Miss Bettie, and she was *sooo* beautiful and I want to go see her again, please can we go back?"

Sam looked at me with scorn. "You dummy, Miss Bettie isn't real. I mean, she *was* real, but she's been dead a long time and *you did not see her!*"

Mother stepped in. "Sam, you know we do not call anyone a dummy, and we do not yell at people. Apologize to your sister right now!"

He mumbled "Sorry, Sarah Jane," but I knew he didn't mean it. I accidentally kicked his shin under the table, and he jumped, but kept his mouth closed.

Deciding it was up to her to issue the lecture, Mother continued. "Sam is right about Miss Bettie, love. She did live in that house, but it was long before you were born. Her father built it over a hundred years ago, I told you that last night. She lived there from the time she was a little girl until she died. Sometimes people think they see or hear things in the house when nobody else was there, and you probably heard some of those stories, and your imagination made you think you saw something too. You know you have a big imagination, and that's okay, but ghosts aren't real."

When she said that, she dropped her gaze, refusing to look me in the eye. "But Mama, you've seen her, too, I can tell you have! And you told me and Sam not to leave the ballroom because Miss Bettie wouldn't like it, so how can she not be real?"

My father, who taught physics at Rice Institute, put on his strict scientist face. "Your mother was just joking about that. And you get that wild imagination from her. When she was about your age—"

"I can tell my own story, John, thank you very much!" Mama's cheeks turned that pretty pink color that meant she was either embarrassed or mad. I knew she wasn't embarrassed this time. "Sarah Jane, you and I will have a nice long talk tonight, but now we have to get ready for church."

As I sat in our pew at Palmer Episcopal Church and admired the prisms of light from the stained glass windows, I wondered why the minister could talk about The Father, the Son, and the Holy Ghost and nobody told *him* ghosts weren't real. I decided to keep that question to myself. Grownups could be very strange.

My mother met my father when they were both students at the Rice Institute, which later became Rice University. Mother studied English and history and Dad studied physics and math. They couldn't have been more different, but it was love at first sight for both of them. They were married at Palmer Episcopal, just across the street from the university. Dad earned a Ph.D. while Mother worked as a reporter for the Houston Post. After Sam was born, she stayed at home and wrote stories for magazines. She was a story teller, and while there were always plenty of books in our home, we loved her bedtime stories best of all. She told us about our pioneer ancestors, who came to Texas when there were still wild Indians roaming the plains, and about their ancestors, who lived in ancient castles in Scotland and Ireland. The stories we loved best had ghosts and goblins and giants and fairies. Dad would grumble, "You shouldn't be filling their heads with that Celtic nonsense, Elizabeth," but she'd just smile and carry on with the story. Sam finally decided he was too old for bedtime stories, and sided with Dad. Anything that can't be seen or proven scientifically isn't real, and that was that!

That night, instead of telling me a bedtime story, Mother told me a secret. "You and I are more sensitive to things than your father and Sam are, and when we really want something to be true, well, we just might see that thing, or that person. My mother and her mother before her were like that, too. Yes, I did see Miss Bettie, when I was a little girl. After the Shriners bought the house from the Brown family, my mother worked in the sewing room in the house, up on the third floor, and I got to go with her once in a while. She and the other ladies remembered the Brown family, and they talked about them when they thought I wasn't listening. Their favorite topic was Miss Bettie, and I paid careful attention when they brought her up." She paused, and a look crossed her face as though she were in a far-away place and time.

"Things were different when Miss Bettie was young. Ladies of her social class were supposed to be meek and modest. They learned to play the piano, took lessons in how to dance gracefully, to do fine needlework, and how to manage a home. They never went anywhere without an escort or chaperon. But Mr. Brown was a free spirit, and he encouraged his children to be the same way. Miss Bettie was the only one who was—she did as she pleased. She had plenty of beaus but never married. She traveled all over the world, without a chaperon, and brought back beautiful things, fine china from England and the best Irish crystal, hand-painted silk fans and ceramic vases from the Orient, paintings and tapestries and antique furniture… They say the house was very nice when her parents were living, but Miss Bettie renovated it and made it even better. She was a painter too, a professional painter, and she took lessons from famous artists in Europe. She never exhibited her paintings or sold them, though. Most of them were displayed here at Ashton Villa. She liked to paint angels and cupids, and she hung some of those in the big parlor they called the Gold Room. After she died, most of those things were packed away or divided up among the surviving relatives. Her family just couldn't keep up with the repairs, and none of them wanted to live there, so they sold it to the Shriners. There are plenty of people, though, who believe, that Miss Bettie never left."

"What makes them believe that, Mama? Did they see her too? Was she angry because her house got sold? She didn't look angry to me, only sad."

"No, she wasn't angry. When I saw her, I thought, like you, she was sad. There are stories about strange sounds, a piano playing, footsteps coming from empty rooms, but nobody felt scared, just surprised. People have seen a hazy shape of a woman in a fancy dress looking from the window of Miss Bettie's room. Maybe she was just wishing the old house could be brought back to the way it used to be."

"Oh, Mama, I sure wish it could be. Maybe we could buy it and I could learn to paint and play the piano and we could have big dinner parties—wouldn't that be the best thing ever?"

Mama smiled, looking around at our little West University bungalow. "That would be the best thing ever, love, but I wouldn't count on it. You can still learn to do those things Miss Bettie did, some of them, anyway. How about we start you on piano lessons right away?"

I did learn to play the piano, and to paint, and, like my mother, I fell in love with literature and history. Sam followed in our father's footsteps, graduating from Rice with a Ph.D. in astrophysics. He had a firm belief that ghosts and other supernatural phenomena can always be explained by science. I went to Rice too, majoring in anthropology, with a particular interest in historical archaeology. While I learned and practiced the scientific method, I knew that some things defy rational explanation.

We visited Galveston Island every year, mostly to swim at the west beach, but sometimes we went downtown to shop and look at the old houses. Many of the Victorian beauties fell to the wrecking ball during the "urban redevelopment" of the 1960's, but the Shriners managed to save their temple, even though it was falling into disrepair. They finally sold it to the city of Galveston in 1972, which then leased it to the Galveston Historical Society for ten dollars a year. It was restored and refurbished, the rooms returned to their original purpose, complete with many of the original furnishings and accessories. Miss Bettie's painting of naked cupids was displayed once again in the Gold Room, where her piano had pride of place. When the home was opened as a museum in 1974, my family was there for the first tour, and I felt like I was in heaven, walking through the rooms Miss Bettie had lived in, looking at the beautiful furniture and decorative pieces she had picked out with loving care.

Although I kept a sharp eye out for the mistress of the house, I didn't see her. I did notice that the crocheted spread on the bed in Miss Bettie's dayroom was rumpled. The docent straightened it, but when we passed by the room at the end of the tour, it was rumpled again, even though nobody but our tour group was in the house. Mother and I exchanged a glance, and she had a twinkle in her eye.

In 1980, as an undergraduate at Rice, I enrolled in the Archaeological Field Methods class. The professor was Dr. Frank Hole, a renowned expert in Middle Eastern archaeology. He was a formidable figure, but we still giggled at the appropriateness of his name. To my surprise and immense delight, one of his graduate students, Texas Anderson, was doing historical research and excavation at Ashton Villa, and our class assignment was to assist her. I felt like my life had come full circle.

Texas contacted descendants of the Brown family, and they sent her dozens of letters and photographs of Ashton Villa in its heyday. We had set up a work area in one corner of the old Shriner ballroom at the back of the house where, long ago, I had danced with my father. I opened one of the large envelopes and pulled out a black and white photo that took my breath away. The Brown family was seated around a large dining table heavily laden with elaborately decorated china, elegant silverware, candelabras and floral arrangements on the lace runner in the center of the table …and at the lower left corner was a young lady with long blond hair flowing down her back, dressed in a magnificent gown that had to be blue. She was looking at the camera, but it seemed like she was looking directly at me. Hello, Miss Bettie!

I read the letter that came with the photo, written by one of the Brown grandchildren:

"This was taken at Christmas, 1870. It was before I was born, but my father told me about those special times. What he liked best when he was a child was the frozen treats molded into the shape of

chickens and ducks. Father said all their meals were formal and food was plentiful, oysters and shrimp and red snapper from the Gulf, meat, roasts and steaks and turkeys, vast serving bowls full of fresh vegetables, a different wine with each course, and all kinds of cakes and pies and puddings."

I showed the photo and letter to Texas. She read through the letter and said, "Let me show you something. I've been wondering what these things were for." We walked into the kitchen, she opened a drawer, and there were two sets of copper molds in the shape of—what else—chickens and ducks! We looked in the china cabinet and butler's pantry and found several matches to the place settings in the photo. I loved the way my chosen field could make history come alive. Little did I know that the best was yet to come.

I spent many hours in the Rosenberg Library, reading stories about Galveston in the 19th century in the *Galveston Daily News* on microfilm, finding bits and pieces about the Brown family as it grew and prospered, descriptions of the New Year's open house held at Ashton Villa each year, about the shopping trips the ladies made to New York City, marriages, funerals, and the like. Miss Bettie made her first big splash in Galveston society in 1876 at the Galveston Mardi Gras celebration. She played the role of Queen Cleopatra for the newly-formed Mid-Day Revelers Krewe, resplendent on a golden throne, surrounded by Nubian "slaves," her neck, wrists and fingers dripping in golden jewelry. According to the *Galveston Daily News*, the twenty-one year old Miss Rebecca Ashton Brown was the belle of the ball. Soon she was the talk of the town, and remained so until her dying day.

I read books about Galveston and its inhabitants, ranging from the scholarly to the light-hearted. In one of the latter, I learned that Miss Bettie smoked cigarettes when that was an unacceptable habit for a lady, and that she had two teams of horses to pull her fine carriage, one all black for daytime, the other white for nighttime excursions. She would race other drivers or just gallop at full speed down Broadway for the fun of it. She spent months at a time in a Paris apartment, and there were rumors that the rent was paid by a married gentleman. She hobnobbed with European royalty and studied painting with an Austrian court painter. She was as much at home, and as well-loved, in Aspen, New York City, and London as she was in Galveston.

The more carefully researched tomes reported that many of the scandalous tales about Miss Bettie may have been started by an abusive, alcoholic brother-in-law who didn't like her interference on her sister's behalf. He publically declared that he would ruin her reputation, and perhaps he tried, but he probably only succeeded in making her sound more interesting. I certainly found her fascinating.

I enjoyed the archival and historical research, but I was ready to literally dig into the history of Ashton Villa. The first part of the excavation wasn't too exciting. Much of archaeology is dogged hard work, in the library, the ground, and the lab. Excitement and romance isn't the point; learning about the past through the artifacts and other traces left behind by those who lived it is the goal, not finding buried treasure. We examined the blueprints and insurance maps of the house and grounds, locating a bronze fountain and the original brick walkway. And we discovered that half of the ornate wrought-iron fence was buried under three feet of fill.

While the home had been built with indoor plumbing, a brick-lined privy had been erected at the edge of the stable for the use of the servants. Our team carefully measured out the plot of land where the outhouse would have been and did some probes in the most likely area.

There were no visible remains above ground due to an event that affected every home on the island: the terrible hurricane on September 8, 1900, that took as many as ten thousand lives, covered the entire island in several feet of water, and destroyed or damaged most of the structures in the city. Ashton Villa, on a high part of the island, had water up to the middle of the stairs to the second floor, and the Brown family, servants and neighbors spent an anxious night watching it creep higher and higher. Before the worst of the storm hit, though, Miss Bettie and her mother took a step that likely saved the house from being swept off its foundations as many other homes, whether stately or humble, were. The front and back of the house had French doors, and they opened them wide so the sea could flow through. The next morning, she and the other survivors waded through the muck and picked up buckets full of fish and other sea creatures.

Later that morning, Miss Bettie set off in her carriage, waving her lace handkerchief to friends as she searched the devastated city for people in need of food, shelter, or other assistance. Miss Bettie was eccentric and colorful, and some of her actions may have scandalized Galveston high society, but she had a big heart and a generous nature.

Not long after the storm, the whole east end of the island was raised, using sand dredged from the Gulf of Mexico. Many of the remaining homes were elevated on stilts as an extra precaution for storms to come. Because of Ashton Villa's location, not much fill was needed. This was a good thing for our excavation team. The probe located the outline of the brick-lined privy vault not too far below the surface, and when we took the top layer of grass and soil away, we found a pristine layer of sand almost three feet thick, sealing what lay below like a time capsule.

Old privies that were no longer used for their primary purpose were often filled with household garbage, and that's what we were hoping for. We made quick work of removing the sand, then troweled carefully through the darker level beneath it. Dick Gregg made the first find, and after it was mapped and photographed *in situ*, he held it up for us all to see. It was a wine bottle, deep green with iridescent flakes glittering like jewels in the bright sunshine. As the day went on, more bottles, whole and broken, green, amber, clear, cobalt blue, rose from the earth, along with shards of fine china, animal bones representing the choicest cuts of meat, prisms from chandeliers and fancy oil lamps, marbles, tiny china dolls, a silver fork missing a tine, pieces of wine glasses, thin and delicate. No ordinary garbage this, but the spring housecleaning of a well-to-do family, dating to the last two decades of the nineteenth century, sealed between the brick bottom of the privy and the pure sand deposit from just after 1900.

By the time the privy vault was emptied, we had recovered forty-nine whole or nearly complete bottles that had contained fine wine or ginger beer, and several amber bottles embossed with the words "Udolpho Wolfe's Aromatic Schnapps." The Browns seemed to prefer fine wines and cognac to hard liquor, as there were few bottles representing that category. I'd been studying late nineteenth-century medicine as part of the research, and I smiled, remembering the advertisements for Dr. Wolfe's concoction. It was a "medicinal beverage, a superlative tonic, safe and effective for many ailments of infants and adults"—and it was ninety-four percent alcohol.

There were snuff bottles and perfume vials, a hand-blown syringe and prescription bottles, pressed, etched, and hand-cut decorative glassware, and colored window glass. Among the ceramics were fine hand-painted china, high-quality transfer-painted earthenware, and a gorgeous china spittoon, banded in gold and garnet stripes. Several bottles had contained Pond's Lily Water for the ladies' delicate complexions. When I held one of the perfume bottles, I caught a faint whiff of jasmine and roses, Miss Bettie's favorite scents.

Two of my favorite finds were items that I discovered while water-screening the soil that was packed around the other artifacts. Both, I felt sure, belonged to Miss Bettie. One was a fragment of pierced ivory, part of a fan blade. Did it break when Miss Bettie tapped a too-ardent suitor, or did she drop it during a spirited dance and snap it beneath her stylish dance pump? Archaeologists are supposed to be rational and follow the scientific method, but I was, after all, my mother's daughter. I kept these thoughts to myself, of course.

I hurried through the last bucket full of soil, oyster and clam shells, not expecting to find anything of importance. For some reason, one particular shell stood out. I picked it up, a tiny clam shell, barely an inch wide, and turned it over. Something dark showed under a light film of dirt. I carefully ran some water over it, and there was a perfect rosebud, each tiny petal and leaf painstakingly painted onto the shell. The paint was black, but I suspected that it was originally brilliant red, and I knew exactly who the painter was. I looked up at the window of Miss Bettie's bedroom, and just for an instant I swear that I saw a lady in a Victorian dress, turquoise in color. She was holding an ivory fan. She flicked her wrist, there was a glint of gold from her bracelet, and in an instant she was gone.

Years have gone by, but Ashton Villa still stands proudly on Broadway Boulevard. Tour guides still talk about Miss Bettie, and that bedspread still gets rumpled, coins rain down out of thin air, and visitors see glimpses of a lady in a turquoise Victorian dress looking through an upstairs window or slipping through the trees surrounding the house. There are even websites devoted to the haunted places of Galveston Island, and Miss Bettie always gets a mention. Eventually, one of those ghost hunter "reality" shows may try to summon her with its electrical toys and its demands to "show yourself, let us know you're really here."

If that happens, I know they are doomed to be disappointed. Miss Bettie has too much class to participate in such tasteless exhibitions. She will show herself only to those who understand that there is more to heaven and earth than can be proved by the scientific method.

About Meeting Miss Bettie

This story was inspired by the many stories of the haunting of Ashton Villa by Miss Bettie Brown, and by an archaeological excavation conducted by Ph.D. candidate Texas Anderson in the early 1980's. Her dissertation is titled *Cognitive Structures, Status and Cultural Affiliation: The Archaeology of Ashton Villa*, which can be found in the Fondren Library at Rice University.

The author of this story, Shirley Wetzel, was also a graduate student at Rice, and assisted in the historical and archival research, the excavation, and the analysis of the bottles and other glassware. She did indeed find the tiny clam shell with the painted rose. Now a librarian at Rice University, she still loves history and archaeology, especially when they are combined.

THE HONEST CON MAN
BY JAMES R. DAVIS

Monday, August 13

"So I should know the odds when I play the lotto?" The prospective client, a scrumptious, matronly blonde in expensive western wear, sipped Sangria. She stroked the Pekingese in her lap, her Manhattan accent making her sound a little bored. "I don't see how that's related to investing. I mean, it's only a dollah a play. I don't do it much…maybe if I have an extra twenty at the liquor store sometimes. The odds are always different, anyway. I should bother to stay current?"

Ralph Masterson, President of the CWA Insurance Company, shook his head. "Oh, indeed not." He laughed with a deliberate note of irony. He placed a Texas Lotto fact sheet on the Louis XIV dining table and drew Pamela Levinstein's attention to certain lines highlighted in orange. "Not that one could. This purports to give you that information, but you'll dig to find the truth in this document, I'm afraid. They really don't want you to know, because the odds are simply awful."

"Oh?" She invited the dog to jump to the floor, then leaned over to see the fact sheet better. It enhanced her cleavage, like the sun peeping over the horizon at dawn. Ralph persuaded himself that the view was truly amazing a few feet beyond her shoulder, where a picture window framed her River Oaks mansion's splendid landscaping. He gave her a closer glimpse only as a courtesy.

After a few seconds, Pamela pushed her glasses up on her

nose and concentrated on the columns of numbers. Ralph silently applauded Pam's moves, then got back into his patter. "For each dollar ticket you buy to play the lotto, your odds are one in seventy-one that you'll win *something*. Look."

He showed her a table he'd drawn. The odds were 1:75 of winning $3, then increased to 1:1,526 to win something like fifty dollars. "Thereafter, the odds get very small indeed, though the payoffs can be enormous. But even those numbers are incredibly deceptive." The thought seemed to weary him.

"Deceptive? They seem straight-forward enough. There's lots of ways I lose money entertaining myself." Pamela's husky, self-mocking voice hinted at those other, unnamed vices. She smiled at Ralph. "What am I missing?" She poured herself another glass of Sangria from a cut crystal pitcher, then one for Ralph. She placed a napkin under it and pushed his drink across.

Ralph took a sip while he collected his thoughts. "Let's take your astute observation about entertainment value. My guess is you've played a little roulette. Las Vegas, Atlantic City, or perhaps Monte Carlo?"

"I enjoy rolling the dice from time to time. There's no shame in that."

"No, of course not! Everyone has a little sporting blood." Ralph calmed his breathing. He was about to shock her, and he wanted to be ready to close the deal in the aftermath. "But let's look closer. You'll recall there are thirty-seven spaces on a roulette wheel: eighteen red, eighteen black, and the house's favorite, the number zero. And there's lots of ways for a gambler to bet. For instance, you could place a bet on one of those thirty-six numbers, and the odds of winning would be one in thirty-six, with a payout of thirty-five to one. Simple, right?"

Pamela nodded.

"But there are many more chances to lose if you do that. It's safest by far to bet on either red or black. Then the odds of your winning are just a tiny bit lower than fifty per cent. Lower, because—remember that zero? If the ball lands on the zero, only the house wins. But, still, the odds are almost even."

Pamela picked up the thread. "If I bet a dollar and win, the house pays me a dollar *and* returns my original dollar. If I lose, they keep my dollar."

"Right. Each time you bet a color, you either double your money or lose it all. The house has a tiny advantage, but it's not a bad way to play.

"Now, contrast that to the Texas Lotto, where the odds of winning a three-dollar payout are one in seventy-five! And that's not the same as saying that the payout is three to one. It isn't. They actually pay you two dollars for your one-dollar bet, and return your original dollar. That's a two to one payout. If the lotto's odds were remotely like Las Vegas roulette, the ticket you bought with one to seventy-five odds of winning would have a payout ratio of very nearly seventy-five to one."

Pamela tilted her head, studying Masterson. He liked the feeling. He'd done the head shake twice, so now he sighed deeply and dropped his gaze.

"It's obvious that you know how the gaming world works," she said, "but you seem to have an extremely low opinion of the lotto. You're polite enough not to say so, but I don't think you approve of gambling in general. Why is that, hon?"

Ralph did his sad-eyed victim thing. "I grew up in total poverty. My father worked in the scrap metal business and made just enough to keep us under one roof without starving most of the time. Not always, because he was an addict. He didn't make the kind of money it took for a drug habit or booze. He played the numbers."

He sneaked a quick glance at his prospect and dropped his voice to a near-whisper as his 'confession' went on. "At first, he'd lose a couple dollars a week. But it grew to the point that many weeks, we had to skip meals. His paychecks disappeared, sometimes within hours of when he got them. The bastard broke my mother's heart, and I hated him." Masterson clenched his teeth as he shared that last confidence.

Pamela listened, rapt, her eyebrows knit with concern.

"So believe me, I know how destructive gambling can be. Most of my customers used to be lotto addicts, after they started out spending only a couple of dollars a week. That's why I founded this company. I want to help people beat the habit; and I want to stick a finger in the eye of the lotto promoters at the same time. They put out a game that's simply unfair, and they're taking billions of dollars away from the people of this state, especially folks who can't afford it." Trembling with emotion, Masterson lifted his glass and drained it.

"I'm so sorry. But I'm not like those other clients you mentioned." Pamela finished her Sangria as well and poured another glass. When she raised the pitcher inviting Masterson to join her again, he declined. "I'm not an addict," she continued. "I just like a little gaming from time to time. I can cover my losses. I wouldn't expect the lotto to be an even-money game. I mean, they have to run the commission and pay the staff. And they're supposed to put money into public education, too. But those odds… that's outrageous."

Masterson laughed, again with a tinge of irony. "The public doesn't know it, but the odds of winning in one try at a roulette table in Monte Carlo are thirty-five times better than the odds of winning anything from the lotto when you buy that ticket at your liquor store."

Pamela pursed her lips, which were stained with purple from the fruit juices and red wine. "Next time I'm in Vegas, I'm going to have a lot more fun."

Forcing his eyes away from Pamela's delightful mouth, Masterson got to the heart of his presentation. "Ah, yes. You've seen what they claim in their ads: the glamour, the fun. The ad campaigns exaggerate the big win possibility, while they downplay the terrible odds for the *second* biggest payoffs." Masterson took out a pen from his coat pocket and pointed to the second line on the Texas Lotto facts sheet. "If you pick five of the six numbers drawn, your odds of winning are one in nearly ninety thousand. The payout ratio's about a thousand to one. Roulette is ninety times better than this!"

Pamela saw his point. "You pick five out of six lotto numbers correctly, most people would think it was worth big bucks."

"And that's wrong. But they make it hard to compare." Ralph allowed himself a little dramatic license. "It's deceptive, if not downright criminal."

Now for the fun part. He waited, and it began.

"It *is* like throwing money away, isn't it."

Bingo! Ralph's heart warmed. When prospects understood how dramatically poor were the lotto odds, and how deceptively conveyed, his pitch was downhill from there.

Pamela went on, her voice rising. "Even if the gambling gods smiled on you, you'd have to buy *thousands* of tickets just to break even!"

Time to plant the hook. "So I take it you believe the house—meaning the lotto commission—has too great an advantage in their games? I agree. And that's exactly why we at CWA are so successful at selling our short-term risk insurance policies." Masterson leaned back, awaiting the inevitable response. It came at once.

"But that's insane! How could your company possibly stay in business insuring lotto players against losses?"

He laughed again, a chuckle meant to convey how much he shared her perspective. "Losses? Good heavens, no. We insure against *winnings*."

One week earlier

Detective Sergeant Harry Harman looked at the pink message slip on his desk. "Call DA Watson ASAP," it read. The word "Masterson!!!" was written beneath the callback number and underlined. "Humph," he said to himself. His lips twitched into a smile, though.

Harman was 53, and he'd worked his way up the ladder at HPD to a desk job supervising investigations into gambling crimes. No more raiding adult video stores, no more listening to hookers whining in the back seat, no more confiscating a room full of slot machines while somebody screamed at you in Vietnamese. He was grateful for a chance to stay until retirement, and he had applied himself diligently once he got promoted to this job. So, yeah, he knew all about Ralph Masterson.

Two years ago, Harman had taken part in a white-collar crime task force that tried, among other things, to put the man behind bars. In tracking down cold leads on a major fraud case, Masterson's name had come up connected with Sonny Pines, one of a multitude of con artists flushed out by the Enron debacle. Pines turned out to be a Masterson copycat who did it wrong. The feds were busy with Arthur Andersen accountants and such, so Harman's task force took a look at Masterson's deal, which involved volume sales of gift cards for just about everything.

Unlike the copycat, who was basically a fence, Masterson had skated. The prosecutors refused to take a bill of indictment against him to a Grand Jury. No one who'd purchased the cards in quantity would testify against Masterson nor against the shell company that had handled their transactions. The sellers were satisfied, too. As Harman's dad would have said, no harm, no foul.

Harman didn't think this reluctance was because of threats or intimidation, either. No, Masterson was simply a great con man, in addition to having great business skills. Harman had talked to his customers; Masterson had totally convinced the people who bought his gift cards—for prepaid meals, telephone service, spa treatments, hotel accommodations, rounds of golf—that their purchases made economic sense to all parties involved.

He'd presented the opportunity to buy his cards with seemingly sincere pleasure, too. He was frumpy and avuncular, an older, trusted well-to-do friend who was just tickled that he'd gotten the chance to bring them such a win-win deal. And like all the best cons, when the skeptics dug into it one layer deep, they found it to be honest.

First, the seller of the merchandise or service made sales that the business probably would not have made except for the gift card, even if the seller took a haircut on them. This amounted, then, to a form of advertising.

Second, the gift card giver had a convenient way of showing the recipient that they cared, and at a reasonable cost, another form of advertising, if you like.

Third, the recipient had "money" to spend on that seller's merchandise, money that was in his or her wallet already earmarked just for that purpose.

No one realized that some cards were lost or destroyed before they were ever used, even once. No one objected to the fact that the gift cards had expiration dates, because those, too, were reasonably far into the future. If you didn't use the card in time, whose fault was that?

On its face it looked trivial, but Harman had eventually established that Masterson made an enormous profit from those oversights and tolerance. And that the transactions were totally legal.

Oh, Harry had searched and searched for a weak point in Masterson's scheme, but he couldn't find one. Masterson was simply taking advantage of this chink in a commonly used payment system. Harman finally tabled the inquiry, but he fully expected that there would be another one someday... For in the course of investigating the gift card scheme, Harman had heard rumors—rumors he couldn't substantiate, yet—that Ralph Masterson was hungry. He'd been hungry all his life. That he was fast on the uptake and determined to accumulate a fortune, one way or another, it was said. Not a million or two, but hundreds of millions of dollars before he stopped.

Harmon suspected it was more than greed or a hoarding complex for Ralph. His instincts told him Masterson would never stop, no matter how much money he made. He was in it for some other reason, something he'd probably deny.

Harmon also knew in his cynical old soul that Ralph had to be skating close to the edge. He was only one man, juggling all these big-money deals left and right, and insisting on full control. Wanting to get one over on the world would lead him right over that edge some day, and into jail.

Putting the guy away would be hard. Masterson did, in fact, do a ton of charity stuff, trying to get gambling addicts to come in for treatment, running TV ads late at night for a gambling addiction hot-line. These were actions that had, according to some local pols, earned Masterson a long rope, if he ever needed one.

Masterson's role in the 'invisible money' underground economy was what Harman really wanted to crack. But the con artist maintained his records in his head, not his computer; and without evidence of fraud, the investigation ground to a stop.

Harry's phone rang. "Harman."

"Sergeant, this is Cliff Watson. I'm an assistant DA. We've received allegations that one Ralph Masterson's running a fraud scam. You familiar with this man?"

Harman noted that Watson had said 'we' instead of 'I'. Apparently the DA himself had a strong interest in this. Harry felt the chill of a political wind blowing in his direction. "Ralph and I are acquainted, but we're not close. I've tried to nail him in the past, but he's as smart as they come, and a very careful businessman. Anyway, I don't usually work white collar crimes. I'm in Vice, specializing in illegal gambling."

"That's why I called you. The State doesn't like anyone else being in the lotto business, and Masterson's running an alternative lotto play. It's gambling, and we want him put out of business. You're our best chance to nail him."

It's funny, Harman thought, that whenever anyone talks about gambling, they seem compelled to use the word 'chance'. "Sure, I'd like a chance to help out," he said. "I got somebody who can find his weak spots, if anyone can."

As soon as the call ended, Harman hit the buzzer on his office intercom. "Hey, Marge, you know Pamela's extension?"

꙳

Monday, August 13, again

"I buy a lotto ticket for a dollar, then I pay you another dollar to insure that the ticket I bought will be a *loser*? Why would anybody do that?" Pamela paced back and forth in front of a heavily gilded and carved buffet. "Wish I had a cigarette," she added. "My vet doesn't want me smoking in the house."

It was a good sign.

Masterson continued, on familiar territory. "That wouldn't be sensible at all, I agree. At CWA, we're totally against the idea of playing the lotto, ever. It's like throwing your money away. Instead, to save our clients from that gambler's itch, we sell 'Can't Win' insurance. You select the numbers that you *would* have used to bet on a particular Texas Lotto game, and instead of paying the Texas Lottery Commission a dollar for that ticket, you pay us that same dollar to insure that those numbers *won't* win. If we're wrong—of course, we've been wrong— and if that set of numbers would have been a winner, we pay you for the 'pain and suffering' you experience for not having played."

"But how much do you pay? I mean, if I didn't buy the ticket that won five million dollars, you wouldn't, you couldn't, pay five million dollars on my policy?"

"Of course not, though we would meet our obligation, whatever it was. No, only the Texas Lottery Commission could make a payout like that. We pay a *benefit* for the pain and suffering of having missed out on winning. It would be the lesser of one million dollars, *or* half of what you would have won, had you actually purchased the ticket with your numbers on it. If your numbers would have won three dollars, which is the smallest payout the Texas Lotto makes, we would pay you a dollar and fifty cents. If you'd have won five thousand dollars, we would pay you twenty-five hundred. But if your ticket would have won more than two million dollars, we would pay you only one million. That's set out in our policy terms." Masterson flipped through the items in his briefcase and pulled out another document. It was a brochure, and "Policy Terms" was printed in red bold-face on the front of it.

Pamela sat across the table from Masterson again. Her manicured fingers played with the flyer. It was another good sign when they wanted to touch it, Masterson thought; she was definitely intrigued.

"But how can your company afford it?" she asked. "The Texas Lotto takes in millions. They build big jackpots to pay big wins. You sell but a tiny fraction of that much in policies. Yet if I paid you a dollar for an insurance policy against my numbers winning, and if I pick the right numbers, you might have to pay me as much as a million dollars. You can't possibly sell enough insurance policies to even break even if that happened. Or maybe you could once, but never again."

"Actually, we do sell a lot of policies. We sell about ten thousand for each drawing. And most of the time we do have to make payouts. But, on average, we take in about ten thousand dollars a game and pay benefits of roughly two, that's all.

"Plus, our operating costs are very low. That helps us build reserves. We're an insurance company, and we're strictly audited to prove that we maintain enough capital. Your contract tells you exactly what we could be liable for, and state regulations insure that you're able to collect." Masterson gently took the brochure and folded it to the correct page, then pointed to the bottom line. "Here's our latest audited reserve balance. It's well in excess of two million dollars. We make a nice profit in this business, and that's where the investment opportunity could be. I foresee a day when we're going to be looking for silent partners. Not today, not this month, maybe not this year. But soon."

Masterson gave Pamela the brochure, an audit statement, and an additional brochure that castigated gambling as a mental health issue. It also explained how his 'Can't Win' policies could be used to help beat the addiction.

"Seems like a lot of trouble for playing a game. Or not playing it."

"Maybe. But it's not unusual for clients to ask for many policies, especially at first. If a habitual gambler adds up what she spends on lotto tickets each month, and understands there's so little upside, she may appreciate the predictability of losing with us, as well as the possibility of a small gain." He knew he'd set the hook with that last jerk of the line.

"What gain?"

Masterson's expression became solemn. "You know, at CWA our reputation means everything. We couldn't be successful if we weren't known for honesty and for making quick, uncontested payments of benefits. When we make a mistake, we are more than pleased to pay. But we go farther than that."

"Yeah? How?" Pamela's face wore a mixture of curiosity and skepticism.

"Here's what we do. To all the other clients who purchased 'Can't Win' policies on that same lotto game, we pay a *duplicate* benefit if someone else would have won. And we distribute that second payout to *them*, to maintain their goodwill. For example, if your hypothetical policy required us to pay you fifty thousand dollars, we would pay a goodwill benefit of fifty thousand dollars to all the other policyholders of record on that game, distributed according to how many policies they held. If there were ten thousand policies, we would pay those insureds five bucks for each. I know that doesn't sound like much, but it's five times what they paid for their policies to begin with."

Pamela was floored. "You pay people whose numbers *wouldn't* have won, too?"

"We try to keep our clients happy. If nobody's numbers would have won, we earned all our policy fees, and the clients got what they paid for—a set of numbers that we guaranteed would lose. Their results are exactly the same, whether they paid us or bought Texas Lotto tickets: nothing. But if *any* of our policyholders picked numbers that would have won, they are *all* paid. They share the goodwill benefit, without increasing their risk in any way."

Pamela took a moment to absorb this. Ralph let her stew for

just the right amount of time. Finally he said, "How many policies would you like to buy?"

One hour later

"He's one slick operator," Pamela Blomberg reported to Harman. No longer the wealthy, seductive River Oaks matron from Manhattan that Masterson had met, she was a 50-year-old cop—and one of HPD's best undercover operatives. "He never even suggested it was *like* gambling. In fact, he went out of his way to describe how playing the lotto's a serious addiction for many folks. He gave me an anti-gambling brochure. If I was into playing the lotto myself, I'd buy a policy for me, just to see if they work."

"You were authorized to buy as many policies as he'd sell you. How much did you set the department back for?"

"Oh, he suggested that I only buy five thousand for any one Texas Lotto game, at least at first. He said I should see how it worked out for me. If I was satisfied, I could always spread the action by setting up automatic purchases for however many I wanted to buy. CWA also has an option for you to roll over all or any part of your account balance into more 'Can't Win' policies, the next time there's a drawing."

"Pretty slick."

"I didn't want to seem too eager, so I bought a thousand and said I'd make future purchases based on how I did."

"So the department's now a thousand bucks lighter. Good call, by the way."

"I tell you, Harry, if the guy was a stockbroker instead of an insurance man on the fringe, I'd seriously consider moving my investments his way. You can't help but trust him."

"Yeah, but don't. A lot of people think he's dirty."

"What do *you* think?"

"I haven't decided. The Texas Lotto boys sure don't like him. He goes out of his way to throw his anti-lotto bias into their faces. He pays for and produces anti-gambling, especially anti-lotto, public service spots. He makes anti-gambling presentations to any group of citizens that want him to, and he describes lotto games as the worst form of gambling around. Hard to argue with any of that, though." Harman's tone took on a hint of amused respect for old Ralph.

"It's a wonder the Commission boys haven't paid somebody to bust his kneecaps." Pamela's opinions about violence were not just a matter of idle chatter. She'd worked Vice herself for a dozen years and had history behind her.

Harman still thought they were chasing a rumor, but someone higher up the food chain definitely wanted Ralph Masterson shut down. Who? he wondered.

Who had a vested interest in protecting the gambling monopoly the State of Texas held? Somebody in Austin, in the state house…or somebody allied with the Commission? Maybe one of the vendors who ran the games. Somebody with another monopoly—the printers? The software guys? Whoever it was, they were determined to stop anybody else from nibbling away even a tiny piece of their take.

Harman looked at a stack of papers with calculations. He'd been scribbling notes all day. "How does Ralph make a profit when he has such a generous benefit schedule? Have they ever defaulted on a claim? Has there ever been a complaint lodged against CWA?"

"I'm not sure his payouts are all that generous," Pam said. "Let's wait and see. It's too early to answer the rest of your questions."

"So all we have now is that his insurance company's acting like a gambling house, by selling insurance with large payouts when the company guesses wrong. There's no way we're going to satisfy the DA's office with that. All insurance companies work that way. They just don't call it gambling."

By late afternoon, Harry had rounded up a small conference room and a traffic court clerk named Oscar to assist. He and

Pamela refined their research on CWA, while Oscar did data input. The insurance company was privately held, so they had little access to its current financial data. Harry verified the audited reserves information, but he'd already realized where the money had come from to found CWA: Masterson's sale of gift cards. A perfectly legal—in fact, a preferred—maneuver, insuring complete control rested with Ralph.

Pamela called the State's Insurance Commissioner's office. She verified that CWA maintained capital reserves amounting to more than $2M; and that it was owned entirely by one Ralph J. Masterson. No complaints about its operation had been filed in the two years of its existence, and its payouts did indeed average about $2,000 on sales of about 10,000 policies, per game played.

What was odd, however, was that CWA appeared to have a negligible profit margin. Its reported reserves had neither grown nor declined since its inception.

Pamela tapped her pad with a pencil. "Either there's an embezzler in Masterson's insurance company, or he's got more operating expenses than I can account for. It's like some accounting black hole. It doesn't look like they make any serious money at all." She handed Harry her notes.

"Maybe he's got a set of books that he shows the Insurance Commission, and another set he keeps in his head that shows he's making a lot more sales…" Oscar was catching on fast.

Harry snapped his fingers. "I know! What if he's not paying the benefits he says he is? If you bought a policy and your numbers turn out to be winners, you'd damn sure know what you're owed under your policy…but if you lost, would you know about those 'goodwill' benefits? The more I think about it, the more I wonder if those are a sham. How could you know if anybody else got one, and for how much? You'd never be able to keep track of whether you were entitled to one. Maybe we could get him on fraud if he didn't pay the losers as well as the winners, like he said he would."

Pamela shook her head no. "Masterson gave me an access code and a URL where CWA posts information about all policyholders for the Texas Lotto game I'm insured against. I checked it."

"And?" Harman read the results from Pam's shrug.

"I was down for a thousand policies, and I could see what numbers I was playing. I could have selected any numbers I wanted, just like the real lotto game, or allow his computer to select numbers for me, same as the Texas Lotto Quick Pick. There were over a hundred other policyholders listed, with over seven thousand policies between them. I could see the numbers they picked. It even showed that my account had a balance of zero so far."

Pamela pushed another sheet of paper at Harry. "Here's the printout he gave me, showing my sets of numbers. He couldn't change a winner into a loser to avoid paying a benefit to me. I don't just see how there's room for a scam, Harry."

But Harman wasn't convinced. "Everything you saw could be bogus except the numbers you insured. I sent Oscar to buy ten policies against the same game you played. We'll track both your policies, and—"

Oscar interrupted. "Yeah, I saw the whole place! CWA has teller windows in the lobby of their building, like a bank, where anyone can buy a policy. There's a big anti-gambling banner on the wall, and two posters saying the Texas Lotto's a rip-off. It all looked legit to me."

"Good job, Oscar." Harman caught himself biting a nail, and stopped.

Later that afternoon, the three investigators—Oscar had wormed his way into the case completely by now—again looked at Pamela's account information on the CWA website. Oscar's information was already in their system, too.

The number of policyholders had now grown by 38, and total policies in play were up by more than 1,000. The next Texas Lotto drawing was Wednesday night.

Thursday, August 16

By 7:45 a.m., Harry, Oscar, and Pamela were gathered in their conference room around a computer screen, studying the Texas Lotto game results on the CWA website.

The numbers picked the night before by both HPD insureds were shown, as well as information about all the policies within the pool that played.

The number of policyholders had reached 1,255 before the purchase deadline; they held 12,433 policies in aggregate.

Pamela prepared a summary sheet of the results.

Winners	*Category*	*Odds*	*Payout per winner*	*Total*
		Payout results from Lotto		
0	6 of 6	1:25,877,165	$8,000,000	$0
1	5 of 6	1:89,678	$1,471	$1,471
8	4 of 6	1:1,526	$53	$212
149	3 of 6	1:75	$3	$447
158				$2,130

If the 158 policyholders who should have been winners, meaning CWA had guessed wrong, had purchased actual lotto tickets instead of insurance policies, they would have collected a total of $2,130 from the Texas Lotto Commission. Ralph's 'Can't Win' policies would pay half their "missed opportunity" winnings, for a total of $1,065.

Out of Pamela's one thousand policies, fifteen sets of her numbers would have won $3 each, but she had no other winners. Had she actually played instead of buying those policies, she would have received a payout of $45 for her $1,000 cost. When she looked up her balance with CWA after the drawing, she expected to see a measly $22.50 credited to her account.

Pamela uttered a startled yelp. "Look!" she said. "My account's got over a hundred dollars in it!"

"There must be an accounting error," Oscar said.

"I should say so. CWA owed me twenty-two fifty, not even close to a hundred dollars plus. I received four times as much as I expected!"

"Or maybe Masterson was on to you. Maybe he manipulated the results to keep you interested," Harman proposed. "Let's check the official Texas Lotto website and make sure that they show the same winning numbers. That'll also show whether their payouts matched this chart."

All the numbers matched.

"Okay, so let's figure out how your benefits got so large."

Harry and Oscar ran the numbers independently. After CWA paid the $1,065 'pain and suffering' claims on the 158 policies where the numbers were winners, then according to Ralph, CWA was obliged to make an additional goodwill payout of $1,065 to all losing policyholders in those games, who were technically owed nothing more.

The total payout should have been $2,130. The claims paid as recorded on the website confirmed it: all the 'goodwill' benefits had been paid, too. The numbers checked out to the penny, including Pamela's $108.15.

Harry was more intrigued than ever. "And he made eighty per cent profit! Most gambling houses, hell, most businesses of any kind, would kill for a margin like that." He stared into space. "I wonder if he really *would* like a silent partner."

Oscar laughed, but Pamela just raised an eyebrow. "Come on, Harry, last night's take was pure chance. Sooner or later the odds are going to bite him in the butt. I wouldn't want my name on his company as an owner or investor, silent or otherwise."

Oscar had another idea. "What if some other gambling boss is trying to move in on his action? Maybe he's paying protection, 'cause they got the muscle to force him out if they wanted to."

"Or maybe they already have. Could be that Masterson is just a front for some really bad guys." Harman said. "Pam, get on that, okay?"

Oscar then logged into his account. The balance was $.85.

None of his policies had been winners. One last inspection confirmed that he could see Pamela's account status and her payouts, too. It was all transparent.

"I don't get it!" Harman said. "This is the craziest scam I've ever seen. Even the losers got eight per cent of their money back. Everybody, and I mean *everybody*, does better with CWA than if they had simply bought lotto tickets."

Pamela announced that she would play the 'Can't Win' policy game again any time, and with her own money, thank you very much.

Suddenly, Oscar spoke up. "Oh, I found out that Masterson has enemies here in Houston as well as in Austin. He drives a fancy car, but it gets stolen or damaged a lot, and he's reported two burglary attempts this year, one last."

"No successful burglaries? No cash missing, nothing like that?"

"No..."

"O.K., let's see what happens if a CWA policy covers a big winner." Pamela drew another chart.

Payout results from a big winner				
Winners	Category	Odds	Payout per winner	Total
1	6 of 6	1:25,877,165	$8,000,000	$8,000,000
1	5 of 6	1:89,678	$1,471	$1,471
8	4 of 6	1:1,526	$53	$212
149	3 of 6	1:75	$3	$447
158				$8,002,130

Next they calculated what Pamela's account balance would have been in this situation. She was absolutely stunned.

Since the hypothetical payout was greater than $2M, Masterson's company would have had to pay the policyholder $1M, assuming only one insured was that lucky; and then CWA would pay 'goodwill' benefits of another million. That additional

$1M would have been paid out at the rate of $80.43 per losing policy. Pamela's account balance would now be sitting at $80,455.50! "Christ!" Oscar was stunned. "He'd go bust the first time that happened, Harry! It would totally wipe out his reserves. Nobody would have to *put* him out of business; they could just walk in once his company crumbled."

"That can't be right," Harry objected. "Masterson's too good a businessman to hang himself out to dry like that. We're missing something here."

Pamela tossed out other scenarios. "Maybe he's selling off some of his action, though I can't imagine who'd buy into that. Forget what I said about muscle wanting to move in on him. They'd want muscle to keep him away."

Harman sent Oscar to CWA's building. He was told to go to the teller window and withdraw his 85 cents, closing the account. Oscar returned shortly and reported no problems at all. He'd seen dozens of other people doing exactly the same thing, along with many who bought more policies. It looked perfectly normal to him.

Pamela called CWA and asked to talk to a customer service rep. She asked what she could do with her new account balance. "Can I simply withdraw it in cash? Will I be paid with a check, or can you send it to my PayPal account?" She hung up. "They'll be happy to give me my money either way."

Harman had to make a report. He called the DA's office. "Cliff, about Masterson…"

"Yeah? The DA's all over my ass. He wants this nailed shut within the next two weeks. You gonna have it wrapped up for me by then?"

"Hell, it's nearly wrapped up now. But you can't satisfy the elements of the crime. He's not running a gambling business. His company sells an insurance policy that insures *against* winning the lotto! His customers are satisfied. No harm, no foul."

"What've you been smoking? You know he's diverting money from the State. In the long run, it comes out of your pocket and mine if the Commission can't meet its revenue goals."

"There's nothing illegal about helping people quit throwing their money away, even if they've been throwing it at the Governor."

"The Speaker's promised to reconcile the budget from those funds!"

Watson had just confirmed his suspicion, thought Harry. The DA was taking heat from way upstairs. Now he had what he needed. Harry was a bit of a salesman, too—maybe not in Masterson's league, but he held his own. His tone was dismissive. "Oh, the Commissioners won't lose money for long because of Ralph. Every time there's a drawing, he risks going belly up. Sooner or later, he'll get smacked down hard."

Watson would have none of it. "The DA can't wait, Harry. He wants to make an example. What about charging Masterson with filing a fraudulent document with the Commission? Can you at least give me that?"

"I can't justify spending any more money on this. If you want to fund more of this effort, I'll hire a white-hat to dig under the covers to find how it works. You get the DA to approve a five grand retainer fee for my guy, and I'll have results within your time frame. But remember, the guy still could be clean."

"I hear ya, Harry. I'll get the funds approved tomorrow, so stay on it. Make me proud."

Harman stewed a moment, then brought up his contact list on his smart phone. He scrolled through the M's to "Marshal." Jerry Marshal had once been a professional con man, a good one. When the police cuffed him after a six-year run at the game, he'd "volunteered" to become a white-hat for them. Harman dialed.

"This is Jerry."

"Harman, with HPD. You interested in five large for a consult?"

"Hell, yes. What and where?"

Monday, August 20

Harmon sat outside the Uptown Park Starbucks watching his coffee get cold, but he didn't want another cup. Marshal had pocketed the retainer fee check and gone over the evidence with him regarding Masterson's business model for an hour or so. Now Harry took a tangent and brought up the gift card scheme, the one that had put Masterson in his headlights before.

"Here's what bothers me. Suppose I'd known a little more about the invisible money underground economy, could I have made a case back then? Maybe I'm not looking at this right."

"The 'invisible money underground' is an optical illusion," Marshal said. "All it means is that a guy uses other people's money to fund his ventures. And he does it without those other people knowing about it."

"Still, the venture could fail, and all that money would be lost."

"Yeah, but who would know? That's why it's called invisible. Look, tell me exactly how these gift cards work."

Harman described Masterson's system. "When Ralph sells you a restaurant gift card, from outside it looks like the sales proceeds are paid to that restaurant chain. You present the card after a meal, and the restaurant simply deducts the tab from whatever balance is on the card. But it only looks like they're checking their own records to determine the value balance on the card. In fact, they're electronically checking Masterson's bank account, using Masterson's computers to determine what the discount is, and then getting a funds transfer to the restaurant's bank account."

"What's his cut?"

"He keeps six per cent for having sold the card and for use of his computer system. On a twenty buck tab, Masterson's account transfers eighteen eighty to the restaurant's bank account, and he keeps the dollar twenty fee." Harman sipped his coffee and pushed it away. It *was* cold, like this damn case.

"So the transaction isn't between the customer and the restaurant?"

"No, it just looks that way. It also looks like the restaurant re-ceives the full twenty dollars when the diner pays for the card, as if the money's already in its bank account, earning interest until it's used. But in reality, Masterson holds the money in his *own* bank account, and *he's* earning interest on it. If the card's lost or destroyed, or if its limited life lapses, Masterson then claims the unused balance as pure profit."

"Any idea how often that happens?" Marshal was following Harman closely.

"On average, nationally, only about seventy-five per cent of a gift card's face value is ever used. Masterson makes most of his profits that way. That's a great example of the invisible money un-derground. He makes money using other people's money, with-out their knowing it. It's fucking brilliant, if you do it in bulk."

Again, Harman realized that he couldn't help but admire the man. "O.K., Jerry, coming back to CWA…from what you know now, is this a scam of some kind?"

"What you have is a case where nobody other than the lotto boys can claim to have been wronged," Marshal replied. "Everyone was fully informed of their risks. The outcome was exactly what they had been promised, and they all came away without gam-bling their money away. It felt like they were making the smartest bet in their lives. I'm telling you, you'll never take this guy down."

Harman disagreed. "Masterson is too smart and too good a businessman to be risking it all on every roll of the dice. I know it sounds like he's making a killing, but to him, even a few mil-lion dollars is small potatoes if it comes with big risk. Taking big financial risks is what he advocates against. He grosses about a million a year from CWA if he insures two games a week, and if it isn't stolen from him somehow. But, hell, his gift card busi-ness makes twice that, and he can let other people run it for him. Plus, he never runs the risk that it'll go belly up overnight. On the other hand, it's no way to end up with hundreds of millions, like he supposedly wants. The man's a puzzle. If you say he's legit,

I'll believe you. But I'm going to keep trying to figure him out."

Wednesday, August 22

"Looks like they caught the guy harassing Masterson," Pamela announced. She was packing up her things. She passed Harry the incident report. "He's a thug who works for, hold your breath, the Texas Lottery Commission. Claims he was working off a personal grudge against Masterson, and nobody else was involved. Guess he wants a job when this is over."

"Really. Well, Jerry's coming by. Let's see what he has to say."

Marshal arrived, and Oscar brought him a cup of coffee as an excuse for sitting in on the meeting.

"Don't feel bad for the guy," Marshal said. "His company's taking down close to eight hundred thousand a year here, net. But that profit just disappears."

"We know CWA doesn't appear to make any money, but there's no reason why it shouldn't. And no matter what happened to the missing profits, Masterson is so risk-averse, so anti-gambling, that I simply can't see him working this deal seven days a week when there's a chance that he'll get knocked out of the game overnight if he insures the wrong numbers. There's something else going on here. What have you found?"

"Not a damn thing you didn't already know. But you need to start thinking like a gambler, Harry. Masterson's deck is stacked more in his company's favor than you realize. You keep worrying about where he'll get the money for a big claim. But with annual sales of just over a million policies a year, the odds of having to pay that big claim are only one in nearly *twenty-six million!* He can expect to strike out just once in twenty-six years. And that only means that there's a good *chance* of a hit in that time frame, it's not a sure thing. For that kind of money, I'd take the risk myself!"

"But given Masterson's style...I don't think he'd take that

chance, even if the odds were he'd only fail once in a *thousand* years." Harry was still troubled, but he'd spent the DA's money, and Jerry Marshal had done the best he could.

He called Watson to give him a final report.

"We've wrapped up Masterson for you, but you're not going to like it. You've got no case. He's running a legitimate insurance company. Sorry, but that's the way it is."

"Listen to me, Harry. My boss won't accept that."

"No, you listen. The Texas Lottery Commission is going to stop this campaign against Ralph Masterson, as of now. Why? Because one of its employees has been harassing him for the last two years, and that self-same thug is now sitting in the Harris County Jail for it. Now, it could be that the lottery boys didn't put him up to it, but Masterson could make a very public and persuasive case to the contrary. Not good."

"Oh."

"So drop it. Anyway, for what it's worth, I'm convinced he's an honest man."

Harry hung up and glanced at his watch, then grabbed his jacket. He left HPD headquarters, driving the few blocks to CWA's offices. His timing was perfect, for Masterson was just exiting the building garage in his Porsche.

Four car-lengths apart, they both drove up to Loop 610 North, to another office building. They parked.

When Masterson entered, Harman slipped in behind him, putting a big potted plant between them in the lobby. Luckily, Masterson entered the elevator alone. The doors closed, and Harman ran to follow the lighted number display.

A moment later, Harman stepped out on the sixteenth floor and looked around. He was determined to witness what was going on. He tiptoed down the hall and stopped outside the only open office door.

What he heard in the next two minutes convinced Harry that he'd made the right decision in telling Watson to back off. The

Texas Lottery Commission was obviously *not* a victim of Ralph Masterson's scheme. He was probably a benefactor, if truth be known.

For Mr. Anti-Gambling, Anti-Lotto Ralph Masterson had found a way to deal with the risk that an insured might win big.

Masterson handed over 158 tickets to the clerk at the Texas Lottery Commission's Claim Center and received $2,130 in exchange.

About The Honest Con Man

"The Honest Con Man" originated as I was cashing a 5 out of 6 winning Texas Lotto ticket for just over $1,800.00. Considering the odds, I felt cheated.

Then I began to think of a way to get back at them.

FLY AWAY
BY NATASHA STORFER AND BECKY HOGELAND

muckraker_mary [06:00am GMT]: Once upon a time I was a journalist. It came with last-minute trips to violence, murder, rioting, or puppies down wells, all tied up in a bow of late nights and a workaholic boss. I loved it. It didn't leave much time for family or romance, but it was a rewarding career. Perhaps someone was affected through my little articles between paper pages. Maybe I made them think, cry, or smile.

My questions weren't trained. I was born with an internal yearning for answers that always seems to lead to more questions… confirming the old saying about the more you know, the more you understand you know nothing.

My fingers tightened my straps. Joe double-checked the lab equipment he'd attached by carabineer to a separate rope before bonding us by our gear with a quiet click. Perched quietly on a limestone rock, Grace watched, looking like part of the scenery in her green Park Ranger polo.

Joe looked into my eyes. "Ready?"

My head bobbed in a weighted nod, avoiding speech due to the constraints of my chin strap. I flicked on the helmet light and looked towards a hole surrounded by black wrought iron fence.

"All right. Tug or shout out if you feel uncomfortable."

The limestone seemed sturdy enough, though appearing chalky in its light golden color. Once my head dipped below the opening, sounds changed. The walls echoed my breaths between the crunchy rasp of feet each time I found the next foothold. I looked up as I passed the protruding rock. The hole had seemed shallower from above.

The line connecting Joe and me remained mostly taut, giving me comfort that if my foot slipped, I wouldn't scrape the sides free-falling 'til I hit water. A call reverberated from above.

"You O.K.?" Joe's voice seemed far away.

I pulled at the chin strap before answering. "So far, so good! How far are we above sea level again?"

"Here?" The black spot of his head haloed by light called from above. "About six hundred feet. But you should hit water in less than fifty feet. The water table's higher."

As the light gleamed down, I perched my arms and legs on rock, a move my yoga teacher would be proud of. Without looking up, I called out. Sound reverberated off walls, vibrations making my words tangible.

"I'm almost there. I'll need the equipment in five minutes or so." I felt very much the 'field lab assistant' while shimmying down the tube. Enjoying myself more after seeing the destination. A deep breath of cool moist air brought tingles to my skin. Once again my eyes sought the minuscule dot of light above, more a habit born of looking toward someone as I spoke than out of any need.

"I'm ready for the kit!" Between the limestone ledge and other smaller rocks peeking out of the sides, the sliver of light from above was greatly diminished. But my light afforded a good view of stone undersides, as well as the descending rectangle of equipment. The container touched the fingertips of my outstretched hands.

"One more foot!" I gripped the rough plastic sides of the water-proof container. "I've got it!" After attaching the handle to my gear and carefully opening the lid, I drew out a cellophane-covered packet. I closed the lid and extracted the little sanitary tube from its protective plastic wrapping. Somehow this had seemed easier when not balancing fifty feet down a small hole.

"Can you keep the line tight a little longer?"

"Will do!" echoed down the tube. Muted voices from above flowed like a gentle stream of white noise down the shaft. I assumed that someone visiting the park was intrigued by the open gate. I focused my attention on the task at hand. The frog squat stretched muscles I didn't know existed. While dipping the tubes into the water, my cursed overactive mind conjured all sorts of imaginary wildlife lurking below the dark surface. When I had finished, I flipped open the case lid, mated the tubes with their corresponding foam slots, and withdrew Petri dishes.

In front of me, lit by my helmet light, sat a colorful array of limestone, sandy something, and clay. What kind of solid sample did Joe need? I concluded it was inconsequential and took a little of everything. After closing the lab equipment a final time, everything was ready for the climb up.

"Joe?" Still silence answered. Come to think of it, the soothing sound of muted voices from earlier was gone. Not even a whisper. Ready to head up, I realized the safety line had moved to the front of my thoughts.

"Hey, Joe! Did you go to sleep on me? Grace?" My call echoed up, unanswered. I tugged on the line to get their attention, immediately regretting it. A slithering hiss announced the rope's descent! What was going on up there?

Acutely aware of the missing spot line, I unfurled from my odd position and carefully began the long trip up, free climbing. I took a moment to pause halfway at a pseudo-ledge, listening to a small piece of broken limestone bounce down the edges of the hole and land in the water with a splash. Though I mentally chided my thoughts towards the exit, my misbehaving mind continued to play a looping reel of 'worst case scenario.'

After what seemed like an eternity, I passed the light's first choke point but became paranoid about calling out. I had no idea how the two people working above had disappeared. My brain construed my own breathing sounds as overly-loud, a roar discernible for miles.

Above, the small distorted circle of light grew to a point where I felt safe reaching to flip off the switch on the helmet light while my other limbs kept me wedged against the walls of the hole. A line of sweat tickled along my back, attesting to the warmth of the day, my exertion, and a bad case of nerves. Soon I'd be out, and Joe would get the lecture of a lifetime. Inspired by this thought and my fear of falling to the bottom again, the last few feet didn't take long.

I felt like a prairie dog peeking out of the hole. The target of my current wrath nowhere to be seen, I turned my gaze farther out to see Grace running towards me. Worry and fear distorted the Park Ranger's features as she offered a hand up.

"I'm so sorry, I shouldn't have left. I just didn't know what to do." The petite woman's strength belied her size as she hauled me up.

My body sagged with fatigue and gratitude. I hadn't noticed my legs trembling until I tried to stand. The cramps in my arms and back made me wince.

"Where's Joe?"

"They took him. Some fellas came, flashed official-looking badges, and 'escorted' him away for questioning about something. I tried to follow, but I lost sight when they turned onto the main road in their black car."

"Who were they?" By now I needed a drink and answers. Answers ranked higher.

"I'm not really sure, to be honest. Maybe FBI, some specialty unit or other? Joe told them no one was down the hole and I was about to head in." Grace ran a hand through her curls, making some stand up, damp with sweat.

Based on her erratic answer, I assumed her to be more than a little rattled. After sharing a few unladylike words under my breath, I called Joe's cell and heard a polite message about leaving my name and number after the tone.

Why would he lie about my being in the hole? Who took him? Did the samples have the answers? My hand strayed protectively to the kit still attached to my gear.

"I'm calling my boss."

Among a stand of trees off to the side, I occupied a bench and pounded out my frustrations on my cell's little buttons. Rebeka took forever to answer the phone. A whole three rings.

"Who did you send me to Austin with?" My voice cracked, desperation in my tone, showing more than I cared to admit. Generally calm in a crisis, for me to be this emotionally attached to a situation defied the norm in my line of work, after the first year or so.

I shrugged it off as dehydration and took a swig of water while listening.

"Joe? He's a professor in the Chemistry Department at Rice University. He's in my local group that does volunteer work with kids. Seems a nice man, and quite brilliant, honestly. What's up? Don't tell me he tried to hit on you." I could hear Rebeka's eyes roll though the phone.

"Beka, he just got hauled away by some people the park contact described as FBI."

There was a moment of pause on the other end. "What's the name of the park employee?"

"Grace. Grace Finly. I'll ask her a few more questions before I head home." But there was more. "Beka, I have the samples."

"Well, sounds like you hit on a bigger story and a handful of evidence. Let me call my contacts in that area. For now, head home and bring the samples. I'll give you a call when I have something nailed down." There was a quick click, and I was quite sure Rebeka was already onto her next phone call. That woman had more contacts than the President.

"Grace?"

Yes, Mary?"

The fey-like lady didn't look too good. In fact, she probably needed to stop pacing, drink some water, and close her eyes a moment. I fished out another lukewarm bottle of H2O and guided her to the shaded bench.

Grace spoke, her trembling hands balancing the water. "I've never seen anything like that."

"I have, but generally not when on a water conservation story." My quiet laughter, spiked with irony, failed at humor. "How well do you know Joe?"

"I've met him maybe half a dozen times. He seemed nice enough, very interested in what he's doing. He knows more than I thought at first. You know the type that never really leaves school? He's a little like that but more hands-on. Most grant holders send others out for field work, but he seemed to enjoy getting out and seeing things for himself."

"What do you mean?"

"Google him. He has a doctorate in chemistry, and more. Degrees and papers written on things like physics, biology, power transmission…" Grace looked thoughtful. "All his hobbies are what my brothers avoided like the plague in school. And he wouldn't hurt a fly, he's really passionate about the environment. He's even a vegetarian."

The vegetarian part had come up when we talked about lunch plans. My stomach rumbled. I'd fix that, then head home.

"I'm sure it's just a mix up, or maybe someone he knows filled out a grant request all wrong." I tried to reassure Grace, though I didn't believe my own words. "Here." I gave her my card. "If you remember anything or just want to talk, let me know. I need to head back to Houston. Are you going to be all right?"

Grace nodded, apparently much better after a drink of water, our chat, and some time in the shade. I assumed she'd be fine and left to pack the gear and equipment. The ride back to Houston would need to be quick to beat rush hour.

The press of traffic on the Loop was always annoying, but today the flashing traffic boards announced an accident in the area. Just my luck. I maneuvered among the zipping cars and had almost reached my apartment when the phone rang. I put Rebeka on speaker-phone with the press of a little button.

"Mary?"

"Hi there, boss-lady. What do you have for me?"

"Nothing that makes sense, really. Joe's being held on un-released charges by a group I've never heard of. Look, can you get those samples to the lab? They let me talk to him a moment, recorded the conversation, of course. He seemed worried about the grant money and his employees. Can I email you the directions and owe you dinner?"

I sighed, hoping Rebeka's ears couldn't hear it over the ambient freeway noise. "You already owe me eight dinners and almost as many lunches. How about I do it because I'm nice and didn't have anything else to do?"

"You're a doll, hon. If I find out anything else, I'll pass it on." The quiet on the other end lasted a moment. "There. The directions are sent. I'll let them know you're coming and call you if you need a key card." Rebeka was good at thinking ahead like that.

"Thanks. I always did want to go to Rice. Take care, and I'm sure I'll talk to you soon."

"Anything for you. Ciao."

My gaze rested on my current passenger: a little dingy, plastic box. Could it contain any answers? The first step to finding out was to download the map into my car's GPS system.

✢

Could they make this any more confusing? Between the parking and the security, I'd never get this stuff into the lab. Rebeka had called back, armed with a phone number and a name for Joe's post-grad assistant: David.

Ironic laughter and a desire to hit something curled up within me. What a tame conservation story had become seemed funny for almost a moment. The humor passed quickly as the questions in my mind accelerated just enough to pile up and cause mental road block before I entered the lab.

David was height challenged but made up for it in girth. His smile reminded me of my Uncle Fred.

He seemed nice, cheerful, and willing to open the door after seeing my identification. "This all just seems a big mess now, doesn't it? First Joe almost loses the grant he's been working towards for years, then this tangle." My escort tsk'd and handed me some safety gear. "Here, you need a lab coat and glasses. I'm glad you're wearing appropriate shoes."

We entered a small room, surrounded by the humming of computer noise and equipment. I identified the scales and other equipment I'd used years ago in school. Other items were quite beyond Chemistry 101.

"Here we are." David perched on a rolling chair, holding out his hand for the sample box.

I handed it over, then restrained the urge to pace, feeling oddly light and antsy without the container.

"I'll place them on the robot here," he said. "We have a pre-prepped sample tray. The robotic arm takes a little of each sample before placing it in a vial." He paused. "This will take a while. You may as well sit and relax. Do you need to call anyone or do anything?"

"Sure. I mean, thank you." I smiled apologetically, mentally blamed a long day for my lapse, and flipped open my laptop.

"Do you have a Wi-Fi here?" If not, I'd be on phone network. I cringed a little inside at the thought.

"Sure do. We have a password, so I'll need to log you in."

"Thank you!" Most colleges thrived on a faster connection than the rest of the world.

Once I was on the network, my normal excessive work email streamed in with a few clicks, along with a few scattered personal items. Spotting one from Grace, I clicked on it.

Mary,
Thank you for helping me today after I was so unreliable when they were taking Joe. I looked up the license plate number on a park camera hoping to find out where I could inquire about him. Only the plate isn't in the system. All I got was a link to the 'Internal Affairs Alliance', and a few odd looking posts by people with conspiracy theories. I thought you may know more as a journalist.
Thank you,
Grace

The Internal Affairs Alliance? That sounded like something someone who plastered their head in aluminum foil might come up with. It was probably just a typo in her license plate search, but I still forwarded it to Rebeka.

With a little beep, my computer announced incoming mail. I clicked to accept it and numbers began to stream down the page.

"Um, David? Does this happen in the lab often?"

He wheeled over in his lab chair with ease and turned to view my screen. The look on his face broadcast his response. No. It was unusual and probably bad.

"Those are analysis numbers. See? Your computer is using Windows, so it's Microsoft Access compatible. Something triggered the software to open and spill information into a database."

"Analysis numbers?"

"Yeah. Come over here and look." He glided back over to his station with a deft push of a toe, and I followed.

"Look here. The columns are different samples, rows based on contaminates, minerals, etcetera, in parts per million."

His hand waved a mechanical pencil in front of his screen and I tried to keep up. The data was very similar. My mind stumbled around the clues as I pulled my laptop closer.

"The numbers are the same. Aren't they? Is the file somehow being sent from that machine?" I scrolled up.

David started typing on the station machine frantically. "I'm a chemist, not a systems analyst. But I'm pretty sure Joe didn't have this set up this way on purpose. Why would he? The numbers will be public knowledge in a few months anyway, when he submits them for publication."

It sounded to me like someone needed to see these numbers before they were published. "I don't know much about water samples. Is there anything here that looks off?"

David snorted at my question.

"We're testing hundreds of substances based on typical household products and a few others Joe was concerned about. Let me take a quick glance. Maybe I can spot something." Numbers scrolled down in a blur as David's practiced eye glanced over the spreadsheet. His hand stopped, fast.

"It's here." The cursor flickered over a number. "I don't understand why he was even testing this, though. This is a byproduct of nuclear energy facilities. There's one south of the testing site, but everything is supposed to be put in containment far from the reservoirs."

Struck by a sudden urge to stick aluminum foil on my head, I resisted and asked another question. "Do you know what's causing this machine to send numbers to another station?"

"Honestly? I have no idea. I'd have to ask one of our network guys."

I wondered if that department owed Rebeka a favor. "Is it O.K. if I ask someone to look at the computer?" David looked uncomfortable, so I shrugged it off. "I understand. It was kind of you to help me this much on such short notice."

David's relief was obvious; my frustration was less so, though still as real.

Discreetly, I saved the file to my hard drive before closing the laptop and exaggerating a yawn. "I'm sure Joe will be very grateful for your help."

The lab tech grinned as I spoke. "I would have come in even if I wasn't promised game tickets. But they did make it more pleasant."

I should have known Rebeka would call ahead with a bribe. They worked so very well.

"I'm sure. Well, I need to head home to get some sleep. Boss has me all over the place this time of year."

"I'll let you out."

The sun had gone down while I'd been chatting with David. The paths of the college were lit by the glow atop lampposts now. I kept my vision forward and my steps quick as I focused on getting to my car. My tunnel vision intensified the surprise as a hand landed on my arm, twisting my body. I stumbled, inhaled to scream, and a hand covered my mouth.

"Shhhhh…" A breath near my ear tried to calm me but had the

opposite effect. "Damn! That was my foot. Mary, it's just me, Joe. I was just trying to get your attention without being too loud."

He released me and I turned with a scowl.

His words hadn't made it any better. From the look on his face, he probably placed me somewhere on the danger scale between "scorpion" and "blind date." And he might be right. For some reason my palms went damp looking into his gray-green eyes. But the need for answers eclipsed my feelings.

"Joe." My voice was hushed among the call of crickets and katydids. "What the hell is going on? Were you really taken by some government organization? And why did the samples I brought in have traces of..."

The professor's hard look silenced me. "I've talked to your boss and promised answers..."

He paused and I prompted. "And?"

"When it's safer."

I took a slow breath and released it, mentally counting to ten before Joe continued quietly.

"Look, I've talked to Rebeka. She said she'll leave something in a place you'll understand. It should give you some answers, but honestly, the less you know right now, the safer you are. I'll give you some time to think. If you decide you want to know more, I'll be at Intercontinental Airport." He put a note in my hand. "On this flight."

We glanced at each other before we parted in different directions. I knew if I turned him in, I'd lose my chance at unraveling this tangle. And he knew I understood the rules.

My first stop was my apartment, thinking maybe Beka had dropped something off. The key turned in my lock with no resistance. I pushed, sending the door open and then pulling it back toward me as it hit something on the floor. Stepping tentatively, I looked about.

A DVD was looping through a silent repetition of my cousin's wedding, the TV screen's flickering images illuminating a scattered mess. My body went still, listening. A lull passed; no one jumped from shadows or strode forward with an arrest warrant. So I did the most stupid thing possible. Pepper spray in hand, I kept going.

A hallway floorboard groaned under my foot, the sound stealing my breath. After a pause, I continued. The bedroom was littered with clothes piled outside their drawers. I found it oddly helpful as I packed. No way was I sleeping here tonight.

I crept towards the front door, locking it in passing. Not that it seemed to matter. The trip to my car was quick, and I was on the phone before closing the door.

"Where are you?" Rebeka sounded agitated. That wasn't like her.

"Leaving my apartment. When I got home, it was unlocked. Someone went through my things." With a flick of my wrist, the key turned in the ignition. The engine roar pierced the late evening serenity.

"Have you called the police? When can you be here?" Rebeka's agitated reply was out of character.

"No. And as soon as I can." I revved the engine to turn into the street.

Rebeka continued in that odd tone. "Good. You have some visitors, and I left a thank-you in your desk."

The odd replies triggered a bout of heartburn. "No offense, but I didn't put you on speaker, and I can drive faster with two hands."

"Bye." The click was immediate.

The trip took an eternity. Normally ten minutes from the office, I made it in eight. But my mind kept time by heartbeats, elongating reality to a surreal journey through time. I parked on the street rather than in the parking garage and hefted my laptop bag. Hopefully, this wouldn't take long. But there was no way I was parting with the evidence on my hard drive.

I flashed my key card and headed up two flights of stairs. The office was busy, as there were always employees getting ready for the next publication. A few I'd never seen before were loitering near the water cooler. After flashing a wave and a smile, I made a beeline to the boss lady's office.

I knocked. A muffled 'come in' prompted me to open the door. Entering, I saw that I wouldn't be talking to Rebeka alone. The two suits moved toward the door, blocking my exit with their bodies. The distinctly gun-shaped bulges in their clothes and their inky-lensed sunglasses did nothing to help my nerves.

"Mary, good to see you. I'm so sorry about all of this. Look, I know you've spent a lot of time on this article, but I think its best tabled for now." Professional and to the point. And so very unnatural. "I've talked to these gentlemen, and they realize that you're in no way connected to Joe's research beyond highlighting the government's efforts to keep our water supply free of contamination, and advising how each person should do his part. They've read your notes and articles, and they're happy with what they saw."

"Of course." I matched her tone for tone. What she really meant was I was free and clear. As long as nothing went to print.

"I have a few assignments in your desk to choose from. You've earned a choice—and probably a vacation—but I'm not that nice of a boss." The normal Rebeka peeked through her ironic smile. "Think it over, but be quick. We have a paper to get out."

With a nod she dismissed me and I left her office, trying to calm the trembling of my hands.

When I arrived at my desk, I did indeed see several files. Rather than start sifting through the pile, I opened the drawer. Inside was a bag of chocolate. It was a game between the two of us, a 'welcome back' that generally held something besides just sweets. Rebeka loved an imaginative bribe.

I paused just long enough to look through the folders, selected a few, and left the office with my surprise. Once in the car, I opened the candy bag. After popping a chocolate into my mouth, I pulled out a plane ticket and an iPod.

I placed an ear bud in my ear. Beka's voice sounded firm as I hit 'play.'

"You're officially on assignment. And you're officially to

disappear until all of this blows over and you're safe. Do you understand me? The ticket is to Mexico. We're having border issues, and it's a hot topic. You're to use alternative contact channels. I still want stories, understand?" The recorded voice paused. "The envelope is so I know you are all right. It has cash, a company credit card, and a couple of ways to contact me. But if you use the card, you'll have to move. It's traceable." There was another pause and a little bit of background noise. "All I'm really doing is buying you time for Joe's brain and your wits to get us out of this mess with some answers and solutions. Until then, you're on assignment, I know nothing beyond what you've told me, and I have no idea where you are. And if you did tell me fantasy stories about some secret organization, I told you I don't run a tabloid. Got it?"

I got it.

An hour later, I looked down at the city's lights with its hub-and-wheel layout. It looked like a web, lights dancing as dew would under moonlight, twinkling as if a light breeze vibrated the delicate weave.

Turning to Joe, vegetarian, professor, and outlaw, I spoke for the first time since we left the airport.

"How the *hell* did you get out of wherever they stuck you?" My tone must have showed how close I was to cracking, because he talked fast.

"There was a car accident, otherwise I'd probably be somewhere answering questions or hearing false charges against me. It was rush hour in Houston, and something was bound to happen. For the first time, I was glad it happened to me. It may have helped a little with distractions."

I could see the strain of child deviant in his expression. "Are we there yet…are we there yet…I need to go potty!" played in my head until he spoke.

"In the confusion of police, media, and curious civilians, I quietly blended in and found a friend willing to drive me to the lab," he said. "I knew you'd eventually arrive."

"Who were those people? Who are you?"

His smile twisted a little. "The Internal Affairs Alliance believes in putting a 'best face forward' for the government. Accidents happen, people get disgruntled, and rallies can get violent. Anything tarnishes the government's image, and IAA intervenes. Generally, there's a word of caution, maybe an exchange of money, and everything's fine. But then you have people like me, and they resort to different...methods. I probably wouldn't have been killed. But they would have found something odd in my lab, planted drugs or supplies to make their case. It's harder to talk behind bars and even if you do, your credibility is shot."

I raised a brow, and he got the hint about the other question.

He sighed and ran a hand through his shaggy blond-brown hair. "Me? I'm a scientist. I love questions. But even more, I like answers. So when people put things between me and an answer, I just become more intrigued."

That sounded too familiar for comfort. But I listened, the answer being more important than the twinge in my brain.

"In searching, I found some people affected by the IAA. In general, the ones that are talking were 'the ones that got away,' so to speak. I didn't give them enough credit. Look, I never thought they would do anything more than normal government hemming and hawing when I found the first traces of contaminates. I admit they tried to pull my grant after the numbers started surfacing, but I had no idea you would be in any danger." He lifted a hand in the air, as if being sworn in. "I promise. If it hadn't been you in this mess, it would have been one of my co-workers. I'd never do that."

He looked out the window as we rose through blue-bottomed clouds, avoiding my gaze for more than a moment of silence as I took it all in.

Rebeka was most likely part of it somehow. But if I learned she really was, I'd probably put her in jeopardy, so I left that question unasked. "There's more, isn't there? You knew I'd come for the answers alone, didn't you? And you knew I had access to channels for highlighting what was happening. Most importantly, you knew I couldn't walk away without answers."

The answer was quiet, but no less profound. "Yes. Will you help us?"

I pulled my travel sleeping mask down and relaxed into my seat, hiding a little from the world as I answered. "Yes."

A few days later, in a dingy motel that asked for payment by the hour, I sat on my bed with my laptop for company and avoided thinking about the man sleeping in the room's other bed. Chaotic thoughts tumbled as my eyes scanned the bright monitor in the dim room.

Driven by necessity, I continued to type:

muckraker_mary [06:10am GMT]: The same curiosity that made me a good journalist has landed me in a place where I can no longer post my legal name in print. I became a pseudonym here, a pen name there. Yet one who still existed to answer questions. Going into hiding didn't dim the light inside me, but instead fueled the flames.

After time I looked about and saw a web. Touch points of humanity that interweave and depend on one another for stability. And I saw the dark side of the web: the predator, viewing humanity as the fly.

This time I was able to dance along the delicate strings and send messages to people who could make a difference, ones who would act rather than hide. Together we've created a place for ourselves outside the web with a view of its dangers and the ability to warn those who wish to act to tread lightly. But will I ever again tread the mundane paths I used to take for granted?

BATS, BONES AND BEETLES
BY CHARLOTTE PHILLIPS

"I'm not trying to pry, Eva, but if you want to talk about it, I'm a pretty good listener."

Liz *was* trying to pry, and I didn't know how she could possibly be a good listener. Between her constant chatter and her dog's incessant yapping, there wasn't room for anyone else in the conversation. It didn't matter. I was sure she didn't want to hear the truth. It was far too boring compared to the scenarios she'd been dreaming up. The fact was, my friend Beth thought I needed to get away for a few days to relax and had hounded me until I agreed to spend a long weekend at Liz's place in the Texas Hill Country. Beth had not mentioned the yappy dog.

So that's how I ended up traipsing along a trail in Old Tunnel WMA—the smallest Wildlife Management Area in Texas—with a friend of a friend, a stranger really, and her four-legged "snookums." The idea was to relax in the welcoming arms of Mother Nature—with her spider webs, millions of insects, and bats. My idea of a relaxing weekend involves good books, a healthy man, a warm fire in the fireplace, and maybe a kitten or two—no bats, no spiders, no creepy crawlies. But I'm told you shouldn't knock what you haven't tried. So, I was trying.

"Spike! No!" Liz had momentarily forgotten her self-image as a strong, butch lesbian. She was screaming like a little girl. The sight of her pint-sized dog heading for the forbidden bat hangout had completely unnerved her.

"Chill, Liz. It's early. At this hour there are no rangers running around with citation books. Spike will be back in a minute."

"Rangers aren't the problem. That tunnel is crawling with flesh-eating beetles." Liz was already climbing over the fence that defined the boundary between the permitted nature trail and the forbidden bat zone. She shouted over her shoulder, "They'll eat Spike alive!"

I'd read the same brochure she'd read and managed to miss the part about yappy-dog-eating-beetles. When I'd perused the document, it said dermestid beetles lived on the floor of the tunnel and ate, among other things, bacteria that lived in the bat guano, a printable word for shit, and bats that fell from above. But, assuming the beetles could consume a jumping, yipping dog, wouldn't they also be able to eat Liz? I hopped the fence and ran after her.

As we got closer to the tunnel entrance, we were met by the pungent odor of ammonia. Spike saved us the full experience by emerging in the nick of time. Liz grabbed him by his rhinestone collar and proceeded to swat at him as if he were covered in vicious beetles. I didn't see any bugs, but I was more interested in the orange high-top sneaker Spike had dragged out of the tunnel. Something protruded from the opening, and beetles definitely clung to it.

While Liz continued to swat at imaginary bugs on the now-aromatic Spike, releasing a fine cloud of bat guano into the air. I would have felt sorry for the dog if he'd just been quiet for five seconds. I kicked at the sneaker to dislodge the freeloaders. When that didn't work, I picked it up and batted them away. The protrusion looked like a short piece of human leg bone that had been gnawed off by something with small, pointy teeth. I peered far enough inside the sneaker to see that the leg bone was held in place by its connection to foot bones.

My inspection of Spike's grisly find was interrupted by a B-movie scream. Liz scooped up Spike and hugged him to her chest. Spike momentarily ceased his yipping, creating a creepy silence. I looked around until I found the source of the scream—a teenage girl, eyes wide, one hand covering her mouth, the other pointing at me—or at the orange high-top. I held the shoe out toward her, and she did a slow-motion, pirouette faint to the ground.

We raced to the girl, and I tucked the sneaker out of sight before attempting to revive her. Liz proved more competent than me at mothering, so I stood back. "Hey, Sweetie. Just lie still for a minute. You kinda fainted." Liz smiled and gently brushed a stray hair behind the teen's ear. "I'm Liz. This is my friend Eva. Who are you?"

"Angie."

"Okay, Angie. Can you move your fingers?"

While Liz stepped Angie through the routine, I listened to an approaching runner and turned just in time to see a young hunk in green T-shirt and shorts jump the fence and call to us. "Hey, what's going on over there?" He looked good enough to eat. Perhaps I could find a way to relax after all. That green getup would work, too. He could be Ranger Rick, and I could be a very naughty camper.

I waited until he was close enough to hear me, then told him, "I don't know yet."

Liz jumped to her feet and rattled off her explanation. "Spike ran into the tunnel and found a sneaker. Angie screamed and fainted."

While Ranger Rick processed that lack of information, Angie added, "They killed Nick."

Ranger Rick took a giant step backwards. Perhaps he wouldn't make a good ranger after all.

Liz and I asked questions at the same time, which confused everyone. I suggested that I should handle the questions. Liz, who knew I was a PI, nodded, and I took over.

"Angie," I spoke slowly. "Who's Nick?"

Angie opened her mouth to speak, but choked up. I suggested she pull herself together and give us some information so we could help her. A little tough love never hurt anyone, right? Liz started to mother the kid, which only made her tear up more, so I pointed out that Spike had slipped away. Liz instantly forgot about Angie and ran off calling for Spike.

I gave Angie an imitation of *the look* I had seen so many times from my aunt during my drama-queen years. It worked like magic. Angie sucked in a deep breath and tried again. "Nick's my best friend."

"Good. And why do you think he's in trouble?" I didn't want to use the 'D' word lest it trigger another flood of tears.

"It's those drama brats. Nick wants to join the club, but they're so mean. They make everyone go through initiation, even when they know they don't want you. Nick promised to get home by six AM, but he didn't."

Ranger Rick stepped back into the conversation. "But that just means he's a little late. It's only eight now. He could be home, and you wouldn't know it because you're here. Why *are* you here?"

Angie started to tear up again. "Because the initiation was here. Nick had to meet the club at the tunnel at midnight and prove he could spend the night in there, by himself…and…and you found his shoe!" The sobs started in earnest.

I picked up the orange sneaker to show it to Ranger Rick. Before I could say one word, the color drained from his face, and he raced for the tunnel. I, too, was wondering if there were more bones. I told Angie to stay put and followed. The odor was stronger than I'd anticipated, and I nearly turned back, but I spotted multiple sets of footprints in the soft floor, and curiosity spurred me on.

My would-be ranger was just a few feet inside, staring at a nearly complete skeleton. The specimen, obviously of the classroom type, had recently been hanging in a dusty corner. Most of the footprints continued into the tunnel. I followed them a bit farther to a stage prop corpse, decorated with what appeared to be ketchup blood and honey ooze. The beetles were feasting on the decorative features.

Todd caught up with me and asked, "What's going on here?"

"So, I'm guessing you're not a ranger?"

"No, ma'am. I'm a wildlife biologist doing research here."

He wiped his hand on his shorts and held it out. "Name's Todd."

Damn, he'd ma'am'd me. That was the kiss of death. I shrugged it off. "I'm Eva Baum, a Houston PI, here on vacation." I shook his hand and continued. "So far, we have a poorly executed hoax. The creepy setting, complete with bats flapping overhead, guano raining down, and bugs swarming across the floor of the tunnel is rather original. The skeleton back there is probably from the high school biology lab, and this fake corpse has been liberated from a thespian prop room."

I pointed out the footprints. Most ended in a riot of activity around the fake corpse, but two pair ventured further in, and one of those returned. The light from the entrance didn't carry far into the tunnel. I cursed myself for not carrying a flashlight. What kind of an idiot heads into the forest so unprepared? "I don't suppose you've got a flashlight hidden on you somewhere?"

Todd wiggled his eyebrows playfully, "I don't believe so, but feel free to search me, ma'am."

"If you call me ma'am one more time, I'm going to turn you over my knee and spank you. My name's Eva."

Todd thought about that. He seemed tempted by my offer. "Yes ma', um, I mean, Eva."

"Tease." I smiled. "I might like a rain check on the search. Right now, I'm fascinated by these prints."

With the lack of light, we couldn't really see much, but we inched along until we found the third grisly attraction. This one was more organic than the first two. "Oh, oh."

"Is that real?" Todd asked.

"It smells real. I think we just contaminated a crime scene."

"Damn." Todd sounded concerned, but continued walking around the gooey mess. He pulled a small flashlight out of his pocket and moved the light back and forth across the odiferous, jellied mess of what remained of a human being. A human being who would be difficult to identify. The beetles had done a number on fingers and toes, the head was shaved, clothes removed, and a larger animal had mauled the face beyond recognition.

"Hey! You said you didn't have a light."

"I offered to let you search. You declined." He circled the area one more time.

"Please stop what you're doing." He'd effectively obliterated all the original footprints with his nervous pacing. "Let's get out of here." I shoved him back towards the mouth of the tunnel, trying to exactly retrace our steps to minimize the damage.

I looked over at Angie. She was sitting on the ground with her arms wrapped around her knees, rocking back and forth. I whispered into Todd's well-tanned ear, "Let's go see what else we can get out of Angie."

"No offense, Eva, but don't you think we should call the sheriff?" Todd asked.

"Sure. But there's no reason not to ask a few questions first."

"I'll tell you what. You wait here with her. I'll run back to the office and make the call. We can turn the whole mess over to him and, if you like, I can show you around the park."

I had no intention of "turning the whole mess over" to anyone, but I wanted some time alone with Angie, and a park tour with the hunky Todd could turn into an interesting afternoon, so I agreed. I spent a few seconds enjoying the view as Todd jumped back over the fence and ran up the trail, before returning to the girl.

I talked Angie to her feet, and we paced back and forth while I rubbed her thin, pale arms for added measure. I did my best to keep her talking.

"Did you see Nick yesterday?"

"Yes."

"Good. Was he wearing orange sneakers?"

"No way!" She looked at me like I was quite dim. "Yesterday was yellow shoe day. He sticks to the plan."

"He wears different color shoes on different days?"

"Of course. We follow the code."

Of course. Doesn't everyone? "So, what color should he be wearing today?"

"Green." She glanced at me to make sure her dim-witted student was paying attention. "Yellow, then green, then blue."

"I see. So he wouldn't wear orange for a few more days—right?"

That got Angie's attention. "How did you know that?"

"It was a guess. I'm a detective—I solve puzzles for a living. I'm guessing that after blue comes purple, then red, then orange."

"Wow. You're good."

"Yes, I am, and I'd like to help you solve this puzzle. Can you tell me if there's any reason at all for Nick to have worn orange high tops last night?"

"No. He would have told me if he was changing the pattern."

I looked at Angie's feet. Sure enough, she sported neon yellow Crocs. "How do you know Nick isn't home yet? Could he be sleeping?" And, I wondered, why hadn't Angie been home long enough to change her shoes?

"No. He promised to text as soon as he got in. He never breaks a promise."

Hmmm. Cell phones. If Nick's phone was nearby, we might hear it ring. "Why don't you try to call him, just to make sure. We don't want to waste the sheriff's valuable time."

Angie raised her arm so her wrist was in front of her face, pushed a button on her watch, and with trembling voice, said, "Call Nick." Her command was answered by a ringing phone—from inside the tunnel. She fainted again, but this time, I caught her and made a mental note of the great acting job. The faint looked real enough, but I could feel she wasn't out. I was tempted to drop her, just to see how she'd handle the surprise.

Liz and Spike returned, followed by Todd, who had a blustery sheriff in tow. I gently lowered Angie to the ground. Liz heaved the yipping Spike into my arms, shoved me aside, and started another round of mothering on Angie.

The sheriff barked his first orders before he hauled his ample butt over the fence. "Eva Baum, step away from the group." My quality time with the girl was definitely over. I took two steps away from Liz and Angie. Sheriff Big Butt wasted no time in getting to the point. "Lady, we'll have none of your shenanigans on my turf. The way things work around here, you interfere with *my* case, I toss *you* in the slammer. Got it?"

"Got it. Have we met?"

"You're damn lucky we haven't. I know all about you. My cousin works for the Houston Police Department."

"Great. What is this big case I need to keep out of?" A PI has to be clear on these matters.

"Any police matter in the whole damn county is my case, and you will keep your nose out of my business." He continued walking toward me, jabbing his finger in my direction for emphasis. "Now step away from my witnesses."

I couldn't resist. I put the ammonia-perfumed Spike in his arms before taking one more step away and saluting.

"What the hell is this?" Big Butt tried to return Spike, but I'd been warned about interfering with his witnesses and wouldn't take the dog.

"Your main witness, Sheriff. Spike found the shoe."

Hunky Todd stepped in and took control of Spike. "Sheriff, if I may. This is Spike. He belongs to this young lady." He handed Spike to Liz. "Spike ran into the tunnel this morning and returned with an orange high top sneaker." Todd looked around for the orange high top, and I pointed toward it.

The Sheriff hustled over to inspect the sneaker. He used a pen to stand it up so he could peer inside. "Christ."

"Probably not." I was just trying to help the sheriff narrow down the possibilities.

His colorful response was interrupted by the arrival of two young deputies who greeted their boss from the tourist side of the fence, but seemed uncertain about whether to proceed. The sheriff ordered them over the fence. He instructed one to interview Angie and Liz. The other was to bag the evidence and keep me from interfering with the interviews. He then asked Todd to show him the bones in the tunnel.

The mention of more bones sent Angie into a fit of uncontrollable sobs. The girl was good. Liz set Spike on the ground and returned her attentions to Angie. Spike chased after Todd and Big Butt. At first the chaos seemed to throw the two deputies off their game, but they came around quickly.

My guard ordered me to stay put, so I sat down. While the officials went about their business, I removed a pencil, notepad, and business card from my pocket. On the back of the business card, I wrote a note to Angie, then listened in on the interviews. I was rewarded with last names and phone numbers for Angie and Nick, the name of the school, drama club, and club leader. I got it all written in my notepad before my guard headed back in my direction. I turned the page and drew a quick caricature of the sheriff.

"Hey, what are you doing?"

"Just drawing to pass the time." I tore off the caricature page and handed it to him. While he laughed at my work, I tucked the important notes back into my pocket. The young deputy grinned from ear to ear when I told him to keep the picture of his boss. I could always draw another one. I wrapped my arms around my knees and attempted to gaze up at the young deputy with a look of innocence. Unfortunately, the sun picked that moment to target my unique bracelet and the glint of sun on metal caught the deputy's eye.

"What's that?"

"What's what?" I asked. When speaking to THE LAW, it's always good to make sure you understand the question before answering.

"What's that thing on your arm?"

"My bracelet?"

"Yea. I ain't never seen one like that."

"It's Japanese. It's a *manriki-gusari*."

"Are you telling me those tiny, little Jap gals run around with all that metal on their arms? That thing looks like it weighs more than half the Jap gals I ever met."

"Do you meet a lot of Japanese women around here?" I tried to change the subject. I'm careful to never tell a bold-faced lie when talking to the law. I wore my *manriki-gusari* as jewelry, but the truth is, it's a handy weapon. However, it's much more useful when the element of surprise is on my side. I didn't care to explain its uses to this young cop.

Unfortunately, the boy wasn't budging. "I ain't no idiot, now. You tell me what that thing's for."

"Okay. I use it to catch bad boys."

The deputy looked like he wanted to laugh at that. While he was making up his mind, Todd and the sheriff emerged from the tunnel. As they strolled toward us, the sheriff slapped at his clothes to remove the film of white dust covering his pants from cuffs to mid-thigh. That put a cloud of bat guano into the air that caused poor Todd a coughing fit. He managed to wheeze out a request for the sheriff to cease and desist, explaining the source of the dust.

"Guano? Son, are you trying to tell me I'm covered in bat shit?" Big Butt hiked up his pants for emphasis. "I'm not falling for that."

"Sheriff. There's three million bats in that tunnel, and their guano is full of bacteria. You can wear it, or you can breathe it. Wearing it is better for your health."

"Shit." He was catching on.

While Big Butt was distracted with this monumental decision, I took the opportunity to get close to Angie. I put my arm around her shoulders, told Liz and Angie to move away from the dust, and slipped my business card under Angie's watch/phone band.

"Miz Baum! I told you to stay away from my witnesses."

"Sorry, Sheriff. I was just trying to get the child away from the toxic cloud."

"We'll take care of her. Taylor, have the kid's parents pick her up at the station. I want to talk to both of them. While you're at it, send a car to the boy's house. I want him and his parents at the station when I get there." He pointed at my young guard. "Jake, you stay here and make sure no one disturbs the scene. I'll escort the rest of our witnesses out of the park and return in about an hour with your relief."

With that, we trekked back up the trail to the parking lot. The sheriff took the opportunity to make sure we all understood the rules and planned to remain in the area for the next twenty-four hours. He had to compete with the yapping Spike every step of the way.

By the time we reached the parking lot, I'd had about all I could take. I told Liz I'd understand if she needed to rush Spike off to the groomers, and reminded Todd he'd promised me an interesting afternoon. Todd's grin told me he understood what I wanted, and a park tour was definitely not on the list. He gallantly offered his muscular arm and I took it, thinking of all the fun ways we could pass the time while I waited to see if Angie would call me.

The wildlife biologist knew a thing or two about women. I was recovering from my third Todd-induced coma when my phone finally rang. While I enjoyed my relaxed state, Todd retrieved my phone and pushed the speaker button.

Before I could croak out a hello, Beth's voice assaulted my ears. "Do you really not know how to take a vacation? You can't keep out of trouble for one weekend?"

"Hello, Beth. How are you?"

"I know that tone. You're in bed, aren't you? Your friends are working to keep you out of the pokey, and you're enjoying a roll in the hay with some…"

"Wildlife biologist—and you're on speaker phone." I interrupted Beth's rant. "Todd, meet Beth. Beth, Todd."

Todd dutifully responded, "Hello, Beth. Nice to meet you."

"Wildlife biologist. At least that's original."

"Thanks. What has Eva done? Is there a SWAT team outside my house?" Todd sounded amused.

"Who knows. Liz called in a panic. The sheriff showed up at

her place with a warrant for Eva's things. It seems Eva's footprints led straight to a not-so-fresh corpse. He found her gun permit and is convinced she illegally carried a concealed weapon into some park. He's planning to use that to lock her up."

I laughed at that. "The sheriff is going to be disappointed."

Beth ignored me. "Todd, you sound like an upstanding citizen. Don't let that evil woman lead you astray. Do not let her talk you into hiding her gun."

"Gee, thanks for that vote of confidence, Beth." I indulged in a cat stretch. "You'll be happy to know Todd is not in any danger. Not from my gun, anyway. It's in the usual place."

"Seriously? You don't have it with you?" Beth sounded surprised.

"Of course not. I'm on vacation. Remember?"

"Good. Please promise me you'll stay on vacation and out of that sheriff's way. He sounds like a pill."

Before I could respond, my phone beeped, indicating someone else wanted to speak to me. "I've got another call, Beth. I'll ring you later. We can talk then." I switched lines before Beth could continue the lecture.

"Miss Eva, you have to help! That woman lied to the police. If they search her house, they'll find out the truth."

"Angie?"

"Yes. She's a lousy mother. Can you help?"

"Angie, I want you to take a few deep breaths and gather your thoughts. Then start at the beginning." I took the phone off speaker so I could have a semi-private chat. Todd took the hint and headed for the shower. "I'm especially interested in how you know what anyone else said to the sheriff."

I waited while Angie made a point of letting me hear her take three deep breaths before she launched back into her story.

"Okay. Those cops kept us at the jail, like, forever. They kept acting like I was a criminal. My mom wanted to take me home, but we had to wait for that mean sheriff guy to get back. They brought Nick's mom in, and she, she said mean things to me, asking me what I got her baby into this time and stuff like that. She kept after me until she saw my mom. Then she started yelling at the cops, demanding to know what was going on, why did they haul her in, they had no right, and her baby would wake up and not know where his mom had got to, acting like Nick's some helpless little baby, and she's worried about him. But she wasn't worried enough to check his room before she told them he was there. She swore he'd been home asleep all night and was still asleep in his bed.

"Finally the sheriff showed up, and that witch insisted on going first even though my mom and I had been there longer. They went into an office and closed the door, but she shouted the whole time, so I could hear everything she said. She lied, lied, lied. I don't understand why they didn't search her house for Nick. Do you?

"Then they let her go, and I thought the sheriff would finally ask his questions and let me go home, but no. That's when all those drama brats walked in with Jason's dad, the big shot lawyer, and Joe's dad who runs the funeral home and, of course, the sheriff just had to talk to them first, so my mom and I sat there some more and…"

"Angie, please remember to breathe."

"Okay, but the sheriff talked to them right there in the lobby. And even though he was all nice and everything to them, Jason's dad wouldn't let anyone answer any questions. He told the sheriff they were just kids, and whatever was wrong was probably a harmless prank that could be put right in short order. So the sheriff said they had twenty-four hours to come up with a good explanation of how some dead person moved herself from the funeral home to the bat tunnel and why anyone, even a dead person, would want to spend eternity lying in bat shit being eaten by bugs. Joe's dad whacked Joe in the back of the head. Then the sheriff just let them all go, like it was no big deal.

"*Finally* the sheriff said he wanted to talk to me alone, but my mom said no, so we went into his office together. Did you know they found three bodies in that tunnel? That's what the sheriff said, anyway, and he kept demanding I tell him how they got there, like I have a crystal ball or something. He said I'd be in big trouble if I didn't come clean. Can you help me?"

Our one-sided conversation was accented by pounding on Todd's front door and a loud, "Sheriff! Open up!"

Todd emerged from the bathroom and raised an eyebrow at me. I told Angie I would call her back and suggested Todd answer the door before the good sheriff kicked it in. The sheriff entered bellowing. I was beginning to wonder if the man had an inside voice. I pulled the top sheet around me before Todd returned to the bedroom with the sheriff and Jake in tow. I waved. "Hello, Sheriff, Jake. I didn't expect to see you again."

"Cut the crap. Get up and show me your things."

"If you insist." I stood up fully intending to flash the boys, when he changed his mind.

"Sit down. You know what I mean. I want to see everything you had with you this morning in the park."

"That might be a problem."

"Why?"

"A funny thing happened while I was, um, napping. A good-hearted cowboy woke me up and offered to launder my clothes. I agreed, and I haven't seen them since."

The sheriff eyed Todd from head to toe. "Cowboy?"

I thought about neighing soft and low, like a very satisfied pony, but didn't know if he'd get the joke. "Show him your hat, pardner."

Todd blushed a deep red that showed off his beautiful blue eyes.

Jake commented, "You should be blushing. Don't you think this kind of behavior will hurt Lulu?"

Excuse me? Lulu? Who the hell was Lulu? I turned to Todd for a response.

"Don't listen to him. That nut case hasn't let me talk to her for two weeks because she thought she saw me with some other woman at Wal-Mart. Why would I take a woman to Wal-Mart?"

"Where are Baum's things?" The sheriff was not a patient man.

"In the dryer."

"Everything?"

"Yes, sir."

"Where'd you put her gun?"

"I didn't see a gun."

"Are you sure?"

"I conducted a pretty thorough search."

"Three times," I offered.

"She has a weapon, sheriff." Jake wasn't a dummy, after all. "She had it wrapped around her arm in the park."

"He means my bracelet, sheriff." I carefully picked up the *manriki-gusari* and slipped it on.

"What the hell kinda weapon is that?" The sheriff asked Jake.

"I don't know, sir. She said she uses it to catch bad guys."

"It works, too." I stood then, letting the sheet fall to the floor. I walked toward Todd while slowly unwrapping a few feet of chain. When I got close enough, I looped the chain behind his neck and pulled him in for a kiss.

"Enough!" Sheriff Big Butt resorted to empty threats. He jabbed his finger in my direction and said he did not expect to read about me or any of my exploits on the front page of the local paper. He hoped I understood. Then he turned on his heel and marched out with Jake following like a lap dog.

I ruined his big exit, "Hey, sheriff, I heard you already solved the case. Who were the unfortunate victims?"

The sheriff turned and puffed up like a blow-fish. He was mighty proud and willing to answer my question. "Not that it's any of your beeswax, missy, but there was only one victim. One victim, one wired-up old skeleton, and a fake body, a left-over prop from the high school's last play. The only victim was Miz Anna Lipschitz. She recently lost a long battle with leukemia. Our local pranksters apparently didn't think that was traumatic enough for her family, so they stole her body from the morgue and dumped it in that tunnel. When the time's right, they'll be making amends. For now, the family just wants to lay her to rest."

That was a long speech for the sheriff and letting out all that hot air caused a small problem. He grabbed his pants in time and hiked them back up around his waist. Then he took the opportunity to lecture me one more time. He jabbed a finger in my direction a few times as he informed me his little town didn't need the likes of me around, stirring up trouble. He suggested I leave—soon. Then he marched out, making sure to slam the door behind him.

I kissed Todd on my way to the shower and asked if I could pretty please have my clothes back. I explained that I needed to talk to Angie's parents and would appreciate a ride. The kid might need a lawyer.

"The kid from this morning? Has she done something wrong?"

"I hope not."

Alone in the bathroom, I couldn't resist a little snooping. I didn't care for me. Todd and I were obviously not headed for a meaningful relationship, but I hated when guys used me to cheat on their significant others. How hard could it be to simply say you appreciated the offer, but weren't available? A quick scan revealed two toothbrushes, two hairbrushes, and a host of feminine care products. Damn. I wanted my cowboy to be the white-hat kind.

I asked Todd to drop me off at my car, but he wanted to tag along. I wasn't sure that was such a good idea, but I did let him chauffeur me.

I didn't return Angie's call. I wanted her to stew a while longer, and I wanted my visit to be a surprise. That gave me the best chance of getting at the truth quickly.

Angie's mom answered the door. I explained who we were, that Angie had requested my help. She looked dubious but invited us in and escorted us to the kitchen where Angie was setting the table for dinner. The scent of warm bread caressed my nostrils, and my stomach growled its response. We were instantly invited to join them for dinner. It took every ounce of will power I had, but I declined.

"Please, sit down. I'm interested in knowing why my daughter believes she needs a PI."

"That makes two of us." I sat at the head of the table. "Angie, please join us and tell me why you lied at the tunnel this morning."

Angie shot a look at Todd and said, "I didn't lie."

"You asked for my help. I can't help you if you don't tell me the truth. I'm not sure I can help you if you *do* tell the truth. If you don't want Todd to stay, he can leave, but your mom has to stay."

Angie politely asked Todd to leave and sat down without ever looking at her mother.

"Sorry, Todd. If you don't want to wait, I can call a cab when we're done."

The ever-gallant Todd promised to wait even if it took all night, and made a graceful exit.

"Okay—tell me why you made up that story about Nick. You knew that sneaker wasn't his."

The girl twisted a napkin around her fingers. "It is so Nick's. I'd know his sneakers anywhere."

"Especially if you lifted them out of his closet."

Angie threw the napkin on the table and yelled, "You're not helping!"

"That's because I don't yet know what the problem is. I know you dressed that skeleton in Nick's clothes and put it in the tunnel. You probably stole the skeleton, but that could be a small problem. The bigger problem is Nick. Are you covering for him? Is he running away? Did you kill him and make up a ridiculous story to place blame on the drama kids?"

Mom stepped in then. "Hey, lady, you can't come in here and accuse my daughter of murder. I think you should leave."

"I want her to stay, Mom. I didn't kill him, and he didn't run away. He's with his dad. I didn't steal the skeleton, either. I have permission to use it for my science project."

"And your science project involves dumping the bones in a public place and making false statements to the police?" It didn't seem logical to me, but I've heard tales of declining education standards, so I had to ask.

"No! My science project is about whether or not those beetles eat bones. I weighed the bones before I put them in there, and I was going to weigh them once a week all month long. I didn't think about other animals taking big bites. My project's ruined."

"That doesn't explain your story about Nick."

"Most of it's true. That clique did plan to haze him last night. Nick figured he'd turn the tables by disappearing. We found a way to get to the road from the far side of the tunnel. I dropped him off at the park entrance, drove to our meeting spot on the road, and waited. He went into the tunnel at the front with everyone watching, then worked his way to the back. It took longer and was messier than we thought, but I got him back to his dad's without anyone noticing, They left early this morning for a two-week vacation."

"Did you have anything to do with the other displays in that tunnel?"

"You mean the real body? No way! Yuck! That had to be Jason and Joe. They're always doing dumb stuff and getting away with it because their fathers go fishing with the sheriff."

"Hmm. That's why I'm worried about you. The sheriff seems to have a bee up his ample butt and is looking to charge someone with something. If you gave the deputy the same story you gave me, you made false statements to the law. That's a crime. You were also out driving after midnight."

"No, she wasn't. She always makes curfew."

"I'm sorry, ma'am, but your daughter snuck out of the house after curfew last night. The drama club prank started at midnight, and she's still wearing yesterday's shoes."

In typical mom-of-a-teen fashion, she refused to believe her child would do such a thing. "Is that true, Ange?"

Angie declined to answer and simply hung her head.

"I see. We'll talk later." She turned her attention to me. "You don't have to worry about the sheriff coming after Angie. His bark is much worse than his bite. This is a small town. We're like family. Besides, I'm the high school principal, and the sheriff has kids of his own."

"Ah. That takes care of everything except the why. Why would you make up a story about Nick being MIA? And don't bother lying. I know it had nothing to do with the other kids. It's about Nick's mom. Spill it."

"I can't."

"Why not."

"I promised Nick."

"What did you promise?"

"To never tell anyone that his mom makes him buy drugs for her."

I let that hang in the air for a good minute. Mom was stunned but sharp enough to keep quiet. It worked. The kid spilled her guts. "She's a lousy mom, the worst. She's always drunk or high or, you know, with men. Nick wants to live with his dad, but his mom says if he ever tells the judge that, she'll plant all the drugs in Nick's room and turn him in to the police. She only wants him for the money his dad has to pay. I hate her."

"So you set this up, hoping the police would search her house looking for Nick and find her stash?"

"Yes."

Mom could keep quiet no longer. "Why didn't you just come to me?"

"Mom! I promised! You taught me to keep my promises, and now I broke a big one. Nick will hate me."

Mom wrapped her arms around her daughter's shoulders. "No, he won't."

I stood to leave. "I'd say I'm not needed here."

"I'd appreciate it if you kept this quiet. I promise you things will be put right."

I agreed and returned to Todd's car. He seemed disappointed

when I asked him to take me to Liz's place, but now that I knew about Lulu, things were different. About halfway there, Todd broke the uncomfortable silence, "Everything okay with that kid?"

"Yes," I said. "Everything's wrapped up neat as a pin." *Too neat*, I thought. Something was bothering me, but I couldn't quite put my finger on it.

"So, you'll be leaving soon?"

"Yup. Sheriff's orders."

Todd didn't try to talk me out of it. Maybe he was thinking about Lulu and feeling guilty. I hoped so.

I didn't have much to pack. The job shouldn't have taken more than a few minutes, but it seems life is never calm *chez* Liz.

As soon as I entered the apartment, Spike zoomed into action. He darted in front of me, barking, of course. When I didn't stop, he zipped back and forth in front of me, zoomed between my legs, ran in circles around me. Clearly he wanted my attention. I stopped and asked the dog what he wanted. He sat with his front paws on my toes, whined, and batted at the pink bow between his ears. Pink. Clearly Liz had issues. Spike was begging for my help. I couldn't resist. I removed the bow and stuck it in my pocket. The grateful Spike back-flipped off my toes, ran back to give my jeans a lick or two, then ran for cover when he heard Liz approaching.

Liz was full of chatter about her experience with the sheriff, her hope that I wasn't in trouble, and that I wasn't mad at her for calling Beth for assistance, her desire to make it up to me by taking me out to dinner. I had to eat something anyway. I was famished.

The small diner was abuzz with news of the day—proof that the small town phone tree is still more efficient than CNN. Most of the chatter was about Anna Lipschitz and her poor family— hadn't they been through enough? One woman was incensed over Todd's infidelity with a stranger and her inability to contact Lulu with the news. Many felt a need to voice their opinions about how those boys ought to be ashamed of themselves, and what they'd do if their kids took part in such nonsense. Seems small town America is full of woodsheds.

A woman showed up with a stack of papers fresh off the press—the town had a weekly. I bought one just to see if I'd made the front page and needed to high-tail it out of town. Luckily, Anna, her heroic cancer battle, the services schedule, and her grieving family took most of the front page honors. The teenage pranksters also made it, in a story about the recent crime wave. Todd's shenanigans were delegated to the gossip column on page three, as was the news that Liz was hosting out-of-town company. Amazing.

I suggested we pay up and leave before the rest of the crowd got to page three and was able to link Liz's out-of-town guest with Todd's mysterious tryst-mate.

This time, Liz didn't argue with me when I suggested it was time for me to head home. And that's where I intended to go—just as fast as my little car would take me.

Which doesn't explain why I was standing in the bottom of a freshly dug grave, using my ice scraper and crow bar as shovels to dig deeper. You don't really want to know how my mind works. It's frightening—I have some sort of warped superpower that forces me think like the bad guys. So, once I figured out what'd been bothering me, my superpower kicked in, and I, because I'm me, had to know if I was right.

So there I was, scraping away layers of freshly dug dirt, soft enough that the crow bar was useless. I tried, several times, to place it out of the way, but it kept falling or rolling into me. I tossed it out of the hole. Usually, the dirt at the bottom of freshly dug graves is hard packed, so I was not overly surprised when I'd brushed away enough dirt to reveal the face of a lovely young woman.

"So, which one are you?" I asked her, not expecting a response.

"Anna."

At the sound of Todd's voice, I jumped back, and in the small space, managed to smash my head against the wall of the grave and slid to my butt. That was fortunate, because Todd was holding my crow bar in one hand and slapping it into the other. Clearly, he intended to use that thing on me. As long as I kept my head down, he wouldn't be able to reach me from up there. I got him talking to distract him.

"Does that mean Lulu was in the tunnel?"

"Yup." More smacking.

"Why?"

"Why was Lulu in the tunnel?"

"Why did you kill Lulu? Why did you put Anna here?"

Todd grinned. "Lulu was a pain in the ass. I've been trying to break it off with her for months, but she just wouldn't leave me alone. She'd started telling people we were getting married. Even had a great story about how I proposed. She had to go."

"You couldn't do the normal thing and file for a restraining order?"

"I thought of that. Even threatened it. Lulu said she'd sue me for breach of promise. I just don't have the time or the money to be tied up with lawyers for years. I needed a quicker solution. Those drama brats provided the opportunity. I was working out there when they met at the tunnel to plan their little hazing party. It never occurred to them that someone else might be nearby. One of them came up with the stage prop idea, and they kept one-upping each other until the mortician's kid came up with the plan to use Anna's body. The brat didn't know about the beetles. He just wanted a cool scare factor."

Todd started pacing then, getting himself worked into a tizzy. "I couldn't believe they were planning to put Anna in there." With his attention off me, I was able to unwrap the *manriki-gusari* and get my feet under me. I just needed to keep low to the ground and wait for the right moment. "She was a sweet gal and didn't deserve that fate. That's when I decided I'd just swap Lulu for Anna."

"How did you kill Lulu? And what did you do to her face?"

Todd's face reappeared above. It was twisted into an ugly snarl. "You would make me have to think about that! I don't know what that bitch was made of, but she was hard to off. I put rat poison in her breakfast biscuits. She ate three of them and didn't bat an eye. While she was in the shower, I added Drano to her coffee. That, at least, got a reaction out of her. She coughed, choked, vomited, but wouldn't die. Eventually, I found her heroin, and shot her up good. The bitch still hung on for hours. Finally, she croaked. I shaved her head so she'd look like Anna, after chemo. It was a pleasure to drag a raccoon's claw across her face until her own mother wouldn't know her." He screamed that last part and took a swing at me with the crow bar, still yelling, "You're not going to take so long!"

He stumbled slightly, and I used the opportunity to swing the *manriki-gusari.* It wasn't my best shot ever, but I did get the ball and chain wrapped around his ankles well enough to trip him up. When he fell on his face, I hauled myself out of the hole so the grave was between us, and in the process nearly let him untangle his feet. I yanked the chain tighter. He hurled the crow bar at my head. I ducked away, but it caught my shoulder. That pissed me off. I let him stand up, then yanked hard. He tumbled into the grave and went silent.

At the sound of applause off to my right, I turned to see Jake perched on a nearby headstone. "You really do use that thing to catch bad guys. I'm impressed."

"How long have you been there?"

"Long enough."

"You heard the confession?"

"Yup."

"You could have stepped in."

"Looked to me like you had things under control. I can take it from here, if you like."

"I hate the paperwork part. How about I take my toys and go home. You stay here and write yourself up as the hero."

"I can live with that."

"Good. I've had all the vacation I can take. I need to get back to work."

About Bats, Bones and Beetles

Eva Baum is the joint creation of Mark and Charlotte Phillips. Eva's short stories have appeared in three other anthologies: *A Death in Texas, A Box of Texas Chocolates*, and *Twisted Tales of Texas Landmarks*. Eva's novel-length adventures are chronicled in *Hacksaw* and *The Golden Key.*

The idea for Bats, Bones and Beetles evolved over time. I had watched a TV special that featured scientists' use of beetles to clean bones and I started thinking—*what if.* A few days later, I was searching for "underground" sites in Texas and found the Old Tunnel WPA, with its millions of bats, and, of course, beetles. I couldn't resist.

A wonderful Wildlife Biologist from Old Tunnel was kind enough to answer all my questions about the park and the environment inside the tunnel. It was my intent to thank her by including a wildlife biologist in the story—a hero character. But, characters don't always behave the way they are first imagined.

INVASION
BY L. STEWART HEARL

Tuesday morning dawned cold and wet. Burton Presley drove through the Baytown early morning traffic as rain gave a thrashing to his aged Pontiac. His attitude matched the weather. He had been informed the previous day that all scheduled vacations had been put on hold at work, pending the second NRC inspection. The Hawaiian vacation he had booked months in advance was to be his honeymoon.

Ten minutes later the huge twin domes that comprised much of the South Texas Project Nuclear became visible through the rain. After he parked and passed through the first two security checkpoints, Presley sat in the small employees' lounge eating an Egg McMuffin and contemplating another boring shift.

Just two weeks ago he had been promoted to Operator IV. It meant an extra thirty dollars a week, but his actual job remained the same. He and his co-operator for the last six years, Marty Kleinmetz, were employed to baby-sit the control room of the twin reactors. Their responsibility had decreased by fifty percent when Reactor Number One was shut down after a surprise inspection by the Nuclear Regulatory Commission four months ago. Since then, he and Marty had spent over one hundred hours in various training courses. They now knew more about their jobs and the workings of the nuclear-powered "teapots" than any other operators in the country.

While working with nuclear energy might seem exciting to some, Presley wasn't impressed. Buried deep beneath them, surrounded by enough concrete to build two Walmarts, were the reactor vessels, essentially a pair of giant water heaters. The heat turned water into steam, which turned a steam turbine, producing electricity. Very exciting, was Presley's sarcastic thought. The additional training began immediately after Reactor Number One had been taken offline. It was spurred by the NRC-induced panic that had swept the place after the inspection, no doubt. Presley didn't care. STPN allowed him to train in his off hours and then paid him for it at time-and-a-half. The extra money would help keep his new wife in clothes and food.

Presley was pitching a McDonald's bag and wrappers into the trash when the door to the lounge opened, and Marty walked in looking like warmed-over death. Marty shucked off his dripping jacket and donned his lab coat. Apparently his wife had been unable to remove the ink stain on its pocket left by a leaking pen. Marty flopped down into the chair by Presley's cup of coffee.

"Hey, guy, what's up?" asked Presley.

"Not me. Not yet. Java," mumbled Marty. "Coffee, and lots of it." He poured a cup from the half-filled carafe that sat on the warming plate, then took two quick gulps. He put the Styrofoam cup down on the table across from Presley. "You?"

Presley said, "Kerry kept me up half the night bitching about the fact that I don't spend enough time at home helping her plan the wedding. I tried to tell her, to keep my job I have to do this extra training, but she doesn't believe me. Shit, it's not like she doesn't know where I am or something. This isn't exactly a happening place."

"What did she say about getting your honeymoon canceled?"

"I haven't told her yet. I figured I could talk to Charlie about making an exception. I mean, it's not like we're overworked."

"Great idea. Charlie's gonna override the NRC. Welcome to Fantasy Land."

"Yeah, well, I'm gonna talk to him anyway. What have I go to lose? This trip took a lot of planning and a big deposit. I'm not cancelling yet."

Marty frowned, took another gulp of coffee, and shook his head. "Dreamer. It'll take an Act of God to sway Charlie."

"I know. But I gotta try." Presley glanced at his watch: 5:55 a.m. "Come on," he said. "It's time."

Marty tossed the remains of his coffee in the trash. He followed Presley down the hall and through the last security doors that led to the control room. They rubbed their magnetic cards against the touch plate which both logged them in and verified their security level. The sliding steel door opened. A blast of warm air hit them, a result of the positive air pressure within the room.

Curly Stevenson looked over at them as they entered. Sterile white fluorescents lit the 30 x 10 x 10 foot room festooned with flat panel monitors.

"Anything special?" asked Presley. He couldn't help sounding bored.

"Had a short flux a bit after three, but just for a second or so. 'Side from that, nothing."

"Where's Binks?" Marty asked.

"Left at five-thirty. Had to get ready to go to a wedding or something. Anyway, board's clean. You got it?"

Presley looked at the check list and then at the central instrument panel. Everything looked normal. Everything was green. "Yeah, we got it."

On the planet called Kitane, under a dark turquois sky, in a dimension not our own, the warrior race V'Let was anticipating another great victory. It would be the fourth one this decade, and K'Hor, the Supreme Battle Commander, was confident. Preparations for the invasion were nearly complete.

He stood on the capitol building's balcony, resplendent in his maroon leather pants and the armor-plated cuirass of an Invincible. An immense staging area lay below. Power tracks with monstrous weapons attached for transport stood in columns facing the Main Translation Gate. Tens of thousands of V'Let Invincibles stood in loose columns bordering the tracks. Nearly a thousand feet below him, a hundred thousand Decimators brought up the rear. This day will be glorious! thought K'Hor.

No human had ever seen a member of the V'Let race. If anyone had, he most likely would have described a V'Let as "Big Foot on steroids". K'Hor stood nearly ten feet tall. His heavily muscled body, covered in light brown fur, was now hidden under his battle gear.

A light, cold wind drifted across the arid plain that separated the Imperial City from the dung brown waters of the Hero's Sea. Huge power launches, capable of carrying 500 V'Let each, now stood empty below a rocky plateau. Soon, thought K'Hor, the ships will return to our lands with songs of blood and victory echoing from within their hulls. Soon, the V'Let will add another gem to the Crown of S'Ador, as another race collapses before our might.

He smiled. The Crown was now covered by 73 perfectly cut sapphires, each representing a victory. "Soon, we shall need a larger crown!" he whispered.

"A new crown, you say? Whatever for, Commander?" came a rasping voice from the shadows of the parapet.

K'Hor spun around to lock eyes with By'Ton Circ, First Consul of V'Let. His regal station did little to make up for his smaller stature and irritatingly high pitched voice. K'Hor snapped to attention, saluted.

The salute was returned by the Consul.

"Your pardon, Consul! I didn't know that you were there," said K'Hor.

"That much, Commander, is obvious. Now, what is the meaning of your talk of a new crown? I never suspected that you had designs in that direction."

"Surely I do not, Consul! I was only thinking that the Crown of S'Ador has little room left for additional gems. Soon, quite soon, another victory stone will be set."

By'Ton was slow to answer as he weighed K'Hor's words. Then a hint of a smile crept across his furry brown muzzle, the ends of his lipless mouth twitching upward. "Perhaps another crown will indeed be necessary, K'Hor. Make sure of it. Bring us another fine victory!"

"As ordered, so I shall do. May I have your leave to complete preparations, Consul?"

"A moment more. You do not wear your campaign bars. Why?"

K'Hor was caught off guard by the question. He thought for a moment, as he scratched behind his left ear. "Well, Consul, the bars are most precious to me. I did not wish to risk losing them during the battle."

"I believe that you should wear them to inspire the troops, Commander."

"Then it shall be so, Consul. May I now depart?"

The Consul gestured dismissal with a small twitch of his paw. K'Hor touched his right arm to his chest in a final salute and re-entered the fortress. He was glad to be away from Circ. The creature almost smelled of intrigue, something that K'Hor shunned.

Two guards snapped to attention as he approached the elevators. He ignored the black-clad figures and stepped into the open car. Seconds later he walked out onto the marble-tiled ground floor. Here too, he ignored the guards as he commandeered a ground car. He drove across the open marble courtyard, threading his way through the assemblage preparing to pass through the Main Translation Gate.

He arrived at the building that held the officers' quarters and left the car behind. K'Hor had a house of his own as well, but he was allowed to have this additional space as a Commander. He took the lift to the top floor. The building was empty of personnel because of the invasion staging going on outside. Soon he arrived at his private quarters. The door opened to the touch of his paw. He entered.

He glanced about, noting the decor and the dark colors of the room with approval. He sat down on the corner of a utilitarian bed and opened an intricately-carved wooden chest beside it.

That old fool's days grow short, he thought, as he rummaged through the chest for the missing bars. Beneath a bone of some defeated enemy and other souvenirs from past campaigns, he found the bars in a simple, silver-trimmed ironwood box. He emptied the contents on the bed and looked at his campaign bars.

He frowned. Wearing colorful trinkets into battle made you a target. Didn't Circ know that? Or did he? He pursued the thought… Was that the Consul's intention? The fool! Rage flooded his mind. It will take more than that to stop me!

He shuffled through the bars, picking up the green and yellow bar called the Kil'li'Car. He had received it less than ten years ago for personally destroying an entire fortress on Bonk. And here was the silver and blue Kil'li'Naf, the first bar he had been awarded 30 years back when he was little more than a pup, for routing a troop of Viles on…on…no matter. It no longer existed.

He sighed. Then he spent a few moments affixing the 62 bars that represented his entire military career to his chest plate.

From piss brat to full Commander in 30 years!, he thought. And, if my plan continues to work, I'll soon be First Consul. By'Ton Circ won't appreciate my achievements, but by then he'll be with his ancestors!

When done, K'Hor looked at himself in his full length mirror and frowned. The bars looked foolish and out of place on his steel breastplate. He shook his head and contemplated leaving them behind. But, no, he thought. Let Circ think I'm his pup right up until the time I bite his head off. By then he'll—

The thought was interrupted when the comm unit on his desk chirped and then filled with an image of F'Lit, the Chief Tech. "Commander, the test Translation will be ready in ten minutes. Permission to charge the caps?"

"Thanks, Chief. I was wondering why things were taking so long."

"Just getting everything in place, sir."

"Then charge the caps. I'm on my way."

K'Hor took a final look in the mirror and smiled. Soon, he

thought, very soon. He closed his trunk and left his room, making sure to seal the door behind him.

Five minutes later he entered the Translation area. The other officers and techs saluted smartly. The arena in front of the gate fell silent but for the low-pitched rumble of the generators. He could almost feel the power being stored in the gigantic barium capacitors that lined the 200-foot-wide main gate and, in one corner of it, the 30-foot-wide test gate.

"Ready for Translation, sir!" said the Chief Tech.

It had better be, thought K'Hor. He secretly marveled that they could transmit a gate to another dimension and then simply walk through the opening it provided. His predecessor had lacked the advantage of a test gate, which had been his downfall. Though the world his predecessor had attacked had been surveyed years before it was attacked, they had no way of knowing that their survey had taken place during a period of extreme drought. By the time their gate was constructed and the attack was mounted, the water level had risen on the planet to such a degree that the Main Translation Gate had opened a portal to the planet 500 feet below the surface of an ocean swollen once again. One hundred and twenty-seven thousand V'Let had drowned before the gate could be shut down. K'Hor's predecessor had been one of them. Now, the test gate would eliminate such problems.

"Make it so," he told the Tech.

The Chief Tech activated the gate. There was a very brief flash from the capacitors, and suddenly several large pieces of pipe and some electrical wiring toppled to the floor of the arena. "Test translation complete, sir. Atmosphere and pressure verified."

"Anything else, Chief?"

"That's all I could get during a two pico-second translation, sir. Shall I do it again for a longer period? I could leave the test gate open if you wish."

"No. No reason to tell them we're coming. They'll know soon enough." K'Hor looked down at the sheared pipes and wires on the deck. Before him was a 30 x 10 x 10 foot block of the world that was their destination. The materials before him had been swapped for the empty space of the test gate. "What's all this stuff?" He rolled one of the wide pipe sections over with the toe of his boot, exposing a yellow triangle enclosed in a circle on the underside of the pipe. Water sloshed from the broken pipe onto the floor as it tipped.

The tech glanced at the floor. "These were the things occupying the area that the test gate translated. When the gate returned, so did they."

K'Hor nudged the pipe again. "Perhaps these creatures will make an adequate foe. At least they have some sort of technology. Sound final assembly!"

The control room was silent. The control board was green. Presley turned the page of the novel he was reading. Marty was in the lounge looking for a donut. Everything was peaceful. Then, it wasn't.

A klaxon blasted from the rear of the room. Presley jumped to his feet. He ran to the main control board and stared at it, incredulity painted across his face. Half the board was studded with bright red, flashing LED indicators. The other half of the board was dead with neither green nor red lights. A second alarm triggered, chirping for attention over the blare of the klaxon. Then a third, then a fourth.

Marty came racing back into the control room with a full cup of coffee in one hand and a Danish in the other. He tripped over the edge of a chair, his hot coffee splashed on his hand, and he dropped the cup and the pastry. "What the hell's going on? What did you do!" he screamed over the alarms.

Presley shouted back, "Ain't me, guy. We've lost primary coolant! And, oh shit, looks like secondary's gone as well!"

"Oh, Jesus, Jesus, Jesus! Initiate shutdown! Scram the reactor!" yelled Marty. "And shut off those damned alarms!"

Presley slammed down the override on the main alarm system, and the room was suddenly quiet. He rummaged quickly through his desk drawer and came up with a clipboard. The top sheet on it read "Emergency Shutdown Procedure."

His voice trembling, Presley read aloud, "Number One: engage dampers one through seven."

Marty threw the damper toggles. He watched the gauges for a few seconds, then said in a shaky voice, "The dampers are not responding."

Presley ran over to look at the gauges and lights. One of the cameras inside Reactor Number Two was still working far underground: it showed a strangely distorted image. "Jesus, Marty, Camera One's under water!" he whispered.

Marty shot back. "It won't be for long. Look at the temperature gauge! That water's gonna be steam in about ten seconds!"

Presley stared at another gauge. "The temperature isn't going to be the problem. Look at the pressure. Jesus, four atmospheres and still climbing!"

Almost in unison, the three white phones and the one red phone on the central desk rang.

Five minutes after the test translation, K'Hor stood before the massive Main Translation Gate. Immediately behind him, across the huge arena and outward as far as he could see stood rank upon rank of the Decimators, each armed with a particle beam projector and other lethal weapons. The Invincibles manned thirty nuclear-powered ion cannons, each attached to a power track that guarded the approach to the Main Translation Gate. K'Hor's paws trembled in nervous anticipation as he waited for the main capacitors to complete the charging process.

He engaged his comm unit.

After a moment, By'Ton Circ answered. "Ready, Commander?"

"With your permission, Consul."

"Make it so!"

K'Hor signaled the troop commanders. Instantly, the Decimators began their war chant. It grew and grew in volume until it drowned out even the deep-throated roar of the power tracks. The Decimators stamped their feet. Even By'Ton Circ in his high tower has to feel the vibrations, K'Hor thought.

He reviewed the assemblage. Soon all of this will be mine, and By'Ton will be history! "How much longer?" he asked the Chief Tech.

"Twenty seconds, sir."

K'Hor counted down the seconds in his mind. This was the worst part. Not being the first to cross, but waiting to go.

The Chief Tech looked up at him. "Ready, Commander."

K'Hor gestured to the tech to energize the Main Translation Gate.

For a moment, nothing seemed to happen as the capacitors poured terawatt after terawatt of stored power into the portal. When the charge reached maximum, inside the 200 x 100 foot gate, a dimensional gateway the same size opened between Kitane and Earth.

Neither K'Hor nor the Decimators got more than an extremely brief look at the white wall of super-heated steam that exploded outward from the gate and incinerated them. Those who survived the steam barely saw what followed. The Main Translation Gate collapsed in a thunderous roar and the port closed, but the damage was done.

᳇

The largest flashing red light on the panel stopped flashing and turned green. Marty's forehead dripped with sweat. He said, "That's it. We've completely lost containment! Kiss your ass goodbye, and climb into a body bag!"

Burton Presley shook his head. "I don't think so. Look at the gauges! Exterior radiation sensors are still showing normal background."

"Sure, Presley. And a hundred thousand cubic feet of superheated dirty steam under ten atmospheres of pressure just goes away, right?"

Presley wasn't listening. Instead, he stared at the video

monitors for Reactor Number Two with an expression of total disbelief. "Jesus Christ! Look!"

Marty pushed around Presley and stared at the monitor. "It… it can't be," he whispered.

Reactor Number Two, just seconds away from meltdown after losing both primary and secondary cooling and most of its control systems less than fifteen minutes ago, was no longer visible on the monitor; but the still-working camera readily showed the interior of the confinement chamber.

At its base, where Reactor Number Two should have been, the flooring looked as if it had been sliced cleanly through with an immense surgical scalpel. Only the reactor supports remained.

Marty stared at the screen in disbelief. "Reactor Number Two… Where'd it go?"

Burton Presley looked away from the monitor, his eyes wide and glassy with shock. Then a spark of animation touched his face, and the merest hint of a smile tightened his lips. The smile broadened quickly. "I have no idea where it went…but I know where *I'm* going in two weeks. Hawaii!"

THE WILD, THROBBING DARK
BY CASH ANTHONY

Searchlight beams crisscrossed the deepening blue of a Texas sky. The rise and fall of the high Hill Country terrain hid their source—and wasn't that the idea? They were meant to beckon and tempt.

The lead motorcyclist in the tight formation of three felt no temptation. Jessica Carr didn't believe in much, but she did believe in premonitions, and she was having one now.

Us old people should hearken to our instincts, she thought. She usually didn't feel even middle-aged, though her standard introduction was, "Name's Carr, Jessie Carr. High mileage, as you can see." But it was meant as a joke!

This evening, though, with another bank of dark clouds on the western horizon in her peripheral vision, Jessie felt a general apprehension at the possibility of riding to shelter in thick traffic through a thunderstorm, and it had manifested as an attack of sensitivity regarding her inevitable decline, whenever it might start. After months of drought, the crowd could be in for a downpour just as the concert let out.

"You know, it wouldn't be all that bad to skip tonight's entertainment and go directly to the Badu House," she said into her helmet's headset microphone, as she keyed her C.B. radio. The Badu House was an old bed-and-breakfast in Llano, where air conditioning, a solid roof, soft beds, and clean towels were sure to await. The owners were motorcyclists, too, and usually welcomed responsible members of the 'family' on short notice.

"You don't mean that," came the reply from Beau Marsberg, riding drag. "This is gonna be cool!"

"Claws rule! Whoo-hoo!" The ear-splitting shout in her ears came from the co-rider on George Mandrake's Gold Wing. Mandrake was a local they'd met only a few times previously. "Grab 'em, Claws!" The voice of his passenger was shrill and passionate.

Jessie groaned. She had to admit the possibility that she felt old today was the presence of a teenager, introduced as Meredith Something.

Beau had proposed a day ride to the Hairy Claws concert as a goof. Unfortunately, at the last gas stop Mandrake showed up, along with his passenger with her exuberant, sexy perkiness that made Jessie feel so far over the hill, she was a speck on the dark side of the moon.

Jessie spotted a sign reading "Longhorn Cavern State Park" with an arrow pointing left. It slipped by her Road King, and she slowed and signaled the riders behind her for the turn. They headed south.

Park Road 4 ran along Inks Lake like a roller coaster, the lake too far away to see through the brush. Jessie eventually caught a whiff of it, a mixture of fish scale, wet limestone, and freshwater. Within a mile, the riders found themselves caught in stop-and-go traffic.

"You don't have to say it," Beau said. Jessie smirked.

At last the line crept on, and Beau took the lead. Soon Jessie saw him signal a turn where a sturdy rock sign marked the museum and the entrance to the cave where the Hairy Claws would play tonight.

In the '30s, the Civilian Conservation Corps put unemployed men to work digging the silt and bat guano out of this cavern system, putting in lights and paved walkways, and building signs like this one, picnic pavilions, a land bridge, and an observation tower. D. G. Sherrard, from whom the state acquired the land, had made few improvements that were visible above ground, but he'd been ahead of his time below. During the Roaring '20s, he'd built a floor forty feet down and rigged an elevator to bring bootleg whiskey in for a nightclub where the locals ate and drank in the "air conditioning" and danced to big bands on tour.

But the Great Depression soaked up their money like sand vanishes water, and Sherrard had to sell.

Now the crowds and the money were back; and the company that licensed the concessions was expanding the cavern's fame once more, making the park into a profitable music venue.

The riders passed the museum. It looked unchanged since Jessie's visit a year before, when she'd taken the Wild Cave Tour with a guide through the cavern's basement level. She'd been stalking one of the other visitors and had bypassed the museum's displays of Indian artifacts, geological formations, and newspaper clippings about lost treasure. Maybe she'd read them tonight, make something positive of the event.

Vehicles lined the park road around the museum. Clumps of pedestrians joined a long, long queue for admission tickets every few seconds.

"Got to stop at Will Call." Jessie knew Beau had reserved tickets for seats in the Indian Council Chamber, where they could see the performance close up.

"We're going for the free concert out here," Mandrake said. "'Cause I ain't standing in a line that long to pay for a seat."

Jessie wondered what Meredith thought of coming out to a concert and getting to sit on a rock. She found out right away.

"You don't have to, Georgie," Meredith said on the C.B. "I went to the Hairy Claws website and got tickets two weeks ago when I heard they're doing their latest hits. Their manager promised me a big surprise. I got drink tickets, too."

"Well, that's something at least." George's lack of enthusiasm was audible.

Jessie tsk'ed to herself at the ease with which illegal commerce was done on the Internet. A child Meredith's age buying tickets for booze, without even having to show a fake I.D. She had to have used somebody else's credit card, too. And what was that about the band's manager?

"Yeah, you could probably stay on your bike and hear everything. The park's got natural amplification," Beau said "But you wouldn't get to see them, and really, that's the show."

Jessie was already pretty sure that the Claws hadn't risen to fame because of their musicality. As if to make her a liar, through her helmet she heard instruments being tuned somewhere in the distance. Suddenly it twigged that once the band got going, music would come throbbing up from the ground like artesian water. The chambers under the pavement extended for more than eleven miles, and that was merely what had been explored. There were at least five known entrances through which the Claws' music could escape and pollute the air. Or satisfy their audience, depending on your viewpoint. Jessie regretted she wasn't a fan, for to hear music you loved in a place like this would be wonderful.

They found a space to park the bikes together, backing them in at an angle to the road. She put her kickstand down and tested that it was solid before getting off. Beau checked Jessie's luggage with his hand after he dismounted, making sure nothing had shifted under its stretchy nets, while Jessie checked his.

Mandrake parked his ancient Wing and tore off his helmet, stuck it over his right side mirror, and dismounted. He, too, rocked the motorcycle to be certain the sidestand wouldn't slip. Jessie thought he should have invited Meredith to dismount first. Maybe he preferred his passengers a little green; or perhaps he feared his rat-bike would disintegrate if it fell on its side.

Meredith picked at the D-ring on her helmet, unable to figure it out. She looked to Mandrake for help, but he paid her no attention.

He said to Jessie and Beau, "Did y'all hear the excitement on the C.B. just now? The cavern's closed. They're closing the park, too."

"What?" Beau frowned. "You're kidding."

As the last one to park, George had heard the bulletin on the

C.B. radio that she and Beau missed. Apparently it didn't register with Meredith. "Closing the park? You're sure?" Jessie asked.

George was a hefty, sloop-shouldered blond pushing 40 and a wannebe cop. "Some kind of emergency where the underground river comes out."

"All this rain," Beau said. "The river rose."

A memory of the river's current as it moved around her legs in the 'basement' of the cavern chilled Jessie. The river had been shallow the day of her tour, but higher water marks indicated its depth was well over her head during a flood. She pulled her jacket closer despite the fading afternoon heat. Looking up, she saw that the dark clouds west of the park had drifted closer. She hoped they wouldn't add to the festivities.

"I wonder if it's a body, this much excitement." Mandrake shifted from foot to foot, anticipating some kind of action.

Jessie and Beau had both seen plenty of dead people; they didn't find it exciting. It usually meant grief for someone and often, lots of work for them.

"Georgie! A little help here?" Meredith squeaked, to no avail.

Beau stretched, then drew a hand through his graying hair. A silvery mustache anchored his lean face, a face dominated by blue eyes that missed nothing. "Whatever's going on, I'm taking a walk to stretch my legs." Beau had little tolerance for hysteria, female or male, Jessie knew. He strolled into the broken scrub.

A bevy of official cars went past, lightbars on, sirens blaring. The buzz of concert-goers waiting in line to enter the cavern rose in the background, like cicadas.

"There's the heat," Mandrake informed the two females. "Look, I know a bunch of these deputies. Let me see what's going on. You little ladies can watch the bikes." He strode off.

Jessie hadn't been crazy about Mandrake and Meredith joining their group of two without invitation. She liked him less now. But she knew that despite the lack of urgency in Beau's response, as a retired Texas Ranger he was intrigued by the ruckus, too. So they'd be there a while. She'd met Sheriff Ratner, the law in Burnet County, and he never moved fast.

Meredith's gaze followed Mandrake toward the flashing lights. "Excuse me, but what the fuck?" she asked the air around her, her voice rising with outrage.

Jessie sympathized, but she had no answers. She put her feet up on the King's highway pegs, crossed her arms, and rested against her luggage. She closed her eyes to wait.

"Would somebody please tell me what's going on?" The screech was ear-splitting.

Jessie opened her eyes again. Meredith had gotten the helmet off and puffed up her flattened hair. Her arms and neck were sunburned, but she seemed nonchalant about it, in a manner typical of adolescents. On the other hand, the threat of being abandoned loomed large.

"I don't think you're going to hear a concert tonight." Jessie's voice was mild.

"Shit! I'm sorry, but really."

"With that many cops at a scene, something's gone very wrong."

"Well, shit. I had the neatest thing planned for afterwards, you two would 'a loved it. If Georgie's planning to hang around, it'll be without me. If I have to, I'll get a ride home."

"I expect you can manage that." The tight jeans, the halter top, the white-blonde hair, and Meredith's gangly adolescence made it almost certain. "Might not be a great idea to take the first offer, though." Jessie wondered how she was going to keep a teenager from doing exactly what she wanted, including disappearing with a stranger if she felt stood up.

"I have a curfew, sorta." Meredith's tone was practical, a welcome change. "And Georgie's got a hot date with his girlfriend later on."

"I wouldn't worry. We'll be leaving earlier than when the concert was going to end."

Apparently this was adequate comfort, for Meredith changed the subject. "You look familiar. Are you somebody famous?"

Jessie hoped not. If you were secretly an occasional Avenging Angel, you sure didn't want every crook to see you coming.

"Not really," Jessie replied.

"You are, too," Meredith persisted. "You came to our house."

"I think you're mistaken." Jessie's recent, intense study of facial features and expressions kept her memory keen, and Meredith's narrow-set eyes, short upper lip, protruding teeth, and wide-open brow would have registered, not to mention her freckled cheeks and gamin ears. She'd never met the girl before.

"No, I'm sure." Jessie glanced through the scrub toward the museum. Some of the fans were peeling off the ticket line and returning to their cars. There was no sign of Mandrake or Beau. She studied Meredith, standing hipshot and playing with the ends of her hair, anxiety beginning to tighten her lips. "Where do you live?"

"I stay in Austin. I go to private school there. I got Georgie to bring me out for the concert tonight and to see my dad. He has a ranch thataway"—Meredith pointed southeast, toward Faulkenstein Castle—"called Spirit Haven. He and Mom did a B&B thing for a while, weekends…"

Jessie took a closer look at Meredith. The narrow-set eyes were a faded blue, the chin long and square. And familiar. "Derwood Cannon? That's your dad?"

"Yeah. Meredith Cannon, that's me. I was staying with my granny when you were there, but I saw a picture of you. Dad closed up last year, but he never forgot the play you wrote for them. You know, putting in that stuff about history and that part about Indians and treasure…"

Jessie remembered. Derwood and Edith Cannon had hired her to write her first attempt at keeping a dozen guests entertained for two-and-a-half days. "Hit or Miss, and aptly named. Your mom sent me a royalty check every time they played it," she said. "How are your folks these days?"

Meredith fiddled with her bangs, using that as an excuse to wipe her eyes. "Mom's…gone. She died two years ago."

Jessie touched her shoulder. "I'm so sorry."

Meredith didn't speak for a moment, collecting herself. "You need to help him," she said at last.

"Your dad? Is he all right?"

Meredith's lips pursed with frustration. "There's this woman…"

Meredith would resent any woman who stepped into her mother's life. This sounded to Jessie like simple jealousy. "Maybe your dad's ready to move on."

"It's not that. It's her. She's…spooky. That's even her name, Spooks. It's like she's bewitched him. I can't get Junior to do nothing about it, but he's a fool if he lets Dad give that woman our inheritance. And that's not even what bugs me the most… I know Mom always ran the show. Dad would do anything she asked him to do. But he's totally lost his backbone. And when I try to talk to him, he just smiles. I want to know what's going on!"

"Do you know anything about her?"

"She wants us to call her Spooks, but I saw her driver's license. Her real name's Adria Vadoma Something. Tom, that's it."

"Her last name is Tom?"

"I Googled Adria. It means 'the dark one' in some weird language I never heard of. And Vadoma means 'the knowing one,' like a pagan magician. I think she's bad news. She's going to suck my father dry like a vampire."

For Jessie, the sound of a Gypsy surname in connection with a widower did feel like 'bad news.' She felt an investigative itch.

Meredith's face brightened with inspiration. "I know! Where are you two staying?"

"The old Badu House."

"You should spend the night with my dad. Can't stay at the Badu House, anyway."

"Why not?"

"The Hanovers sold the place. It's closed. Let me call him." Meredith pulled out her cell phone—again Jessie marveled at the carrying capacity of those jeans—and wandered a few steps away.

She returned, smiling. "You'd best go the long way. You get to the highway, turn left and go into Burnet. Then take 29 west, coming back toward the park. If this was all flat land, you'd be surprised how close it is. Georgie could lead you, he grew up around here."

As if summoned by the mention of his name, Mandrake popped out of the undergrowth. "The concert's cancelled. No Claws tonight."

"I can't believe it! I won a backstage visit! I was gonna have ten minutes with Eric Crawford, their manager! And Dawgface the D.J., I was supposed to meet him in person, too."

Mandrake looked at Meredith with surprise, Jessie thought at first—or was that jealousy? "Yeah? Well, you ain't gonna believe this either, baby, but swear to God, I was standing right there when he said it…"

"When who said what?" Meredith asked.

Beau ambled back into the clearing towards the bikes as Mandrake went on, with something like glee.

"The sheriff. A body washed out of the cavern a while ago. And Ratner walks up, everybody gathered round, he didn't hardly look at it, and suddenly he says to everybody—"

And in unison with Mandrake, Beau spoke. "'The ghost did it.'"

"Shit!" Meredith said. She stamped her foot, then paced in a small circle with her hands on her hips.

"What?" Jessie dared to be curious at the teenager's reaction.

"We missed the surprise! This is totally lame. Georgie, let's go."

The three motorcyclists came to an intersection an hour later after the riders were waved forward, stopped, questioned briefly, then made to wait in another long line of disappointed fans and exhaust-belching pick-up trucks. Meredith had rattled off the details about the radio station's contest and how she'd won, but Mandrake interrupted and told her she was a silly kid. She clammed up, miffed.

It was full dark when she waved goodbye from the Wing's

pillion as Mandrake turned south. He tore off without a word
on the C.B. to ask whether Jessie and Beau wanted to join them
for dinner, or to say goodbye. Just as well, for what Jessie wanted
most was an end to their riding day, a drink, and a full, reasoned
report from Beau on the events at the museum lodge. She turned
north on Highway 281.

"Where are we going?" Beau often followed her without knowing their destination.

"I have a fan who wants us to stop over."

"You have a fan?"

Jessie lifted her left hand off the grip and gave him the finger.
Then she pressed the C.B. button again. "This one's choice. It's
Meredith's dad. I wrote a play for his B&B a while back. It's a big
house, not far from here. His son lives with him, and Meredith
got us a room. She wants us to meet his new sweetheart. His
Gypsy sweetheart."

"Oh, like that, is it?"

"Maybe. If I had to predict…" Jessie advised that the Cannon
ranch was on the north side of the park, but with the traffic, it
would be faster to circle around through Burnet. "You want to
stop and eat?"

"I sense there's a chili dog in your future…"

In a booth at the Dairy Queen, Jessie licked the chili sauce
off her fingers. "So what's the deal with the dead body?"

Beau's talent at sucking information and/or rumors out of
a group of deputies, or just now a line of hungry cowboys and
their dates, was tops.

"Guy went to check sound for the show and found the dead
guy washed into a side cave, very recently. No ID, but it could be
lost upstream. The cave's only where they found him, not where
he went into the river."

"Anything unusual for cause of death?"

"Drowning, but he looked beat up, too. The river could have
driven him into walls and outcroppings. The water table's higher

than normal now, and it takes more side paths. Or someone may have roughed him up to make him to go into the cave upstream, not even knowing the river was rising. It rained last night and this morning. I'm afraid they'll play hell finding any trace. Autopsy may show more."

"Not a bad way to off someone," Jessie mused.

"You bet." Ordinarily, Beau explained, a death in the cavern without witnesses would have involved a member of a tour group who had wandered off, or a maintenance worker who'd had an accident. But no one had reported a missing tourist; no one had requested a search and rescue for an employee; no one had heard the victim call out for help. So first, the sheriff would need to identify the DB. Beau allowed one lip to rise in irritation and disgust, making his mustache twitch. "And the level of intelligence among some guys wearing a badge? Sheee. Judging by the saying, 'what you don't know won't hurt you,' these county guys are invulnerable."

"You make any sense of the ghost thing?"

"It was that stunt Meredith mentioned. The Hairy Claws would pretend to play a man—a dummy, obviously—back to life. They have this new song, there's a chorus about defeating a ghost, and the deputies were in on it. They were supposed to look scared when this dummy washed out, and talk about the 'Ghost Killer' getting another one. Now, what's that got to do with law enforcement?"

It was obviously a rhetorical question, and Jessie left it alone. They paid, and Jessie pulled out her yellow rain gear when she got back to her Road King. "Killed by a ghost," Beau said, waiting to offer a hand as she stood on one foot and slid the pants of the rainsuit on. He sounded more amused than disgusted now. "Shall we bust that idea? Of course, it means sticking around these parts a few more days. It's not what we planned."

"O.K., let's see what's in the cards, so to speak."

The bikes carved parallel paths under a moonless sky, with

Jessie in the lead again. Mist speckled her windscreen, then dried. Cannon's place was north of Inks Lake Park, where Indian Springs Road came to a dead-end, near the headwaters of a creek that ran into the cavern system they'd just been riding over. Interesting, Jessie thought. The caves beneath them were formed when ground-water levels dropped. Water dissolved the limestone, but huge stream beds were also cut out of the solid rock. The combination of formation both by dissolving and by river cuts made Longhorn Cavern one of the most unusual in the world.

Past Burnet, the ambient world outside the overlapping cones of their headlights was dark, shadowy dark, and darker. Distant dots of light became brighter and then vanished as they passed pockets of life. The engines thrummed beneath them, the sound rising around them off the pavement and the rocky terrain.

After the turn-off, they hit real rain. The empty two-lane became a winding wet ribbon, spooling out, inviting Jessie to test herself with its treacherous hidden curves and deer crossings. Her peripheral vision registered the rippling, pulsing white stripes on the left and the solid white line on the right, between which she aimed her bike and hurtled into the night, still traveling a mile a minute. She had ridden across half of Texas in the rain over the years and saw it as part of their adventures.

She slowed as they began to encounter mail boxes and hard-to-read street signs. At Indian Springs Road she saw a lettered arch over an open gate to a private road. "Spirit Haven," it read.

Spreading live-oak trees wove a broken ceiling of branches over the long driveway. Jessie kept their speed low as the rain dwindled. Soon the house, a white-shingled two-story with many gables, came into view. A lighted parking lot, bounded by a lime-stone rock wall and covered with several acres of smooth, level asphalt, welcomed them. The clouds lifted, a northwest wind taking them toward the Gulf Coast.

The riders parked beside a wrap-around porch, next to a pick-up truck with beads, graduation dangles, and tiny chains swinging from the rear-view mirror. One bumper sticker said,

"If you ride my ass, you better be pulling my hair." As Jessie dismounted from her Road King, a voice piped up behind her. "Ah, yes. Come, come! We expect." A tiny, older woman threw herself into Jessie's arms, kissed her on both cheeks, then pulled her toward the house.

Jessie stopped her, intent on getting her wet gear off while she sized the woman up. Spooks looked to be Jessie's senior, but not by much; her body exuded youth and sensuality. Where she had grazed Jessie's cheek, she left a trace of a familiar fragrance, one Jessie couldn't quite identify. Her face had a feline slant, her nose was long and straight. Heavy eyebrows framed large brown eyes; and her dark frizz of hair was parted in the center and tucked behind her ears. She wore a long skirt, a loose, belted blouse with multiple strings of beads and a crucifix, and a crocheted shawl, none of which hid her unfettered curves; and many, many rings.

"You tell about body in the cave?" Spooks was nothing if not up to speed.

"Ah, the deputies sent everyone home as soon as it was reported," Jessie said. "How did you find out about it?"

"Spirit guides sent word."

"Are you kidding me?" Beau's voice rose.

"No. Police band radio." Spooks pronounced it "PO-lees", as if she spoke Ebonics. Her sentences had an odd rhythm, too.

By now they had crossed to the porch and entered. The old-fashioned front of the house was joined by a breezeway to a new family room. It was furnished with a big-screen TV and leather chairs where the riders piled their jackets, helmets, and gloves. Curiously, folding tables covered with small piles of paper lined the walls.

In a green recliner Derwood Cannon was getting to his feet. He had aged terribly in a few years and now looked every day of 60. His cheeks were sunk in, and under-eye pouches suggesting liver damage to Jessie pulled his face down. But his faded blue eyes lit up as she approached.

"This is wonderful! How's my favorite writer?"

"Don't get up. Mr. Cannon, this is Beau Marsberg."

"We're old friends, Jessie. I'm Dub, did you forget?" Cannon went to shake hands with Beau but lost his balance. He toppled backward, the chair catching him at the knees.

"Whoa!" Beau, with reflexes like a snake, got an arm around the older man before his head could snap back. Beau let him down slowly, until he was resting in the chair again.

"I'm O.K. A little fuzzy-headed these days, that's all. Spooks, honey, get these people a drink, would you?"

Jessie, who was ready for almost anything alcoholic, cringed as the doorbell peeled the first bars of "The Eyes of Texas." Spooks threw up her hands, as if this was just too much, this answering of the door, and trotted off. Jessie suddenly remembered what the fragrance was: Cool Water, by Davidoff. A men's after-shave.

Jessie heard a familiar voice. "What's up, Spooks?" It was Mandrake. Crap.

"Hey. Where's my dad?" Without waiting for an answer, Meredith ran into the family room. Spooks followed Mandrake in, watching as he hustled over to shake Dub's hand, bumping Beau out of his way.

"Hey, now—" Beau firmly pulled Mandrake aside. "She had a curfew. Didn't you care?"

"Daddy?"

Meredith smelled of beer. Jessie saw her premonition about to realize itself in the fight that would start after the teenager gave her father a kiss on the cheek. And indeed, he reared back to look at her.

"Daddy, what's wrong?" Meredith glowered at Spooks.

"I'm fine, honey, I keep telling you. It's good to see you. How's tricks?"

Hmm. Nothing about the under-age drinking, nothing about riding off with George.

But Jessie noticed a glaze over Cannon's eyes and a hesitant positioning of his hand in space. There was a lot he didn't see. And the room looked tacky somehow. Items were missing, things Jessie would have expected him to have kept from Edith's collection of antiques. A cheap bookcase held her teacup collection, when normally it would have been in her curved-glass curio cabinet.

Meredith spun around to bark at Spooks. "Has he had his supper? His medicine?"

Spooks sent the teenager a look of loathing. "I take care. I listen, I feed, I bathe."

"That's disgusting."

"You don't do it. You go into city."

"Where's Junior?" Mandrake asked. "Off polishing them crystal balls?"

Before Spooks could answer, the doorbell rang again. "Aiie, he need his rest!" She left with a scowl on her face that made her eyebrows a V, her mouth arching downward like an angry trout. Meredith stormed out in a different direction, apparently looking for her brother. Mandrake picked up the TV remote and ran through the channels aimlessly.

Jessie's intuition tingled again when she saw who entered— Sheriff Ratner, seen recently uttering nonsense in the park.

"Hey, Dub," he said, his tenor voice unexpected from such a big, barrel-chested man. "Evening, ma'am." He nodded to Spooks, glanced at Mandrake, and walked over to Cannon's chair. He put a hand on the older man's shoulder and gave it a small, friendly squeeze. "Got something I need you to look at."

Good luck with that, Jessie thought.

Ratner pulled out a smart phone and fiddled with it, then passed it over to Dub, who brought close to his face. He turned his head to the side, studying the image on its face, or pretending to.

"You recognize that boy?" Sheriff Ratner asked.

"Can't say as I do," Cannon replied. He raised an eyebrow in the sheriff's direction, and getting no objection, passed the phone over to Beau, who studied it, shook his head no, then handed it to Jessie.

She memorized the image: the body of a slim young Caucasian man dressed all in black with long hair to his shoulders. A few days' growth of beard darkened his bruised cheeks.

Jessie passed the phone back towards the sheriff, but Spooks grabbed it. She took one look at the body, let out a startled gasp, and grabbed her crucifix.

"You know this guy?" Sheriff Ratner demanded.

Spooks shook her head no.

"You sure? How long you been here, ma'am?"

Cannon spoke up. "We met about eight months ago. She was down on her luck and needed a place to stay, and Junior and me needed some help. She's got her own place now, and she's paying her way. She even knows how to use the Internet. She's become indispensable to me." He smiled tenderly at Spooks.

But her attention was elsewhere. "Man is dead? Spirit flown?" Spooks asked, pointing to the picture.

Ratner said yes and went through the few known facts.

Jessie drifted over to the card tables while Ratner talked. A laptop slept on one of them; a stack of brochures awaited address labels. She picked one up and read, "Vadoma Financial Group, Payment Agent Opportunity." Glancing through it, she saw at once that it was a work-at-home part-time scam, offering "Unlimited earnings! Incredible commissions." Sure, right. Another stack of paper proved to be bank deposit slips. A box of business cards stood open. Jessie took one showing a black palm, fingers pointed up, and under the image, the name "Vadoma Tom, Mistress of Fortune."

At a break in Ratner's recitation, Jessie asked Cannon, "Is all this for the B&B?"

"No, for Junior's job."

"What does he do?"

"People buy and sell things, they sometimes need a third party to handle the actual transfer of money and products," Cannon said. "He does that. At least, that's what I understand. Spooks puts these people from overseas in touch with Junior, and he gets a fee."

"People send him money," Spooks said. "And he send it to other people. Good, honest work. Is just about money."

"He puts it into his bank account, then writes somebody a check, right?"

"Must be sent by Western Union. Is perfectly safe."

Jessie and Beau exchanged a glance. No legitimate company would hire someone part-time to act as an escrow agent nor allow him to use his private bank account.

But Sheriff Ratner's mind was on something else. "We heard that a guy in this band—"

"The Hairy Claws? Sure," Mandrake growled. "Bunch of rich bastards."

Ratner's mouth twitched in irritation. "If you don't mind…" He gave Mandrake a quelling look. "Seems like somebody with the band came out to see you this afternoon, Dub."

Cannon was puzzled. "No, we've had no visitors in ages. Isn't that right, Spooks?"

"Is right."

"Well, see, I think he'd already talked to Junior. Ran into him in town, somebody pointed him out, whatever. But Junior wanted something outrageous in return for access, I don't doubt, so maybe he thought you'd say something different." The sheriff seemed embarrassed. "One of my deputies gave him directions here."

"What did he want to talk to me about?"

"Are you sure Junior didn't mention it to you?"

"I haven't seen Junior all day." Cannon's confusion seemed to grow.

Meredith scurried toward the front hall, but stopped short at her father's words. "But she's always around," she glared at Spooks, "except when she's wiring money to who knows where. When she's tired of Dad, she stays at her own place. Junior does what he pleases."

"Is that right." Ratner's eyes roamed the ceiling as if he expected to find Junior there. "See, the deputy that gave the band guy directions was kinda bored, so he followed him out here, made sure he found the right place. Guy was riding a dual-sport bike."

Spooks twisted one ring after another.

Sheriff Ratner towered over her like a tree.

"What the hell's going on?" A man shouted in another part of the house. Thumps and bangs preceded him, but he eventually flung himself into the room. Jessie guessed his age at 25 but recognized his arrested development at once, too.

He was a geeky guy, the type who lived in front of a monitor, which helped account for his pasty white skin, unruly hair, and anorexic physique. He wore a headset around his neck, ah, yes, the police band radio, Jessie thought, and his all-black attire did nothing to discourage the notion he had one foot in the grave and would trip you into yours with the other. "Who the hell are these people? Spooks, are you O.K.?"

He went over and put his arm around Spooks, pulling her against his body. Together, they seemed to form a united front—from which the fragrance of Cool Water emanated.

Jessie got it: Spooks was Junior's Dark Lady. Every day, Dub Cannon was surrounded by people he shouldn't trust.

"This lady is Jessie Carr," he told Junior. "You were in college when we met. And this is her friend, Beau, um."

Meredith arrived in the doorway again, this time with a stack of mail and a pearl-handled "dagger" for opening it. When she saw Junior and Spooks standing arm in arm, she stopped, hands on hips. "I can't believe this. You moron, she's totally lying to you and stealing from us all."

Spooks stepped forward, one finger in the air in rebuke.

Before she could speak, Ratner's high voice intruded. "I'm Sheriff Ratner, and I'm investigating a homicide." He brought up his photos on the smart phone again and handed it across, through Jessie, to Junior.

In this photo the body was turned on its side. It showed how the young man's hands had been tied behind him with some kind of lumpy dark cord. This was no accident.

Jessie waited for Junior's response when she gave him the phone.

He looked at it half a second, then handed it back, ignoring his sister standing there. "Never seen him," Junior said.

"Well, that's peculiar, but witnesses can be wrong." The sheriff pocketed the phone and seemed to give up. "It's getting late. I should let you folks get to bed."

"No! You should arrest this woman. She's a thief." Meredith pointed at Spooks.

"Yeah, well, you're drunk." Junior's tone was cruel. "Who gave you the beer, him?" He pointed at Mandrake. "Did he get you pregnant, too?"

"It's not my kid." Mandrake's denial was addressed to Spooks, not to Cannon, who seemed inured to his children's arguments.

Meredith absorbed this like a physical assault. Not only anger but hurt shaped her face. She turned to her father, but Cannon didn't see her, and Mandrake shrugged, useless.

Ratner shrugged, too. "It's all about evidence, and we don't have much so far."

"Oh, there's evidence." Everyone turned to look at Jessie. "It's a matter of the details, isn't it?" Jessie motioned to Ratner to get out his phone one more time. He did so. "Meredith, could that be Eric?"

The girl walked over to look. She saw the image and fell back against Mandrake, her eyes rolling up, the dagger dropping from her hand, the mail spilling in a paper cascade.

"I think we can take that as a yes," Jessie said.

Meredith gasped and struggled to get to her feet. "Oh, my god. Was he the one in the cave?" She squealed, stricken.

Ratner gave Jessie an appreciative look. "Knowing his name would be a big help."

Beau picked up the dagger and moved it to a safe spot on a card table.

"Maybe you could schedule a séance," Mandrake was apparently sincere, Jessie observed, with disbelief.

"Hey, it's not illegal!" Junior yelled, his voice rising almost as high as his sister's.

"Son." Cannon got to his feet, pulling himself up to his full height. "Are you in trouble?"

"What? No!" Junior's eyes darted from one face to another.

Jessie looked Junior up and down, her contempt visible. "You're all about money, too, aren't you. You thought Eric was rich. Manager of a famous band, hit songs, tour bus, all that. You tried to shake him down, and he said no deal."

"O.K., who we talking about?" Ratner asked.

"Eric Crawford," Meredith wailed, overwrought.

Junior flapped a hand at his sister. "She admits she knew him."

"I knew of him. He practically made that band."

Cannon weakly summoned his daughter to his side. She ran to him and grabbed a tissue to dab at the sweat on his face.

Jessie circled the Junior like a shark, her leather chaps swishing, her attitude inexorable. "Consider. Somebody saw Eric talking to Junior and knew he wasn't a happy camper when the conversation was over. Ergo, no deal." She spoke into Junior's left ear. "How much did you try to take him for?"

"I don't know what you're talking about."

"Sure you do. He wanted to come onto your land, in fact everything about the band's big number required it. He was willing to pay something, but you tried to rob him."

Junior looked at Jessie as if she were stupid. "If you're the seller, you get to set the price."

"The only way to make that dummy come out of the river when they wanted was to put it in upstream, have someone waiting at the cavern, and time how long it took to float out. Right, Meredith?"

"They would have done it two or three times, just to be sure. Eric was a perfectionist. Everybody knows that."

"Exactly." Jessie drilled down on Junior again. "And when you wouldn't be reasonable about it, and time got short, he decided to talk to your father, who as the actual owner of the land could overrule you."

"I never talked to anyone about a dummy." Cannon remained confused.

"Yes, but not because he didn't come. Isn't that right, Spooks?"

"I never know him."

The sheriff gently wagged a finger at Spooks. "Not the same. He was here, wasn't he?"

Beau leaned over to speak to Cannon, avoiding any suggestion of interrogation. "Dub, what were you doing mid-morning?"

"I took a nap." Cannon's voice was hollow croak. "But maybe I did hear a motorcycle…"

Jessie took up her shark-circling again, this time coming closer but never looking directly at the geek in the center of her orbit.

"And what was Junior doing about that time?" she asked Cannon.

"I…don't know."

Beau took up Jessie's point, his voice still quiet. "Did she make promises to you, too?"

Spooks pointed at Cannon. "I said only truth. I said, is good man, Big Boss. Very nice to me." Then she looked at Junior. "And I help Little Boss make money. Soon get to be Big Boss, and nicer. I make happy, everyone."

Cannon's face fell. He pursed his lips and stared at the floor. "She said her mother used to bring her into our shop in San Marcos when she was a little girl. Her credit card wouldn't work that first day, and her car needed repairs. But she seemed so interested in…my life. I thought she was going to stay with me…forever."

Junior looked ill. "You creepy old fool! You really believed she loved you?"

Something in Cannon's pale eyes retreated to a place the size of an atom.

Jessie broke the silence. "When Eric got here this afternoon, he saw something…" She turned to Junior. "I don't know what, but it was probably incriminating. You stood to lose your home and whatever support your dad's been giving you. And you," Jessie looked at the fortune teller, "would be cut off, too, if Dub knew the truth. You'd hate for that to happen before you'd bled him dry, wouldn't you."

"Seems like letting the guy walk around your land was a lot simpler," Beau drawled. "He'd never have known anything was wrong."

"I, I—" Spooks swirled away from her young lover. "It was Junior, all Junior."

Meredith's eyes narrowed. Hate aged her delicate features. "It was Junior, your dear Little Boss? Give me a break. You come in here and steal Daddy blind, take my mother's things and sell them, run this fortune teller scam. You'll do anything, won't you?" Meredith leaned in close to Spooks. "Oh, and I've got one more bombshell for you. The only reason I came out here tonight is because Daddy's bank account has been frozen. How do you like that?"

"What?" Cannon asked, shocked.

"I tried to use your credit card tonight in Marble Falls, and they told us it's no good. There's no money left!"

"What? Noooo!" Junior cried.

Meredith whirled to face him. "And do you know why? Because this cockamamie scheme she got you into is international money laundering, dummy! The restaurant let me call Sam Vickers, Daddy's bank officer, at home, and he said the Secret Service shut us down today. You put the checks you received into the family account, so we can't get any of our own money out until they decide we can."

In a rage, Meredith seized the dagger and took an ill-aimed swipe at Junior's head. He ducked, knocking Jessie off balance, but his sister found another target. She went for Spooks, the dagger moving in her hand like a cobra's head, back and forth. "You don't deserve another minute's worth of air, you bitch!"

"Meredith, honey, think about what you're doing," Mandrake whined. He made sure to stay well out of the zone of danger, though. "Trixie needs a mother. Best put that down before one of you girls gets hurt."

Ah, Jessie thought. Cannon had asked about "Trixie," not "tricks" when we arrived. A grandchild, no doubt.

"I never know dead guy." Spooks snatched up a stack of checks from the card table, stuffed them down her blouse, and began edging toward the door. "George, you take me home?"

Meredith lowered her voice to an adult tone but the dagger remained in her hand. "Sheriff Ratner, I'll swear to it, she steals."

"I gotta arrest you, ma'am," Ratner said. He grabbed Spooks by the arm, pulling her out of Meredith's range in case she lost it again.

He gave Beau a wave, and in a flash, Beau moved behind Meredith, wrapped his arms around her, and grasped the hand with the dagger in it. "Let it go, and I'll bet the sheriff will chalk this up to stress."

Meredith slowly straightened up and dropped the letter opener again. She took several moments to regroup, but Beau ignored her and swooped to pick it up from the floor. In a moment, she went to her father's side, looking dazed.

The sheriff turned Spooks around, trying to cuff her hands behind her back. "We're gonna check your whole story out."

Spooks was fast, though; she ran straight for the door. Jessie made a diving leap and caught her by the legs, and they both went down in a tangle of gypsy skirts and men's cologne. Rolling on top of the older woman, Jessie pinned her, one arm twisted high behind her back.

"Got her," Jessie said.

Cannon turned away and covered his despairing eyes, while Mandrake collected the checks that had flown free of Spook's blouse. It had been pulled open in the fray, exposing her voluptuous, naked breasts.

Beau stared at them a moment, then grabbed a blanket from Cannon's recliner and tossed it to her. "You lost a button," he said.

A few minutes later, Ratner marched Spooks out toward the parking lot. Jessie and Meredith straightened the furniture that had been knocked around, while Beau checked on Cannon.

George Mandrake thumbed through the checks, squinting at them, lips pursed, as useless as a blow dryer to a bald man.

The engine of the sheriff's patrol car turned over outside, and the room went quiet. Junior schlepped over to his father and stood there looking down at the bald spot on top his head. "Guess she wasn't that crazy about me, either. I never would have guessed she was a killer. Sorry, Dad."

But the tension in the room wasn't gone. Dub shifted in his chair and turned his back on his son. Meredith pretended he wasn't there.

Jessie gave Beau a little jerk of the head, and he drifted toward Junior. She moved to flank the geek before she spoke. "Looking for a silver lining, Junior? That would be premature. See, Sheriff Ratner may not be able to make his case against Spooks. There's that prejudice the Romani complain about, and there's some truth on both sides. I could poke half a dozen holes in a murder case against her without breaking a sweat."

"Surely she won't get off?" Meredith was ready to blaze again.

"No, I don't think so. But they'll have to have a damn good case of fraud, 'cause they'll never get her for Eric's death." Jessie pressed on, talking directly to Junior now. "Which is only just, because she didn't do it. So who could have taken Eric out there and put him in the caves? Meredith would have no reason to kill Eric; the opposite, in fact. Your father wasn't up to it; and during the period Spooks has been here, we've had a drought until the last couple of days. She couldn't have found the headwaters of an underground creek she didn't know existed. But you knew right where to go. It's practically in your backyard."

"That tomfoolery hanging in your truck," Beau added, "makes a good rope."

"I didn't do it!" Junior yelled. "That truck's always unlocked."

Beau moved toward him, but the younger man bolted for the side door.

Jessie realized what he had in mind and scrambled outside after him as he ran around the pick-up truck and jumped into the cab.

In his haste, however, he failed to notice that Mandrake's

Gold Wing was parked behind him. He threw the pick-up into Reverse and ran right into it.

Plastic parts exploded. Metal crunched, glass tinkled as it broke. The motorcycle's mangled frame was trapped behind Junior's rear wheels. After several attempts to get the pick-up free, which just pushed it further onto the wrecked Wing, Junior stopped, jumped out, and kicked the truck's front quarter-panel.

"Damn, damn, damn!" he screamed.

Jessie stood on the stoop and shook her head at his useless fury. Junior was going to need to look for a real job now.

Sticking his head out the side door behind her, Mandrake wilted at the sight of his Wing, now quite destroyed. "Oh, nooooo," he moaned. "My biiiike!"

He ran over to the crumpled fiberglass of its trunk and pried open the lid. He reached inside, pulled out a black Beretta, and aimed it at the house. Mad with frustration, he fired.

It was a standard nine millimeter by the sound of it, Jessie thought, rolling into the shadows. Suddenly everything fell into place in her mind.

Mandrake sprinted across the parking lot toward the main road.

Beau's head and shoulders, framed by the light from inside, filled the side door. He spotted Mandrake running, then yelled at Meredith to call 911 and get Ratner back out there.

Mandrake's downfall was looking back. He saw Jessie coming after him, missed his footing, and tripped, sprawling into the water-filled ditch and sending the Beretta flying. On hands and knees, sandy and wet, he turned his head and snarled at Jessie. "Who made you God?"

"Odd question coming from someone who wanted to know the future so bad." Jessie had drawn her boot pistol, a nifty Smith & Wesson Model 642 Airweight, and pointed it at him; but his eyes shifted, scanning the environment for another escape route. He couldn't believe he was caught.

"You got nothin' on me," he told her.

"Oh, I bet we find where you dumped Eric's bike," she replied. "It was bad enough that Spooks was playing Dub and Junior both, but when you saw Eric ride up here, you thought she'd found yet another sugar daddy, didn't you."

"So how'd you guess?"

"Well, first, for a guy who had a hot date waiting, you weren't in any hurry to leave. Then when Ratner pulled Spooks off the floor, you didn't check out her boobs," Jessie said. "Finally it dawned on me, that's because they were nothing new to you."

She held the gun steady, but she felt a shudder start along the back of her arms and neck. She recognized it as revulsion at this piss-poor example of a man, one whose life she could take, that moment, if she chose. What it must have been like for Eric, she thought, gasping, tumbling, banging into the cavern walls in the rush of water, his heart beating its last in the impenetrable dark...

Her fingers tightened on the Airweight. She raised her hand and took aim at Mandrake's head. Oh, it was tempting.

"The sheriff's on his way back," Dub Cannon called to Jessie from the porch. "Only took him about six miles to figure it out."

Beau came up behind her, his Ruger LCR steady in his hand, and stopped beside her. He stared down at the bedraggled biker. "I got it, Jessie. At ease."

She holstered her pistol. "Looks like the Wheel of Fortune just reversed for you," she told Mandrake. "Don't worry, you can stay in that ditch for a while. A man who's born for the needle will never drown."

About The Wild, Throbbing Dark

Several years ago, when I was doing research on Texas caves for my novel "A Week of Wednesdays" (still in progress), my writing and riding partner Jim Davis accompanied me on a geological tour of Longhorn Cavern. It has many beautiful rock formations, but its history is what intrigued me most.

We found the idea that D.G. Sherrod had created a nightclub that was truly "underground" during Prohibition amusing; and the faded photographs of barrels of illegal liquor being dropped through a hole in the cave's roof and tables set up around a dance floor demonstrated how he managed it, and how popular the place was for a time. A niche in a wall several feet above the cave floor housed the establishment's tiny orchestra, and visiting it on a hot Texas evening must have been a lovely relief from the heat in the days before air conditioning, for the interior temperature is about 70 degrees all the time.

Writing "The Wild, Throbbing Dark" reintroduced me to the Wild Cave Tour, which gives visitors who can rough it an impressive look at areas of the cavern rarely seen. If there's still a kid in you, eager to put on a hardhat and wade through an underground river, you, too, can discover mysteries in this deep, dark place.

TUNNEL VISION
BY SALLY LOVE

Carol Magnusson pushed her long brown waves behind her ears as she rushed to the elevator, the two-way clutched in her hand. She checked her watch, then slid the radio into its belt holster. She was in her second year as the building manager of a Houston skyscraper and this was her first emergency. The photo store's print processor had overheated and sprung a leak, sparking a fire. She willed the elevator to hightail it down to the second floor where she caught the escalator to the Tunnel System.

Her speaker crackled. "Unit One, come in."

"Unit One," Carol replied, "Call it in. Make sure HFD knows the fire is out. I'll meet them at the tenant." She picked up her pace by running down the escalator. As she stepped off the tread, a heel caught in the gap between steps, sending the shoe flying. Carol steadied herself and scooped up the shoe. She put her bare toe down and scanned the tile for the broken heel until she spotted it half-hidden in a shadowed corner.

Carol grabbed the heel, slipped it into her pocket and toe-stepped her way to the photo shop. "What's the damage?" she asked the shop manager.

"Machine's a total loss, but I got to use the fire extinguisher." The young man smiled. "It works great."

Carol checked around the machine, eyeing the green spill mixed with extinguisher foam seeping along the fire-blackened tile. "Everybody's okay?"

He nodded.

"I'll send maintenance to help with the clean-up." After the firemen gave the okay, she limped out and rounded the corner. Fortunately, the new shoe shop was only a few doors down.

Carol loved the tunnels—seven miles of air-conditioned walkways twenty feet below downtown Houston streets. She'd even taken the official Tunnel Tour on her own time. Carol's company leased, managed, and protected the tunnels under her building, manning strategically placed gates with twenty-four/seven security. Other cities had their measly little skywalks a couple of stories high, meandering riverwalks, or subway stations designed by big-name architects. But Houstonians could escape scorching days, strangling humidity, or tropical-storm-force rains by descending to a city beneath the city.

Good thing TRIPLE-G SHOE REPAIR had opened a few days early, or she'd be showing lease space this afternoon on bare feet. As she hobbled to the counter, one of the lease signatories, Garwood Moore, emerged through a sliding panel from the back room.

A fun part of her job included seeing innovations in action. The sensor to detect approaching customers was ingenious. *So that's how it works. Clever idea.* After all, the most important component of a successful service business was a prompt, friendly proprietor.

Carol had been surprised when the son of one of Houston's elite families showed up to view lease space. She was more than a bit puzzled when the business turned out to be shoe repair. Somehow a twenty-something who bunked in the River Oaks zip code didn't fit with a store that replaced shredded laces, shined and re-soled wingtips, or reattached broken heels. But the financial information Gar submitted, along with a Letter of Intent to Lease, proved healthier than most of the other small tenants. Her job depended on keeping the building leased with a maximum revenue stream, not investigating a trust fund baby with a yen to shine shoes. She welcomed the new paying tenant to her section of the tunnel.

Gar was drop-dead gorgeous—black hair, spiky but not punk, red-carpet smile and intense blue eyes—the kind that might entice a woman to forget her pledge to swear off attractive men. Carol had firsthand knowledge of the chaos a Looker could cause. She'd learned her lesson and then some. But it never hurt to add a piece of eye candy to her tunnel section to lure droves of appreciative women.

Gar leaned a tanned arm on the counter as Carol placed the shoe and its detached heel on a cloth pad.

"Aaah, an injured slingback." He rewarded her with The Smile and motioned her past the shoe-shine stand to an upholstered wingback chair labeled, "Barefoot Zone."

"Let's get this casualty to our ace cobbler." Gar turned to the back wall and laid his palm on the partition. "I'll have him put a rush on your emergency." A split second later, the partition slid open just enough for him to pass through.

Carol peered into the dimly lit area behind the wall, unable to make out any details before the sliding door snapped shut. *Must be another sensor.* Although she'd been through the empty space before she signed TRIPLE-G, the owners had politely declined to use the management's construction company. TRIPLE-G had handled its own build-out and inspections. Neither Gar nor the other two owners had invited Carol to tour the finished area. Most tenants couldn't wait to show off their new build-outs.

Gar returned, sat next to Carol and proceeded to regale her with the details of his weekend feral hog hunting trip at his family's South Texas ranch. She had to hand it to Gar, he could tell a story, but his touching her arm to emphasize a point shifted from sexy to creepy as his touches reached seven.

He tapped the Bluetooth earpiece and listened. "Back in a moment." Gar glided through the wall, then returned with the slingback, heel re-attached. He knelt down and slid it on Carol's foot, caressing her arch with an experienced hand.

She managed to ignore the not-so-subtle caress, then stood, tested the heel, and pulled out her wallet.

"No, ma'am, Miz Carol," Gar drawled. "Consider this a goodwill gesture to a damsel in distress."

Carol studied Gar. He'd said the words with a straight face. The guy was good—lots of practice.

Gar hooked a thumb into an expensive khaki belt loop. "And before I forget it, we need access over the weekend."

Uh-huh. A special request. Never let your guard down. "Will you need the AC?"

He shook his head. "Won't be here that long."

Carol turned to see owner number two, Reginald, RG, Graydon, wheeling a box showing a four-color label of a Sun Sparc server. She let out a low whistle and raised a brow. "Sun Sparc. Y'all are bringing the big guns." *Why would a shoe repair shop need more horsepower than a basic PC loaded with QuickBooks?*

A few inches shorter than Gar, with a solid gym-toned physique, RG stopped briefly, offering a respectful nod to the building manager. He ran a hand through his longish, sandy-brown hair and continued. As he rounded the corner guiding the new server, he blew a monstrous pink bubble, flicked a playful glance at Carol, then popped it with his teeth.

Gar flinched at the sound and sent an immediate glare at RG, then a slow smile at Carol. "We're aiming to link TRIPLE-G with additional stores as we expand. This location will be the hub."

Carol held back a laugh at RG's boyish fun and took in Gar's explanation with a decade-and-a-half of experience in the feast and famine world of commercial real estate. She wiggled the foot sporting the mended shoe at Gar and RG. "Thanks again for the quick fix." She'd realized from the first meeting that this trio wasn't your average mom-and-pop operation. They had chosen teak flooring, marble counters, grasscloth wall coverings, titanium light fixtures, plus embedded sensors for nifty sliding walls. These folks would be interesting.

Carol meandered through the tunnels back toward her building, enjoying the mid-afternoon lull. She pulled her ringing phone from a suit pocket.

"Mom, did you remind Dad to pick me up?" her son blurted before she had a chance to say "hello."

She tightened her grip. "Yes, baby, I sent him an email."

"Don't call me that," Jason snapped. "I'm almost twelve. I called him, but it went to voice mail. I just sent another text."

Carol grimaced, trying to keep her voice even. "Give him another fifteen minutes, then call me back." She paused. "Are you in front of the school? Where the circle driveway is?"

"Duh!"

Carol let that one go. Pick your battles, she reminded herself. *Damn, Paul. For once, put your son first.* She didn't blame Jason for being angry. By now the school bus had delivered half his classmates. And the grandparents who usually kept him until she got home were in the middle of a movie matinee. *Damn, Paul.*

Gar waited until Carol turned the corner and was no longer in sight, then turned on RG, fists balled. "I *told* you to wait until *after* closing to bring stuff inside." He grabbed a handful of RG's T-shirt. "Stick with the plan."

RG backed off a step and slapped at Gar's fist. "Watch it, dude. This is an original REO Speedwagon shirt." He smoothed the fabric over his flat belly, then leaned into Gar's sneer. "Don't forget. You need me." RG wheeled the Sparc around the counter and through the disappearing wall.

Gar reined in his temper and studied the third partner, Genna Trotter, a gangly blonde sporting skinny, black-rimmed glasses. She spotted his stare and threw back a reserved smile and half a wave while her fingers manipulated a keyboard. She stopped momentarily, gathered her hair into a ponytail at her nape, and clipped it with a silver barrette. Even the tight black jeans and long-sleeved, knit shirt barely revealed a woman's form. She had a pre-teen shape, all angles and joints.

Genna still held the combined high school/college record in the Hacker Hall of Fame for stealing and distributing the largest quantity of exams without being caught. He thought she had been stupid for posting them for free, but Genna wasn't in it for the money. She was a digital goddess in the hacker world and the rep was enough. He'd keep her, at least for a while, for security, to make sure the software worked as planned.

As awkward as she seemed in social and business situations, Genna worked miracles with computers. Sit her in front of a keyboard, and she'd overflow her earbuds with heavy metal while coaxing three surrounding monitors to sing in harmony. So far, her software savvy had been the key to their monetary success. More important, managing Genna was easy: a wink here, a pat there, and she'd walk a plank for him.

Gar followed RG out the back door into the freight elevator and up to the street-level dock.

"Grab those three first." Gar pointed inside the truck. RG rolled the loaded dolly into the freight elevator, down a level to the maintenance hallway, and into the back door of TRIPLE-G.

"Careful," Gar growled. The pricy, new equipment would launch the trio into uncharted wealth.

RG unpacked the shelving, then began assembly. He remained silent as he stepped through a sea of metal parts. "The shelves will have to support a lot of weight." With a wide grin, he pitched a flathead screwdriver to Gar. "Righty-tighty."

Gar whirled and gave RG a menacing glare, letting the screwdriver bounce on the newly installed carpet.

"I'm just saying." RG screwed in the reinforced braces, then after a quick shake to check for stability, shifted a unit to the wall.

Some months before the two partners had walked off the measurements of the TRIPLE-G space. Beyond their back wall lay a hallway—a mere three feet wide—used as a maintenance corridor. Throughout the day, plumbers, electricians, and construction crews hurried to and from tenants. RG had designed the store around a hidden room especially constructed to hold a series of powered-up integrated servers.

"Come hold this, pard." RG steadied a shelf.

Gar ambled over, making sure his expression reflected his contempt for manual labor.

RG quickly attached the shelf, then moved to the next and the next with efficiency.

Gar ripped open a package of cloths and wiped a fine layer of dust off his hands and custom shirt, then stood back and watched RG tighten each screw. *Righty-tighty my ass. As soon as this room is operational, you'll be history.*

Gar had brought RG in only recently and he was becoming a problem. Some years older than Gar and Genna, RG had the experience the partnership needed for now. And he could configure hardware like nobody Gar had ever seen. The skill sets of the three partners meshed perfectly. Profits split only three ways. Best of all, since Gar was the company's brains and founder, his cut totaled twice that of RG's and Genna's. The only improvement would be a one-man operation and no profit split.

Jason called. "Mom, Dad's still not here."

"Hold on a sec." Carol put aside the Common Area Maintenance (CAM) report and listened to her son's desperate tone. If she hadn't divorced Paul ten-and-a-half years earlier, she'd track down the jerk and strangle him. She struggled to keep her voice calm.

"I'm sure he'll be there any second." She wasn't sure at all. "You know this evening is important to your dad." She knew no such thing. "You guys will have fun at the game." On their last sports outing, she'd had to pick Jason up when a security guard declared Paul too drunk to drive.

Carol closed her eyes and recalled Paul's college courting. She'd fallen quickly under his spell, mesmerized by his thatch of dark hair and soulful brown eyes—a Looker. He had been the most romantic, most attentive, most persuasive—until months later she found herself with a seven-pound, eleven-ounce son that Paul didn't want. Unfortunately, Jason idolized his dad.

Her phone rang. She recognized her boss's caller ID.

"Hey, Carol. Bert. What's the status of the environmental contest?"

She grimaced at her boss's gravelly voice and brusque tone. "Operation Green Downtown has my full attention now that CAM bills have been mailed."

"Be sure you tally each CAM payment."

"Standard procedure." *Perhaps he'd like to come over and stick the numbers in the Excel blanks himself.* Carol had gotten off to a contentious start by expressing surprise when he demanded a paper report—messengered. Everyone else opted for an electronic version. "I've scheduled a meeting next week for the tenant team leaders...and I'm feeding them lunch."

"They don't need lunch," he barked. "The budget—"

"The approved budget included the meal." She didn't remind her boss that the budget had his initials on the approval page. And she didn't mention she also planned to bribe the team leaders with home-baked brownies. She hoped the leaders would whip up support among their co-workers to discard shredded papers, cardboard boxes, and old phone books in the recycle bins distributed throughout the building. If the tenants joined her crusade, her building had a chance to win the contest.

Gar inspected the new server as RG connected cable after cable, then tossed excess parts toward the corner.

"Hey, watch out," Gar shouted, "you'll scar the wall." He'd personally selected the custom panels that made up TRIPLE-G's back wall. The buildout crew had installed a series of interconnecting wallboard covered with black, soundproof fabric. The panels would muffle the noise of the new equipment.

"I'm watching," RG grumbled. "Do you want this done right or not?"

Gar gritted his teeth, wishing he could've set up the system himself. Gar could handle a basic hacker configuration, but he was a minor leaguer compared to RG. He'd be glad when RG wasn't so valuable to the operation. Gar smiled to himself just thinking of the approaching exponential jump in his net income.

His father, Garwood Moore, Sr., had inherited his wealth in land and made his fortune selling pieces to raze for parking lots or turn into another sterile office building. But Gar had no interest in scrutinizing property maps, site plans, or architectural drawings. His greatest pleasure came in examining his growing brokerage statements.

"Will everything fit?" Gar watched as RG walked a second rack of shelving into place.

RG stared back through the steel braces. "I configured the schematic, Ace. It's a perfect fit." He tossed a handful of extra bolts into his toolbox. RG pushed aside a coil of Aluminum Flexible Conduit and a yellow roll of Romex cable. "We'll set the servers up in the next couple of days, then for the tricky part—the electricity source." RG smiled.

"What's so tricky about it?" Gar's question was rhetorical and snide; they had planned this part before signing the lease. After RG connected the electricity to the new servers, his usefulness would be over. Then Gar could cut the strings to the pain-in-the-butt and complete his mission.

Their current digs were a huge improvement over the start-up in Gar's parents' guesthouse. The three allies had stuffed the cottage with wall-to-wall electronics until there was barely room for Gar to crash. The partners padded their bank accounts until the nosy maid happened into the locked bungalow one morning as Gar slept. He had dictated the note saying she must return to Salvador to tend her sick mother. No one would ever find the maid's final resting place. Gar had set out looking for lease space the following day.

Jason IM'd Carol twenty minutes later. Paul had finally picked him up. After a couple of hours redlining a new lease from a particularly difficult tenant's lawyer, Carol gathered up her work papers and left the office. She circled the building in her six-year-old, no-frills Malibu like she did every evening. She peered into each entrance and exit, checking that every access appeared secure. Only then could she leave her building to the protection of night security. She pulled to a stop, shifted her stuffed briefcase to the front floorboard, and pointed the car home.

After finishing a Lean Cuisine supper, Carol heard the key in the lock. She shifted her lapful of paperwork to the sofa cushion, muting the sixth-inning telecast of the Astros baseball game. "You're home early."

Jason brushed past her without a word, flew to his room and slammed the door. *Not again.* She waited a few minutes before knocking. "Jason. I'm coming in." She turned the doorknob and slid into the dim room. Jason lay face down on the bed. His treasured Astros program poked out of the trash.

"What happened?" She lowered herself to the bed and waited. After several more minutes, Jason turned his face toward her.

"It was supposed to be just us, but he brought some girl. She didn't like me. Dad handed me a couple of twenties and sent me for a hotdog and coke."

Carol stifled a frantic gasp. What kind of idiot would send an undersized, attention-starved eleven-year-old into a food court teeming with beer-drinking fans? What better place for a pedophile to threaten or entice his target away. Her breath stopped as she fast-forwarded through every horror movie she'd ever seen.

"When I got back, they were kissing." A tear slid onto the bedspread. "It was awful. They wouldn't stop. A lady behind us complained. They made us leave." He turned away. "I hate him, Mom. I really hate him."

Carol laid a trembling hand on Jason's back and patted him like she had so many times as a toddler. Nothing she could say would make up for Paul's cruelty, so she remained silent.

Sitting at his desk, Gar opened the email from Genna and reviewed the previous quarter's financial statements.

Expenses:

Rent + Common Area Maintenance (CAM): $8,250.

Equipment Repair and Maintenance: $1,023.

Contract Employee, Cobbler: $5,497.

Cobbler Supplies and Materials: $2,971.

Miscellaneous Office Expense—Janitorial Service, Utilities, Office Supplies: $7,409.

Internet Advertising Links: $25,693.

Income:

Shoe Services: $6,675.

Wi-fi Taps: $933,487.

Partner Distributions: $769,821.

Genna bounced to the music rolling through her head while her fingers flew along the keyboard.

Gar tapped her on the shoulder.

She turned. Her eyes brightened as she tugged out an earbud.

"Why was the distribution so low?" Gar rolled a chair close and straddled it, bringing him within an inch of Genna's face. He smiled.

She averted her gaze for a second, then pulled up the financials on the center monitor. "We upgraded to a Sun Modular Server. If we'd increased the distribution, we'd have to finance the unit. RG and I agreed that an easier install would let us gear up ninety days ahead of schedule. I thought you okayed the upgrade."

"How much?"

"Main Server? Fifty-one grand."

Gar squelched a gasp. Of course the two geeks would opt for the Mercedes version. Gar rested his chin on the back of the chair and swallowed his anger for the moment, reminding himself that RG and Genna's innovations had brought six hundred thousand into the partnership since the first of the year…and that neither figured into his long-range plans.

"My calculations say we'll bring in seven figures the first

quarter and double that in a year." She readjusted the barrette on her ponytail. "You know we have to ease into the sites, so that their security doesn't expose us. The primary server upgrade will help."

"What if we upped the override another penny?"

Genna shook her head. "The way it's set up, we go into a site through our links, gain access to a company's payables or directly to their bank accounts. Our program siphons off fractions of cents from each account. We have to investigate each site before we insert our program. We lock onto the sites of small-to-medium businesses. The big corporations have more sophisticated security, so we steer clear. The beauty of the system is that the take is too small for either human or most machines to detect. If we push the system, it'll blow up."

Gar already knew what Genna had painstakingly and tactfully explained. The goal was to increase the quantity of hacked sites, not over-milk existing ones. But his lifestyle required more income than his techie partners. They got off on the process. He, on the other hand, was interested in growing his personal assets. He'd have to arrange it so no one could trace him through the two geeks.

Carol made her customary drive around the building and spotted the same panel truck she'd seen the previous week. Or was it? Her brain had grown numb from spending an hour listening to the interior designer for the El-Lobo Minerals Company whine. According to the man's astute sensibilities, the paint in the chairman's office didn't exude the proper ambience.

She drove into the loading entrance while fielding telephone complaints from dueling lawyers over the setting of a shared thermostat. She stared down the long entrance. The sun's glare through the windshield darkened the shaded dock. Did she detect movement? No tenant had scheduled after-hours access.

Her phone rang. "Mom, Jeremy wants to come over. Can we watch *Avatar* again?"

Lately Jason had ditched his middle-school swagger and

reverted to the sweet kid he'd always been. She made a U-turn and drove home.

Gar waited until Carol's car made the loop and drove off, then flagged the panel truck to return with the last piece of equipment. He stared at the place where Carol's taillights had disappeared. "That was close."

RG clapped him on the back. "Relax, Bubba. You worry too much."

"You'd better be glad *somebody* worries. If you'd worried *before*, you might not have landed in a federal lockup."

RG's eyes flashed as he angled the packed dolly into the freight elevator. He blew a bubble, then popped it at Gar.

Gar followed him with a ferocious stare. *As soon as this outfit is up and running, that dirtbag is gone.*

Back inside the store, Gar marched over and snatched a crimper out of RG's hand.

"You idiot! What if she'd seen the truck? You nearly blew this expansion to hell and back."

"Watch out. You'll tear the gloves. One spark, and we start all over."

Gar jerked his hand away. All RG cared about was the stupid electronics.

Gar kept an eye on RG as he disconnected the existing rack of servers, then placed them in the proper sequence on the new shelving. *Wait until he finishes the project. Wait for the dough to roll in. Wait for the right opportunity.*

RG repositioned the anti-static gloves, exchanged the star bit for the square bit, then tightened the connection.

"I just want this deal to work like it's supposed to, like we drew it up," Gar said.

"You mean like *I* drew it up," RG snapped.

Gar stalked away to the opposite side of Triple-G's backroom and sat in the cobbler's chair, eyeing RG. *That tears it. If I didn't need him...* He shook off the thought. "Genna. Start a log of Carol's trips around the building."

"What for?" Genna removed an earbud. "She can't see back here from the front of the shop."

"Her *car* trips," Gar yelled. "She nearly spotted the truck." *Did he have to spell out everything in sign language?* "She just drove by the dock entrance. Your first item will be Wednesday, May 2, 6:12 p.m."

Carol paged through the monthly utility report listing the building's totals. As part of the green goals of Downtown Houston, Inc. (DHI), the organization produced an annual document comparing the current year usage with previous years. Carol's office kept its own spreadsheet to back-bill CAM expenses. The goal of DHI and the individual building managers was to reduce power consumption. The organization recognized the progress at an annual pat-on-the-back banquet. This year her boss had ordered her to win.

In Carol's effort to win the DHI competition, she'd cleared additional space to hold recyclables for city pickup. She had installed motion sensors in the remaining offices, and only a few had balked at paying their half-share. The tenants seemed excited about this small attempt to clean up the environment. She was sure they would back further efforts. If she didn't win, her boss would make the coming year a living hell. Her building had taken the DHI two spot the previous year—the highest ranking any of the company's properties. Second place had earned her an after-banquet dressing down from Bert in front of her colleagues.

Gar checked his Blackberry messages while RG threaded a roll of Romex electrical cable through the AFC sheathing, measuring the lengths and placing connectors according to the schematic. He stripped the ends, twisted connections into junction boxes and laid them along the concrete floor.

The second shift couldn't be installed soon enough for Gar. In his world, status and influence were measured by possessions. Gar wanted riches fast and didn't care how he got them. He couldn't wait to rub his father's nose in his own wealth and importance. He wondered again if he'd chosen the right partners. Until the second hacker shift was settled in and producing, he was stuck.

"Hey, Hollywood," RG yelled. "I could use a hand." He held up a junction box and waved it over his head.

Gar took his time walking to the far back corner of the shop. Used to giving, not receiving, the orders, he chafed at being shoved into a secondary role. Without electricity, the expansion couldn't go forward. The system had to function seamlessly for his income to see steady growth. He stared at the junction box RG had connected to the adjacent tenant's power line. Gar's palms began to sweat as they always did when he came too close to anything connected with electricity. He considered wiping his damp palms on his pants, then reached for an anti-static cloth and scrubbed his hands dry. "Where are the gloves?"

Barely hiding a smirk, RG nodded toward the heavy rubber gloves hanging off the new shelving,

Gar had pressed for a rubber mat underneath the oversized HVAC system in the computer room. The constantly-running air-cooling system was critical to keep the servers cool. Gar kept himself at least a foot away from any machine connected to a wall socket, especially the mega-servers RG had installed that now sucked up massive amounts of electricity. RG had countered that the rubber mat was overkill, and Gar's fear of electricity was unfounded.

"It's on concrete, Gar, a non-conductor. You won't get zapped."

"I'm not interested in a physics lesson." Gar lashed out, more at RG's amused expression than his words.

"If you hadn't insisted on the River-Oaks-priced furnishings, we would've had enough funds to counter your electricity phobia with a rubber layer."

The mat had been cut from the build-out budget.

RG grabbed his set of insulated tools and set about hooking up the various wires. "We'd be better off hooking the new stuff to our own meter. Sponging off other guys is risky."

"I told you I'm not paying for more power." Gar said. "Our expenses have already siphoned off more money than I'd planned."

"All right. All right, Bubba, penny-pinching wins." RG took the strippers and exposed the bare wires of a Romex cable.

Gar reluctantly held the wooden ladder steady as RG lifted four ceiling panels and handed them down. He and RG had scouted a dozen locations before picking this spot in the tunnels. The space had easy access to a tie-in to the main power supply. RG disappeared into the crawl space.

An hour later, RG emerged dusted in insulation and motioned a thumbs-up at Gar.

"You're sure the new line won't be detected?" Gar stared at the ceiling squares.

RG sent a disgusted look. "If you want, Ace, I'll undo every connection I just spliced and you can redo the job. Or, better yet I'll disconnect everything and we can pay an electric bill ten times the current one." His threw up his hands. "Say the word, dude. Otherwise quit second-guessing every move I make." He replaced the tools, reset the backroom thermostat to sixty and plugged in the racks of servers. RG paused to listen for the anticipated hum as each in turn sucked power from the new connection.

Gar felt his anger rise. *Arrogant sonofabitch. If anything goes wrong, he'll think doing federal time is a vacation.* Gar grabbed RG's arm as he passed by. "Don't ever forget." Gar squeezed the arm—hard. "You could find yourself behind bars with a single anonymous phone call."

RG wrenched his arm away and smiled. "Just call me 'Quicksilver.' I'll slip through their fingers again."

Gar thought otherwise. Some years back RG had taken one too many risks. His plea bargain banned him from using a computer for five years. Neither the FBI or the IRS had discovered RG's *sub-rosa* activity with TRIPLE-G. RG was the perfect third partner. He had more to lose than any of them.

"Take these boxes to the dumpster after Carol leaves." Gar

kicked a box toward the pile. "It'll get picked up tonight."

"Gee, Hoss, I'd never have figured that out." RG rolled his eyes and ripped a box down with the cutter, then added it to the stack.

Carol hung up from Jason's I'm-home-Mom phone call. She returned to the latest utility report from corporate. Despite the push to lower electricity costs—recaulking windows, replacing weather-stripping around doors, and offering to replace old thermostats with programmable ones—the total building usage had ticked up even with an unusually cool April. She still smarted from Bert's previous criticism and planned to do whatever possible to avoid a repeat performance.

After another hour of reviewing proposed CAM adjustments, she answered another call. "Hey Carol. Our electric bill doubled this month." The sandwich shop owner went on. "And we've noticed a burning smell—but not all the time. It seems to be worse early in the morning. The electric company re-read our meter and checked for malfunctions. They claim it's performing perfectly."

"Have you—"

"Tested our equipment? Absolutely. Microwave, toaster, fridge, freezer. All confirmed A-okay. We've never had anything like this happen in the six years we've been in the tunnel."

She replaced the receiver and picked up the radio. "Unit One to Unit Five." She related the sandwich shop problem.

"I'm up on ten stringing computer cable for the psychologists' build-out," the maintenance tech reported. "I won't be able to leave for at least thirty."

She laid her papers aside. Carol grabbed the radio and flashlight, opened the door and bumped into Jason. "What are you doing here?"

He hung his head. "Dad came by to get a burger with me."

"Okay." Carol reeled in her rage, took a few breaths and waited for Jason to continue. She sneaked a glance at her watch.

"Dad got a call." Jason's head drooped lower. "He said he'd have to give me a rain check. He drove here and let me out."

This incident, plus the baseball game, warranted a call to her attorney. But first she'd have to review the rules with Jason and her parents about always asking her *before* he went anywhere with Paul. And she'd need to calm down so she wouldn't come across as a hysterical helicopter mother. "Come on." She handed him the flashlight. "You can help me with a tenant problem."

At the sandwich shop, she introduced Jason to the owner. With the peak lunch-time crowd long gone, the owner stopped in the middle of afternoon clean-up and shook hands with the boy. "What would you like to drink, son?"

Jason looked at Carol for permission.

She nodded.

"Sprite, please."

Jason passed his mother the flashlight.

The owner set up a ladder just outside the back door, within the maintenance corridor. "The odor is strongest back here." He led the way.

Carol holstered the radio and climbed. She pushed a ceiling square up and over, shining a light in the crawlspace. In the maze of wires, she spotted a yellow Romex cable attached to the sandwich shop's electrical conduit. She turned her light in the opposite direction toward the next-door tenant and found nothing similar. Even after a decade of inspecting build-out construction, she couldn't be certain if the wiring had been installed incorrectly or if an old or frayed cable might have created an electrical short, causing the odor. She climbed down.

"We'll get an opinion from our electrician. I'll send him as soon as he's finished on the tenth floor."

"Fine." The owner waved Jason over. "How about a refill for the young man?"

Half an hour past quitting time, Carol and Jason took the elevator to the parking garage. She swung by the exits as usual, then drove into the loading dock entrance. As she eased closer, she saw RG dragging stacks of cardboard to the dumpster. Cardboard was recyclable. Didn't they know about the green push? Carol threw the car into park and removed the keys. "Stay in the car, Jason.

I'll be just a minute." If her building won the environmental contest, Bert might stay off her back for a solid month.

"Hi." She waved as she hit the first step.

RG whirled toward her, startled.

"Sorry, didn't mean to scare you. If you'll put the cardboard in the recycle bins, it'll boost our environmental campaign. Here, I'll help." She took hold of a flattened box labeled AFC and did a double-take. She flashed back to the sandwich shop crawlspace, realizing the Romex cable connection she had spotted had come from TRIPLE-G. *No wonder they've been so secretive. They're pirating electricity from the next-door tenants. But why? Running a shoe shop can't use enough electricity to warrant theft. What else are they hiding?* She had to get security here—pronto.

Carol lifted her radio from the holster and raised it to her mouth, turned and stepped into Gar's chest.

He gave her The Smile, then snatched her radio and threw it skidding across the bare concrete floor. He stuffed an anti-static cloth in her mouth and pulled a box cutter from his pocket. Gar held the blade to her throat, nicking the skin. Blood dripped down her neck. He dragged her, still struggling, through the shop past shelf after shelf of droning, blinking servers and tossed her on the floor.

Even with her limited computer knowledge, Carol knew they were up to their eyeballs in something illegal.

RG followed in silence. He stopped just inside the back entrance, his gaze fixed on Gar's hand.

Genna sprinted around a shelf of servers, wide-eyed, her breath coming in spurts. "What's going on?"

Gar swung the box cutter toward Genna. "Get out. Now."

Genna ran for the freight elevator.

"You had to come snooping, didn't you?" Gar stood over Carol, flipping the cutter blade in and out. "Now look what you've done."

"Mom?" Jason stepped through the back door. "Let's go. We have to—"

"Leave him alone." Carol stretched to grab Gar's ankle and missed.

"I've got him, Gar." RG clamped a hand on Jason's shoulder. "Throw me the cutter. She won't do anything as long as we have the kid." He bent and whispered to Jason.

Carol nodded at Jason, hoping to keep him calm.

Gar closed the blade and tossed it to RG. He snatched it in mid-air.

RG held the boy's shoulder in a tight grip, then stepped in front of him.

While Gar focused on Jason, Carol readjusted her legs, then positioned her feet under her. *Wait. Wait until he looks away.* When he did, she hurled herself at Gar and knocked him to the floor. She rolled away toward the open junction box and tugged the live Romex cable from its connection.

"Jig's up, Gar." RG pushed Jason farther behind him, keeping a hand around his arm.

Carol stood halfway up, still clutching the cable and took a quick glance at the bare wires.

"The hell it is." Gar reached behind him and pulled a gun from his waistband.

Carol sprang up and threw the cable at the gun looming in Gar's hand. The wires contacted the gun and sparked. Gar writhed and twitched, then fell against the shelving.

Carol ran to Jason and spun him around, away from Gar's wide, staring eyes. She pulled him to her and covered her mouth and nose against the stench of frying flesh.

RG kicked away the live wires. Gar sagged into the floor, dead.

Carol turned on RG, hands white-knuckled into fists. By the time she steadied herself on wobbly knees, she noticed the badge hanging against his Grateful Dead T-shirt.

RG held out the badge for her to see as six Kevlar-vested FBI Special Agents rushed in. RG put his arm around Jason's shoulder. "Thanks for your help, buddy. You were really brave."

Carol ran to Jason and held him close.

"Did you see me, Mom? I was really scared, but I acted brave. *He* said so." Jason pointed to RG. Carol looked at the undercover cop for an explanation, but an FBI agent herded her and Jason outside the shop and down the maintenance hallway. Genna sat on the concrete floor against the wall, wrists flex-cuffed.

After giving a statement to the agent, Carol spotted RG walking back toward them. He ushered them toward the maintenance elevator.

"We've been tracking this group for years," RG explained. "They finally made enough mistakes for us to pinpoint their location."

Carol nodded. "I thought I was done for." They rode the freight elevator up to street level. "What did you say to Jason?"

RG ducked his head, coloring slightly. "I told him I wouldn't let anything happen to him or his Mom." He leaned over to talk to Jason. "I'm starving. How about you, buddy? Y'all want to get a bite with me?""

Jason grinned up at Carol. "Can we, Mom?"

Carol inspected RG as they walked to his vehicle. "Is RG your real name?"

About Tunnel Vision

TUNNEL VISION was inspired by my first job with a Houston-based mega-bank where I discovered the underground city beneath downtown skyscrapers. As the meandering tile pathways expanded and more buildings were connected, workers could walk from one corner of downtown to another without enduring Houston's blazing sun or tropical downpours. Within the tunnels are a winding collection of retail shops, restaurants, boutiques, snack vendors, bars and drycleaners for thousands of downtown employees. What would happen if a tenant wasn't satisfied with the shop's revenue?

About the Authors

CASH ANTHONY is a Houston author, screenwriter, editor, and director for stage and short films. Her stories featuring biker-sleuth Jessie Carr have appeared in *A Death in Texas, Dead and Breakfast, A Box of Texas Chocolates,* and *Twisted Tales of Texas Landmarks.* With her partner James R. Davis, she owns and operates The Master Strategy Group and has toured on her motorcycle across the U.S. She is generously sited as co-author of *Motorcycle Safety and Dynamics,* an academic study of the sport. Cash is a graduate of The University of Texas at Austin in Plan II Honors and of UT School of Law. She and her husband Tim Hogan live in Houston with their two cats, Cora and Sam.

JAMES R. DAVIS is a Houston writer, now retired from an eclectic career as a senior executive in the IT, Oil & Gas, and Securities industries. He has co-authored a two-volume reference work called *Motorcycle Safety and Dynamics,* as well as over two hundred fifty articles presented on his website, Motorcycle Tips and Techniques. Jim has also co-authored six murder mystery plays with Cash Anthony.

L. STEWART HEARL is the author of *Hamilton Swoop, Wizard of Greenridge,* his debut fantasy-adventure novel. He is currently completing work on the sequel, *Hamilton Swoop, Wizard at Large* and is the author of *Invasion* and co-author of *GOOD,* short stories in this anthology. A veteran of the U.S. Navy Submarine Service, he has lived in Houston for the past 31 years pursuing his writing and working in information technology. His writing credits also include a monthly column in the Texas Gulf Coast MENSA bulletin (*InforMENSA*) and nationally published freelance articles. Find out more about him at www.WizardOfGreenRidge.com.

BECKY HOGELAND has been a jane-of-all-trades, from "libation consumption engineer" to curriculum designer, and thus brings a wide range of experiences to her work with co-writer Natasha Storfer. She enjoys reading, especially about history, science, and art, and loves music. Her family has taught her to approach life looking for whimsy…and that duct tape goes a long way.

SALLY LOVE Native Texan Sally Love grew up in Austin and spent more than twenty-five years as a financial writer and a public relations/media relations specialist for financial and high-tech companies. She holds bachelor degrees in English and Journalism from The University of Texas and an MBA in Marketing from the University of Houston. She and retired optometrist husband and ace-editor, Lou, live in Houston. Look for more of her stories in L&L Dreamspell Anthologies, *Mysteries, Dreams and Darkness, Mystery of the Green Mist* and *Dreamspell Revenge II.*

CHARLOTTE PHILLIPS is a novelist and short story writer. With her husband Mark, she writes the **Eva Baum mystery series**. Charlotte's short stories have appeared in *A Death in Texas, A Box of Texas Chocolates, Demented Dreamspell* and *Twisted Tales of Texas Landmarks.* She is a graduate of both Houston Baptist University and the Florida Institute of Technology.

MARK H. PHILLIPS grew up reading the classics—especially James Bond novels, Greek mythology, and Batman comics. He is a prolific writer of short stories and novels. His work includes *The Resqueth Revolution*, a horror/science fiction novel, and the **Eva Baum mystery series**, co-written with his wife Charlotte. Mark's short stories have appeared in TFT anthologies *A Box of Texas Chocolates, A Death in Texas,* and *Twisted Tales of Texas Landmarks.* He holds a BA from the University of Illinois and an MA from Northwestern University, both in Philosophy. Mark teaches pre-calculus and political philosophy at Houston's Bellaire High School.

NATASHA STORFER is a graduate of Texas A&M's College of Engineering. After years of working within the limitations imposed by the laws of science, she turned to writing fiction as an outlet for her imagination and creativity. Her writing includes plot and world development for computer games, fantasy, sci-fi, and mystery. The "Mary Muckraker" series has been created in close collaboration with her co-author and sister, Becky Hogeland.

SHIRLEY WETZEL began writing poems and stories as soon as she could hold a pencil. She has had a number of historical articles and personal essays published in academic journals, newspapers, and anthologies, including a story in *A Cup of Comfort for Weddings.* Her short story, "Feels Like Home", was included in L&L Dreamspell's 2008 anthology, *A Death in Texas* and *Twisted Tales of Texas Landmarks* included "Sarah Hornsby's Dream."

CPSIA information can be obtained at www.ICGtesting.com
Printed in the USA
BVOW042023160112

280494BV00007B/12/P

[15]